TEMPTED TO REBEL

BRUTAL BEAUTY

MISTI WILDS

Tempted to Rebel

Copyright © 2025 by Misti Wilds

Cover Design: Raven Ink Covers

Paperback ISBN: 979-8-9902695-4-5

All rights reserved.

Misti Wilds asserts the moral right to be identified as the author of this work.

This novel is entirely a work of fiction. The names, characters and incidents portrayed in it are the work of the author's imagination. Any resemblance to actual persons, living or dead, events or localities is entirely coincidental.

Designations used by companies to distinguish their products are often claimed as trademarks. All brand names and product names used in this book and on its cover are trade names, service marks, trademarks and registered trademarks of their respective owners. The publishers and the book are not associated with any product or vendor mentioned in this book. None of the companies referenced within the book have endorsed the book.

No part of this book may be reproduced in any form or by any electronic or mechanical means, including information storage and retrieval systems, without written permission from the author, except for the use of brief quotations in a book review.

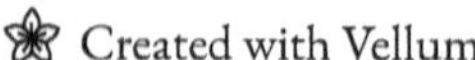 Created with Vellum

Author's Note

Tempted to Rebel is book two of the Brutal Beauty series, a why choose mafia dark romance filled with angst and a growing harem of brothers. You must read book one, *Claimed by Rage*, before reading book two, *Tempted to Rebel*. Book one and book two end on cliffhangers that lead directly into the next book, with the end of the series HEA guaranteed.

Please check the content warnings on my website before reading. There are dark themes woven throughout this book as we dive into the boys' past, and I don't want anyone *SHOOK* unexpectedly. 🩶
https://mistiwilds.com/pages/content-warnings

Chapter 1

Celia

Muffled whispers swirl in the air as wedding guests grow anxious, tired of waiting for the ceremony to begin. I keep my hands folded in my lap and my ankles crossed beneath the pew. Silent. Watching. A shiver rolls down my spine as guards shift before my eyes, transforming from well-dressed men into thugs and brawlers in padded armor and black, faceless masks. A new security detail has taken over the room, and no one seems happy about it. There's an energy swirling around them—a crackle in the air that snaps and pops every time one of their fingers twitch on their guns or they scuff their boots on the marble.

They're waiting for something, just like the rest of us.

Once the few attentive guests catch on to the shift in guard detail, whispers flow more freely, spilling like water through the aisles. One ripple of fear turns into a wave, engulfing the room in panic, and suddenly, people are shouting. Guests reach for their weapons, forgetting that all firearms, knives, and blunt objects were checked at the entrance to the church.

The panic swells in a crescendo that echoes in the rafters.

No one is safe. Old, wooden pews act as barriers, trapping the crowd in neat, little rows waiting to be gunned down. The more agile guests leap from their seats, some seeking answers from known bratva personnel—perhaps a cousin or an uncle—while others rush the closed outer doors.

None of the guards move to stop them.

The heavy wood rattles against chains hidden on the other side, barring them shut from the outside. The sound echoes louder than the voices, and I watch as people shrink into themselves, avoiding the memory of cold iron kissing their wrists and keeping them prisoner. Others, invigorated by the possibility of violence, crack their knuckles and approach the guards with cocksure smiles.

The screaming begins. It echoes through the rafters and pings off of every piece of stained glass lining the Sanctuary walls, ricocheting louder than any bullet. The force of it rings in my ears, making me flinch.

I should have never agreed to accompanying my mother to a bratva event, let alone a wedding for its *pakhan.*

"*Celia.*" My mother clicks her tongue in disapproval. "Compose yourself." Unlike most of the people surrounding us, she's unaffected by the chaos erupting around us, maintaining an icy distance from her emotions.

She has one thing I lack within the bratva: *experience.*

"What's going on?" I crane my neck to get a better look, but in my heart, I already know that something has gone wrong. The wedding is over before it ever began.

Two masked men drag someone out of the room, smearing blood across the polished marble. I stare at the crimson streak as my body turns ice cold, unable to believe what I'm seeing.

A wedding should be sacred. It should be full of love and light—not this. Anything but *this.*

I fight a rush of tears, knowing that they'll only stoke my mother's ire. Why is nothing sacred in this godforsaken city? Why must everything involving my family turn to violence and chaos? Can't there be a single day of happiness, just *one* innocent moment of peace?

A pair of young children, a little boy and a littler girl, hold each other in the row in front of us. The girl whimpers softly while the boy tries to be brave, emulating the stony expressions he sees on all of the adults around him, including my mother.

Forced to be brave when he's still only a child. My heart cracks, and a wave of grief for every child forced to witness these events flows freely through my veins.

"Hey," I murmur, keeping my tone gentle and soft. "Everything is going to be okay."

Their father turns to glare at me, his jaw clenching as he chews on his thoughts before they turn into words. "Adella," he says finally, addressing my mother, "what a shame it would be for your son's marriage to fall apart before it's even begun." His glare pings between the two of us. "Then again, the Monrovias have a poor track record when it comes to their spouses. Perhaps Mikhail should give up before he's either dead or divorced by Christmas."

My mother presses her lips into a fine line. "Watch your tongue, Fiero, before someone's hand simply—" she flashes a three-inch knife concealed within a silver tube of lipstick—"*slips.*"

A vein in Fiero's neck pulses as he swallows and chooses to remain silent. He turns to his children and ushers them to the other side of the pew away from us. When he tries to exit into the aisle, a masked man shoves to his chest, stopping Fiero in his tracks. He argues with the guard until a rifle smashes into his face with a sickening *crack,* a second masked man hauling Fiero away without further warning. Fiero shouts Russian curses even after the doors to the hallway close behind him.

He left his children behind.

The little girl starts to cry in earnest, and I gather my skirts and leap over the back of the pew to reach her. "Hush, now," I soothe, petting both the children's heads. "Everything will be okay. *Shhh.*"

My heart breaks for the children—less so for their father. No one else steps up to claim his kids as theirs, despite my silent searching for a second parent. Everyone avoids meeting my eye. My mother is the exception; her disdain unmistakable. Before we ever arrived, she warned me to keep a low profile. Pretending that everything is fine is her specialty, and after navigating the social ruin that my divorce brought our family name, she's become an expert.

Normally, I would do as I'm told and keep my head down, but today is anything but a normal day, and these children deserve better memories than this.

One of the guards aims his rifle toward the crowd. "Everyone *move!*" He repeats the order in Russian while a half dozen other guards follow his lead and corral us into the four corners of the room, separating us by age and ability. I'm placed with the younger group of women and children, while my mother is split into another group with women closer to her age. A few people argue, but anyone who raises true hell gets pistol-whipped or punched in the gut and removed from the room entirely, following the path of blood. Every time someone opens the doors that lead outside the Sanctuary, we hear the rapid-fire *tat-tat* of a gun or the agonized scream that comes after. I remove my shawl and wrap it around Fiero's little girl's neck, careful to cover her ears. "Keep this on," I instruct, tying a loose knot at the base of her neck, "it'll help with the noise." She looks up at me with wide eyes, and I enlist her brother's help to keep the shawl in place.

Too soon, a guard approaches my corner of the cathedral and sizes up our group like livestock. Fire stirs in my chest with each kick of my heartbeat, and I quickly move to the front of the group and stand in his way before he can grab anyone and haul them off. "Back the *fuck* up," I hiss, bracing myself as best as I can for whatever violence comes next. My entire body shakes from adrenaline and frayed nerves, the careful control I keep over my fear having snapped the moment Fiero's daughter first started trembling.

I might be afraid, but I will *not* let them touch the children.

Clenching my fists as the guard steps closer, I scan him for weaknesses the same instant he scans me for mine. An AK is casually slung across his back like he doesn't intend to use it, but his body is thicker than the others', built from years of training and fighting. If he wants to hurt me, he won't need to use a gun—he has an arsenal at his fingertips.

I can't see his face behind the mask, but his eyes—deep pools of ebony ink—suddenly spark with interest. "You're trouble," he rumbles, the hint of a smile in his voice, "aren't you, *krosotka?*"

Memories from the Baranova wedding flash before my eyes the moment Rage comes into view. Confidence rolls off of him in waves every time his muscles shift beneath his clothes, each movement smoother than silk. A shiver rolls down my spine as he looks me up and down—and I do the same to him, taking in the all-black ensemble and wondering how I never noticed it before.

He walks like a man who would crush the world in his fist if it meant he could drink from eternity.

The moment Ruin carries me across the threshold

into the brothers' domain, Rage finally smiles, and my heart stumbles over itself. Foolishly, a part of me clings to the man I thought he was, the one who promised to take care of me, but I know that version is a well-crafted lie.

A man who is capable of love wouldn't break my heart so easily.

As he steps closer, my breath catches on the snap of fear crowding my chest. The last time I saw Rage, I attacked him, wrapping my hands around his throat and squeezing, like he's done so many times to me, only I dialed it up a notch when I knocked the bastard out, handcuffed him to his car, and left him there to freeze in the middle of winter.

Time slows to a crawl, hovering in the razor-thin precipice between reality and fantasy. As Rage moves, flashes of memory blur with the present. An image of a masked guard from the Baranova wedding flickers in my mind, replacing the man silently stalking toward me with the one burned into my mind—the word *krosotka* falling from both of their lips in that same, hushed reverence I've come to expect.

Rage isn't just *any one* of the armed guards from the Baranova wedding—he's *the* man—the one who approached me and called me beautiful.

The only one who couldn't take his eyes off of me.

At the time, I was struck by his presence. Sunlight filtered through the stained glass windows, painting the Santuary floor in a kaleidoscope of color that he stepped right through, breaking the mirage so that he could get to me. With the mask covering his face, no one could recognize him for who he was, but now, I could close my eyes and blindly pick him from a lineup.

I know this man. I've seen what he's capable of. I've tasted the warmth of his body and all the allure it promises.

But it's merely a pretty picture. A trap intended to capture pretty prey like me.

As Rage stops in front of us, I catch a gleam of gold behind his massive frame. At first, I don't understand what I'm seeing. The room has changed since I was last in it, with all of the furniture replaced by this towering *thing*, all bright metal and harsh lines. A low, padded bench is nestled inside the bars, with a pallet of blankets folded on the floor beside it.

A cage, I realize with a start.

One large enough to fit a human... or two on top of each other.

I fight against Ruin's hold on my body, struggling to free myself. I've heard war stories from bratva members who have been captured overseas, and every single one of them warned against being put in a cage. Because when the door locks, you're at your captor's mercy until you escape... or you die by their hands.

Ruin holds me tighter, crushing me against his chest. "Be still, *krosotka*. You are home." He might as well say *bad dog*, for all his tone implies. *I'm misbehaving.* He handles my struggle easily, wrapping a fist around the rope at my back and pulling. It arches my spine and pulls at both my thighs and shoulders, making them scream in protest. I clench my teeth around the gag in my mouth and shut my eyes tight, praying he'll stop.

Instead, someone grabs my jaw and pries it open, looping their finger through the gag and tearing it from between my teeth. A scream burns in the back of my throat, but I fight it with all my strength. I won't give either of them the satisfaction of hearing it.

"Look at me," Rage commands, dropping the gag in favor of cupping my face. When I don't comply, he snarls and lifts me from Ruin's grasp, taking possession of my body. The tug on my limbs ceases, and I swallow a whimper as sharp relief washes over me.

A tear slips free, sliding down my cheek until it falls.

"You did this," Rage snarls, carrying me in his arms. "This is *your* fault." A sudden clang of metal on metal makes me jump, and Rage clamps down harder to keep me still, bruising my skin in his hands. "Things could have been much simpler if you'd just—" he cuts himself off with a hiss, bending at the waist to set me down. Plush blankets greet my ass, and he makes quick work of undoing the knots binding my feet and arms. As the rope falls away, he fishes a key from his pocket and removes the handcuffs next. I don't bother moving my arms once they're free, so he does it for me, bringing them to the front and setting them in my lap. He then rubs the red welts on my wrists with his thumbs, a pinched scowl on his face.

"Don't take pity on her now," a familiar voice calls out. Rebel appears from a doorway at the side of the living room, stepping into the dim light with catlike ease.

He looks like he always does—casually grunge, with dark jeans slung low over his hips and a soft maroon t-shirt that exposes a sliver of his midriff, the usual mischievous smirk curving across his lips. But his eyes, usually sparking with amusement, remain cold and distant. "She runs away from every good thing she gets. Isn't that right, baby?" He crosses to the side of the cage and raps his knuckles against the bars. "In the end, you're a runner, not a fighter." His voice quiets to a whisper meant only for me. "Sure had me fooled."

I meet Rebel's eyes and silently plead with him. He's always been the sweeter, softer brother—I can't lose him now that every inch of the horizon is shadowed with misery.

If I'm surrounded by three genuine monsters, I don't think I'll survive.

"Keep the cuffs on," Rebel warns, wrapping his fists around two of the bars, his silver rings clinking against the metal, "or she might slip her cage, brother."

"She won't." Rage grips my chin and turns my face back toward him. "She's going to be a good little pet, isn't she?"

He can't be serious. Eyes wide, I search his face for the joke, for the hint of a smile, but there's no crack in the facade, nothing for me to latch onto.

When he pulls out a collar from his pocket, I realize just how serious he is. He loops the black leather around my throat and latches it at the back, setting a dangling, golden heart pendant against my throat. I can't see what it says, but the metal is cold against my skin, contrasting the warmth of the soft leather. Rage slips his hand into my hair and tugs the tie free, spilling long tresses down my back. He combs loose strands away from my face, admiring his *pet*.

For that one brief moment, he transforms back into the man who promised me a future worth living, the tenderness in his gaze giving him away. My heart aches as it clings to this version of him, wanting nothing more than to rewind time and freeze it at that exact moment.

Rebel scoffs and rolls his eyes. "If you're going to fuck her, do it already. Don't do the whole—" he whines in the back of his throat—"*fawning over her* thing."

"I'm not going to fuck her, and I'm not fawning over her." Rage slips the handcuffs over one of my wrists while I'm distracted and cinches the other one around one of the bars to the cage. Tearing the gag free from my neck and dropping it to the floor, he presses the pad of his thumb against my chapped bottom lip. "*When* I give you my cock," he murmurs, brushing the tip of his nose against mine as he leans in close, "you're going to beg for it. Because the only way you're getting out of this cage, *Mama*—" he presses the flat of his palm to my stomach —"is with a baby in your belly."

I shake my head violently and back away from him as far as I can, the cage and the cuffs not giving much leeway. I barely move a few inches before my body bends in ways it was never meant to. "No, please—"

His eyes darken, and my body trembles as it senses danger. The world stills, my heartbeat quieting to a whisper as he speaks. "You *will* bear my children. You begged me to fill up that pretty pussy of yours to give you what you've always wanted, and you don't get to go back on your word. You made a promise—" his nostrils flare— "and so did I." Slamming the cage door shut behind him, he locks it with a key from his pocket and hovers just outside. Lip curling, he reaches for a bundle of clothes on the kitchen island and tosses them to Rebel. "See that she gets dressed."

Rebel pulls a face. "I'm not touching her."

Only a week ago, Rebel wouldn't *stop* touching me.

The whiplash hits hard, but I keep my composure the way my mother taught me. Chin up. Eyes front. Shoulders back. Spine straight. I stare at Rebel while he crumples the clothing in his fists and wrestles with his emotions. The swift change in the dynamic between us is my fault, just like Rage said, because I'm the one who fled after Rebel came to my rescue and saved me from the stranger who invaded my home and took me hostage.

I wince at the reality of the situation. It's not really *my* fault, is it? Rage is the one who is taking everything to such extremes. I'm not the one who installed a cage in my living room or had a collar made for my bride.

If he had dated me like a normal man, asked me to dinner or took me to see a movie, would we be at each other's throats like we are now?

Rebel shoves the clothes against Ruin's chest. "*You* undress her." A silent moment passes between the three brothers before Rebel snatches the clothes back, an unspoken acknowledgement passing between them. "*Ugh,* fine, I'll do it."

My heart hammers like a kick drum as I finally speak up. "I want Ruin's help." I lift my leg, pointing my toes toward the masked brother. "I choose him." He may have carried me inside after Thanatos tied me up and kidnapped me, but I don't think he'll hurt me. I can't trust Rebel when he's so clearly upset with me after I ran out on him. I've only ever seen Rebel's sweet side—I don't know what to make of this version of him.

He's shaking with anger as we speak, and that scares me.

"You think you get to choose—" Rebel snarls—"*anything* anymore?" He laughs bitterly and assesses the clothes in his hand. There are multiple pairs of lacy panties, a trio of skimpy bras, and a handful of different tops and bottoms to mix and match an outfit. Tossing most of the items to the ground, he approaches with a handful of scarlet lace.

My gaze flicks to Rage, but if I think he's going to offer any help, I'm sorely mistaken. His demeanor has shifted from his usual shade of pent-up anger to cool dismissal as he shrugs on a coat and heads for the door.

"Where are you going?" I ask, wincing at the hint of desperation in my voice. Despite what I did to Rage the last time I saw him, we shared a special moment together before everything went to shit. He didn't just agree to fuck a baby into me—he made love to me, promising to provide for my every need if I could just... *let him.*

Then I shoved all of his promises back in his face with a big *F You* in the shape of a little white morning after pill.

But as soon as I swallowed it, I couldn't hold it in. My body revolted, throwing it back up within seconds. It's the reason I didn't hear my attacker climb the staircase and slip into my bedroom—I was heaving my guts into the toilet bowl.

The truth crumbles like ash in my mouth as Rage's icy gaze pins me to the floor. He doesn't answer my question. Turning on his heel, he walks away and *clicks* the door shut behind him, not sparing me a second glance as he leaves. I wait for him to walk back through the door like he did once before—to march right up to me and kiss me, to demand more, to fight for answers.

Why did you do it, Celia? Why did you betray the promise we made each other?

Shivering, I imagine a sinkhole splitting the room open and swallowing me whole. Shrouded in darkness, I could pretend that this is all one extended nightmare. That none of this is real, and I'll wake up tomorrow as bitterly heartbroken and lonely as I was months ago before ever receiving my invitation to *Midnight*—before these brothers walked into my life and refused to walk back out.

But the harsh glare of gold in my peripheral makes it impossible to ignore my new reality. I've chosen this path, and now I have to live with the consequences.

Rebel saunters up to the front of my cage. "Take your clothes off."

Steeling my nerves, I meet Rebel's unflinching stare. I can't solve my problems with Rage right now, but I can address the ones I have with Rebel head-on. Rattling the chains of my handcuffs, I reply, "I'm a little tied up here."

"I don't care." His smile remains cruel. "Take your clothes off, *krosotka*. Now." He grips the bars, allowing me a glimpse of the scanty panties and bralette he chose for me to wear. Neither looks comfortable or the least bit supportive, but I doubt that's their intended purpose. Rebel licks a stripe across his top row of teeth. "Unless you'd rather be naked. I could always throw these away." He shakes the lingerie mockingly.

Glaring at him, I kick off my boots first, struggling to undo the laces one-handed. Then I peel off my clothes layer by layer, my sweater and bra getting caught around my arm, as predicted. I twist and contort my body to pull off as much clothing as I can, then huff and collapse onto the blankets. Undoing the bra clasp at my back with one hand was a bitch, but tearing the rest off is impossible without either removing the cuffs or sawing through the stitches with my teeth. "A little help?" I ignore the ache in my wrist and rattle the cuffs again.

Rebel's glare freezes on my bare tits. The air is cold in their apartment, and it shows—goosebumps trail down my arms and legs while my nipples harden to sharp points. I shiver under his gaze, locking my legs tightly together so that he can't see anything else. I know he's seen me naked—but that doesn't mean I have to spread my legs and give him a show.

He grabs a sheathed knife from Ruin's belt and crouches by my side. "Hold fucking still." Flicking the blade through the bars, he cuts away my bra strap like he's slicing through butter, then he does the same for my sweater. I tear the tattered garments off and toss them into a pile with my leggings and panties. He slips the lace bralette and panties through the bars, our fingers brushing.

Static jolts between us, shocking each other on contact. Rebel hisses like a cat while I recoil like I've been burned. My body shudders at the jolt while Rebel curses up a storm. "Goddammit!" He drops the knife and kicks it toward the wall. "Put some fucking clothes on!"

My temper flares. "I would if you'd give me any!"

Seriously, the bralette barely holds my nipples, let alone my entire boob, and the panties hardly cover anything. I'm grateful they at least stay in place instead of rolling down my hips. The bralette, on the other hand, takes double the effort to pull over my chest with only one hand available. Rebel snatches a matching key to Rage's from a silver chain around his neck and tosses it into my lap. "Fix your damned top then give those back."

There are four keys hanging from the chain, the tiniest being a spare key to my handcuffs. A larger, golden key likely belongs to my cage, and two more silver keys look eerily familiar. "Where did you get these?" I finger the heaviest key and realize exactly what it is—my ex-husband's house key that went missing from my keyhook a few weeks ago. I scratch my fingernail across the grooves in the final key, tracing the cut like I've done hundreds of times over the years, before I knew what it unlocked.

It's the key to my father's safe house. A replica of the original, no doubt, which means that Rebel had to have found mine and made a copy. Did he know what it belonged to before I ran away, or did he figure it out after Thanatos tracked me down?

A smirk curves across Rebel's handsome face. "Where do you think?"

"You *stole* them from me?"

He shrugs. "You invited me in. I couldn't leave without a souvenir."

What else has he lifted over the past few weeks? My face flushes with shame and I silently berate myself for being a stupid, lovestruck girl letting strangers into my home without thinking it through. I figured they were dangerous mafia men—but I didn't think through what that meant in the day-to-day. Rage is easy to figure out because he's suffocating about possessing me—but Rebel and Ruin?

I don't really know them at all.

Once my cuffs are off, I quickly adjust my top and slide my arm through, then pull a blanket over my lap to fight off the cold. I hold onto the keys for a moment longer, wondering when I'll have them in my hands again. This could be my moment. I could make a run for it.

I don't have to look to know that Ruin's knife is still lying on the floor a few feet away. I could hold onto the keys until they're forced to open the door from the outside, and then I could lunge at them, or maybe I can fit my hand through the bars and unlock it myself—

"Tick-tock," Rebel hisses, stomping the heel of his

boot against the cage wall closest to me. "Give them back, Celia."

Frustration licks through my body like fire as I hold out the keys for Rebel to take. Even if I make it out of the cage, there are two of them in the room. I might be able to overpower Rebel if my adrenaline kicks in, but I don't stand a chance against him *and* Ruin.

Rebel snatches the chain and slips it back over his head, the keys jangling until they settle against his chest. He tucks them beneath his shirt, hiding them from view, and rakes a hand through his dark hair. It's gotten longer over the past few weeks, giving him an even edgier appearance than usual.

We stare at each other for long, silent heartbeats while he pinches his snakebite between his front teeth. "You shouldn't have run," he says finally, a muscle in his jaw twitching. "We can handle a creepy stalker. It's not like you were in danger. I would have stayed with you the entire time. All night, if you'd have let me."

Ignoring the irony of having *another* stalker than these three, I shake my head. In truth, it's not the break-in or the man behind it that scares me—it's the three men holding the keys to my freedom.

I run my palm down one of the golden bars, shivering at how cold it is to the touch. *This* is why I know better than to mess around with mafia men. They'll go to any extreme to prove they're right or keep their word. I wonder which of the brothers had the idea first—was it Rage who decided to lock me up so he could be the first to knock me up, or was it Rebel who half-jokingly threw the idea out in the middle of dinner one night?

Shifting my gaze from Rebel to Ruin, I wonder if he could have made the decision or if he merely went along with it. He seems to go along with everything the others propose—is that because he agrees with them, or because there's no detriment to following their lead?

What does Ruin get out of keeping me in a cage?

I want to ask, but I'm not sure I'm ready for the answer.

"Did you find him?" I ask instead. "The stalker."

Rebel picks up Ruin's knife and twirls it between his fingers. "No. But we're on his trail. It's only a matter of time before we gut him." He passes the knife to Ruin, who sheaths it. "Well, before this guy does. I don't like the mess."

Ruin grunts, like he agrees.

I don't know why anyone would stalk me. I'm a normal woman living a normal life—up until recently. "It must have been a random attack," I say softly. I've been thinking about it all week when I wasn't frantically finishing my designs for the upcoming gala and outsourcing their completion. Having a stalker doesn't make sense. "I don't know anyone out to get me aside from you three."

Rebel gets this pinched look on his face, like he doesn't like the implication that he's a threat to my well-being, but he doesn't comment. He disappears into the bedroom directly beside me, leaving the door open —*wait*. I scan the doorway and huff in disbelief.

There is no door. There are empty hinges but no nails and no door to shut. The palm scanner that acts as an automatic lock lies dormant on the wall beside the doorframe. Rebel flops onto his back on an unmade bed and props his knee up, staring at the ceiling. Aside from a strip of LED lights behind the headboard that paint the back wall in a wash of cerulean blue, the room is dim. Rebel flicks through his phone for a moment, and then music booms through unseen speakers, filling the entire apartment with loud drumming, electric guitars, and a mix of male vocalists singing, screaming, and rapping.

I guess our conversation is over.

Ruin stands completely still a few feet away, watching me. As tempting as it is to let this man ogle my tits over the others, I wrap a blanket around my shoulders to keep myself warm and keep Rebel from enjoying the view.

Not that he's looking. His arm dangles over the edge of the bed, a bottle of hard liquor uncapped and hanging from his fingertips. I missed him taking the first swig, but I catch him gulping a few mouthfuls now, then the bottle goes right back to skimming the hardwood floor.

Great. My keeper's going to be drunk *and* irritable.

I stretch out my legs and brush my bare toes against the cold bars. My boots lie on top of my torn sweater, the leggings, bra, and underwear I wore this afternoon crumpled in a sad heap beneath them. "Aren't you going to take my clothes?" I eye my discarded socks eagerly, knowing that any extra layers in this place will be worth their weight in gold. I can probably put my sweater back on, too, at least over one arm.

Ruin doesn't reply, choosing to stand like a silent sentinel instead of answering my question. I guess I should be used to that by now, although I might actually miss his late-night advances into my bedroom after receiving such a warm welcome home from his brothers.

Judging from his silence, it doesn't look like I'll be receiving any firm caresses or growled orders for me to come anytime soon.

Not that I want them anymore.

I close my eyes and hug my knees to my chest, wishing this would all be over. The worst part of all isn't actually the cold or the cage—it's knowing that despite what Fox and Angel told me the night we met, I'm powerless to fight back.

Chapter 2

Rebel

Eventually, every part of my body goes numb. The fizzy tingle in my arms fades. The burn in my throat disappears. The throbbing ache in my chest—the one Celia fucking put there when she *left*—finally lets up, and I can breathe for the first time in days.

It's when I roll over onto my stomach and peer out the open doorway to see her curled into a ball and covered in blankets that everything comes rushing back.

The hurt.

The anger.

The sorrow.

The *pain*.

But the alcohol has done its job—every feeling fizzles out one agonizing second later, and I drop the empty glass bottle to the floor. Celia flinches, letting me know that she's awake. My music stopped playing an hour ago when my playlist ran dry, and we've been sitting in silence ever since. Ruin ran off to his dungeon upstairs—is it still a dungeon if it's on the third floor?—and left me to babysit.

Two weeks ago, I would have jumped at the chance to spend all day alone with Celia. Just the two of us with every flicker of desire my brothers have been stoking inside of her, all ready and waiting for me to ignite.

I would have fucked her hard. Soft. Gently. Rough. Flipped her over the side of the couch and bucked my hips into hers, or backed her against the wall and wrapped those perfect thighs around my hips to punch up inside of her, or laid her down gently on my bed and carved a place for myself so deep that she could never get rid of me.

Because that's exactly what she did when she ran away—she threw me out like a boyfriend she didn't want or need anymore.

Boyfriend. I scoff, rubbing the back of my eyelids. Yeah, right, like we were ever boyfriend-girlfriend. I scowl at the memory of how it felt to consider such a thing—that fluttery excitement when she'd text me back, or the anticipation of seeing her once she got off work and made it home.

How fucking *stupid.*

I'm twenty-eight years old, and somehow, she makes me feel like I'm a teenager all over again, horny as shit and craving whatever scraps of attention she'll give me. I scratch my chest and the wad of keys around my neck clink together, the metal warm on my skin. Yeah, I took her stuff, so what? How did she think I was getting into her house every day? And that second house, the one she kept a secret from us so that she could disappear once she decided she wasn't having fun anymore—

I scowl harder. Thanatos sent us the body cam footage from when he picked her up. The house itself was deteriorating, like it hadn't been maintained in years, and Celia... she actually looked frightened when he burst through the front door.

Of what, Thanatos being rough with her, or of coming home to us?

The former, I can understand, but the latter pisses me off.

What the fuck does she have to be scared of?

I think back to when Rage finally arrived at Celia's house after the break-in. He walked into her bedroom completely put-together, but the moment he noticed that little purple box torn open on her bathroom counter, he lost his shit.

"Do you know what the fuck this is?" He tosses the box to the floor and stomps on it, his jaw clenched tightly shut.

I hadn't bothered dissecting her belongings today, so I wait to pick up the empty box until he starts pacing her bedroom. Turning it over in my hands, I decipher the torn logo.

It's a fucking morning-after pill.

Jealousy courses through me hotter than hell itself, but then relief immediately settles in. If she and Rage have finally had sex, that means that it's on the table for the rest of us.

Then reality hits and I'm crumpling the box in my fist.

She doesn't deserve anything from me until I get a goddamned apology, and even then, I might throw her rejection right back in her beautiful fucking face. Everything feels gnarled and twisted inside my chest, the knife in my back cutting deeper than I realized.

My brother feels the betrayal, too, maybe even harder than me. Once Rage figures out how to speak again, he snarls a half-sentence, "like I'm going to fucking let her."

The cage was Rage's idea, born from a need to keep Celia somewhere we can monitor her at all times. I suggested a tracking chip embedded in her neck—which is still on the table, as far as I'm concerned—but he wanted something bigger and louder so that it's impossible for her to ignore. A microchip, she could pretend doesn't exist.

But a cage?

She'll be as trapped as the rest of us are, unable to escape each other.

I pull a box of smokes from my pocket and pinch one between my teeth. Rage hates when I smoke indoors, but *fuck it*, he isn't here. I light up, taking my first hit of nicotine, and try to relax. Celia hasn't said a word since Ruin traipsed upstairs to his bedroom, and the quiet feels like a buzz of its own, thrumming between the two of us. I'd usually chalk that up to sexual tension. Even my dick twitches, like it knows that she's nearby.

I'm hungry for her. I always have been.

But the tension between us now isn't sexual. It's something I can't name. An energy that's tight and uncomfortable, like an itch I can't scratch.

My life wasn't great before we dragged Celia into the mix, but now it feels unbearable in the worst fucking way. Rage might be okay with possessing her like his favorite pet, but I'm not.

I don't want to force her to be with me.

I want her to *want* me, no matter what our future together looks like. Isn't that what partners do? They stick together through whatever life throws at them?

Celia turns her head to look at me as I blow smoke in her direction. It wafts through the doorway and dissipates once it reaches the main room. Now that I'm numbed to the turmoil brewing inside my chest, I can look at her without feeling like I'm falling apart.

Slowly, it dawns on me that she doesn't look like her usual self. Her hair is a mess, the waves unraveling into a frizzy curtain over her shoulders. There are dark circles under her eyes, and if my own aren't deceiving me, hers are bloodshot, too. There's a pallor to her cheeks that can't be healthy, and I can't find a single trace of makeup on her skin. Not that I'd know what the fuck to look for when it comes to makeup, but despite the drying tear-tracks on her cheeks, her mascara hasn't run, so she must not be wearing any.

Somehow, she's still beautiful to look at. Maybe it's the alcohol talking. Or the light playing tricks on me. Or the sudden, inescapable distance between us, or whatever the fuck that saying is. Distance makes the heart grow fonder? Time does?

Fuck it—she looks good, even all mussed up inside of a cage.

I let cigarette smoke pass my lips in a lazy cloud that obscures her from view. When it clears, she's standing up, no longer hiding beneath a quilt, and I get the full-body experience of seeing her tanned skin wrapped in the scarlet lace I chose for her.

Fuck, she's beautiful.

The bra doesn't stop just beneath her breasts. A band of lace continues down her ribs, ending where the curve of her waist begins. Then there's the panties—boyshorts, technically, but with how thick Celia's thighs are, they ride up her legs and let her ass hang out the back. The lace, although mostly sheer, bleeds in full color where it's bunched between her thighs and across her tits, the peaks of her nipples hidden behind an intricate rose design. It's not bright red, but a maroon that's even sexier.

A mental image of Celia wearing bright red panties beneath a pleated skirt blips into mind, but unlike the woman standing before me, it's pure fantasy that I conjured up while missing our girl. Rage couldn't keep his mouth shut about the red fucking panties she wore to breakfast with him, but I bet she *really* wore them for me.

I was supposed to be on that date with her, not my brother. She chose *me.*

Something's been nagging me since that day, though,

before everything went to shit. I flick cigarette ash onto the ground before taking another drag.

She opens her mouth to speak. "Rebel, I—"

But I beat her to it. "Why'd you ghost me?"

"—what?" Her eyebrows scrunch together, the little divot between them driving me crazy. Were things better between us, I might run my thumb across her forehead to smooth it out, press a tender kiss against her skin, atop each of her cheekbones, then finally on her lips.

But I can't see myself doing that anytime soon. My chest twinges, and I scratch my pec distractedly. "That morning. I was excited to see you, and you ghosted me after I sent you that pic." I lick my lips, picturing the one she sent me. I've stared at it for hours by now, memorizing the way her skin glistens in the shower mist and her smile brightens the whole goddamn world.

My world.

Fuck, I'm such a goner for this girl.

Realization washes over her features. "Oh, Rebel." She grabs the bars and presses her body against them, the tips of her breasts and her kneecaps fitting between the gaps.

I bet I could suck on her nipple if I got close enough.

"I dropped my phone in the shower, and it broke. Rage bought me a new one right before we—" She cuts herself off at first, but then she straightens her spine and looks me dead in the eyes. "Before we had sex." Brushing a frizzy strand of hair behind her ear, she continues, "but I want you to know that I would have chosen you, Rebel, not Rage. I wanted to go to breakfast with *you.*"

If this were a normal day and I hadn't drank nearly an entire bottle of vodka, I'd feel a twisting ache beneath my ribs right about now. The alcohol is fucking bliss, though, numbing me to it. "You would have fucked me, then, right? I would have been the first?" I cling to the idea that Celia still wants me more than my brothers, no matter how foolish that idea is.

I exhale until the tight feeling in my chest dissipates. "I would have made it good for you."

She blushes like a fucking schoolgirl, and I hate how much I enjoy it.

"It was good with him, too."

"That why you tried to kill him?" Shaking my head, I can't help but laugh. "It was so good, you had to strangle him? Or what, you'd fall in love?" I wish I had another bottle to throw back. In fact—I do. Sliding off the bed, I shuffle into the kitchen and grab an unopened bottle from the cabinet. Cracking the top, I take a swig of vodka and hop up onto the island, sloshing a little liquid past the rim. It drips onto my jeans, staining them black, and I itch to take them off. I'm rarely dressed while home, so this is a rare exception on account of how fucked up everything is. I stare at Celia as the burn settles in the back of my throat, the heat quickly fading into a drunken numbness. "Nothing to say?" A bitter chuckle catches in my chest, and I scratch it again, my fingers catching on the silver chain and every single one of those keys.

Celia turns to face me and crosses her arms over her chest. "What do you want me to say? That I regret it?"

I lift an eyebrow. "Do you?"

Her eyes narrow. "No."

I tilt the bottle back and swallow as much as I can without throwing it all back up. My eyes water, my chest burns, and goddamn it all, I just want to feel *better*. I gasp for air once I've killed half the bottle, then slam it down on the granite countertop with a heavy *clink* of glass on stone.

Celia pretends to be unaffected by either our conversation or my drinking, but I can see through her mask as if it were made of glass.

"Something on your mind, baby?" I lick the vodka from my lips and hold the bottle out toward her. "Want a little liquid courage to make this easier?"

"Nothing about this is easy," she mutters, frowning.

I gesture broadly, throwing my arms out beside me. "Hence the alcohol." Hopping down from the counter, I cross the short distance to the cage and slip the neck of the bottle through the bars, high over her head. "Open up."

To my surprise, the tilts her head back and pops open her mouth, allowing me to pour vodka past her lips. She swallows as best she can without choking, but a trickle slips down her chin and drips into her chest.

I'm still staring at those soft, pillowy tits when she reaches her fingertips through the cage and wraps them around mine. I barely notice, suddenly too caught up in the warm depths of her eyes. They aren't brown, not really. They're hazel, shifting colors depending on the slant of light.

Her voice ghosts across my skin like a lover's caress. "Why are you mad at me, baby?"

A shiver runs down my spine. *I* call her baby—not the other way around. We're crossing into new territory, talking like this with each other. I shouldn't let it happen. I should back the fuck up and lock myself in my room—except, I took my door off its hinges after Rage unkindly barred me inside, so I literally can't escape from her. Fuck. Fucking fuck.

I press my forehead against the cold bars of cage and close my eyes. "You know why."

She exhales, our breath mingling. "I wasn't running from *you*, Rebel. I was running from *this*." She taps the gold bars with her fingertips. "Do you really think this is what I want? To be nothing more than a possession?"

My chest tightens. I'm not sure that I want that, either, but I don't have a choice. "This *is* me, *krosotka*." The Russian nickname falls from my lips before I can stop it, reminding me of how this all began.

One little dance turned into so much more.

"It's not you," Celia insists. She struggles to hold onto my hand, her fingertips slipping from mine every few seconds. "This is Rage's doing. You wouldn't lock me up like this."

I tear my body away from hers, breathing hard as I fight her siren's call. Sweet words and an even sweeter voice, but I can't trust her after what she's done. "Not everything is about Rage." I swallow more vodka and wipe my mouth on my forearm. "Until you learn that, *this*—" I gesture between us—"goes nowhere." I carry the vodka back to my bedroom and strip, not caring if she watches me get naked. I'm not doing it for her. I need some goddamn air.

Flopping onto my bed and kicking all of the blankets to the floor, I turn my music back on and drown out the noise.

The kick drum beat of my heart.

The echo of her voice in my head.

The whisper-sweet way she calls me *baby*.

CHAPTER 3

RAGE

MY DAILY TASKS take fucking forever. In five hours, I've settled one territory dispute, kicked the shit out of some lowlife who tried to stiff us for S-tier product, and completed a hefty perimeter check of the Baranova compound and its surrounding territory at Ezra's direct request. Thanatos meets me at the gates on my way back around to the front of the main house, looking grim as hell and like he needs at least one week's worth of sleep. I wasn't there when he dropped off Celia this morning, and now I'm glad for it.

For once, he actually looks his age.

Instead of greeting me, he gets right to business. "We're upping security all over the city," Thanatos says, scratching the stubble on his chin. "Two more women have gone missing, and another body showed up on the beach."

"Burn scars?"

He hands me a tablet with all of the crime scene

photos organized into different folders for each victim. I open the most recent case file and scan every single picture for signs that our killer is none other than *good ol' Dad* stirring up trouble. But although the murderer is clearly fucked in the head, we don't have proof that it's our father. Just a gut feeling that neither Thanatos or I can shake.

That, and the fact that the victims are treated like *shit*.

The latest victim has burns on her calves and forearms, a few nastier ones on the backs of her hands and around her ankles. Some are deep and in a pattern resembling chain links, but a few marks are too indiscernible to make out around the mutilated flesh. Whoever is doing this to people has one hell of a grudge to work through, and if I know anything about my father, it's that he's been harboring massive amounts of hate and resentment our entire lives.

I ignore the way my skin itches at seeing the burn scars on the victim's body and continue scanning the photos. "Was she assaulted?" She's still wearing a little black cocktail dress and heels, which points to her having been on a date the night she died. A quick shake of my eldest brother's head confirms my suspicions. Aside from the violence, she wasn't touched otherwise, meaning that although the assailant might get off on torturing women, the crimes may not be sexual in nature.

"She was alive for most of it," Thanatos continues, sighing heavily, "but she sustained the worst of the injuries post-mortem, if that's any consolation."

"Since when did you become a detective?"

Thanatos has always been more of the muscle than the brains to the bratva's operations—hell, all of us are—so either he's gotten a promotion, or he's taking a personal interest on account of Dad's unknown whereabouts.

He pinches his lips together. "You of all people should know that in order to survive, we have to adapt. I can't take out a target if I don't know how to find him first. Whoever is doing this is on the bratva's radar, so I've been tasked with finding him."

"And have you found him?"

Thanatos clenches his jaw and stares off into the distance. "No."

I change the subject to something much more important. "What about the break-in at Celia's? Any idea if they're connected?"

My brother nods toward the tablet in my hand. "Open the file from last week."

I open the indicated file and swipe through the images to recheck each one. I don't have to scroll far before my blood runs cold. This victim is lying on her front in the damp sand at the beach, her honey-blonde hair fanning out around her shoulders and an expensive evening gown hugging her curves. The warm sunrise highlights her caramel skin—and every burn tearing across it.

My heart fucking stops the longer I stare. This woman could be Celia's sister with how similar their features are to each other's.

"The guy has a type?" I tap the screen until I find the other victims' files, noting how they're all women of roughly the same age and build; pretty girls with winning smiles, perfect teeth, and immaculate manicures. Although they likely come from wealthy families, none of them are immediately familiar to me. Whoever the murderer is, he's either strategically picking women we don't protect as part of the bratva's network, or he's really good at avoiding us until now. "How did he find Celia?"

Thanatos shrugs. "She's a pretty girl. Anyone with half a brain would notice her."

I lift an eyebrow. "I didn't think you liked pretty girls, much less mine."

A vein in his neck throbs. "I *don't* like her."

"But you think she's pretty."

"Objectively-speaking, yes." His dark eyes narrow as he swallows, and for once, he doesn't seem like someone parading around with a major stick up his ass. He looks like a man struggling through an attraction to someone he hates.

"Mhm." I hand him back the tablet, unable to keep a smirk off my face. "You can come visit her anytime, you know. You have access to our apartment."

"I'm not interested in petsitting."

I quickly try another tactic. Regardless of if the murderer is our father, Celia will need updated protection if she's his type. Cage or no cage, she'll be in danger until he's captured. "What if I want to increase our security at the club?"

Thanatos closes his eyes and pinches the bridge of his nose. "I'm busy enough as it is. *Too* busy. I did you a favor by bringing her to you—*twice* now." He holds up two fingers, likely referencing their shared limo ride to *Midnight* in addition to his most recent abduction. "I'm not doing any more."

"I'll pay you, so it's not a favor. It's a job."

"Ezra's working me hard enough as it is." He takes a steadying breath, and by the way his shoulders drop, it seems like he really fucking needs it. "I'm actually surprised that Ezra doesn't have you running laps all over the city after what happened with Katya. We need new blood in our ranks if we're going to keep things running smoothly."

I know about Katya Dolohov's recent transgressions with our *pakhan*—transgressions that she died for. Good fucking riddance, if you ask me. The bitch was bound to die messy, and from what I hear, she got off easy.

"Regardless," I continue, "I want more security for the club. People are going to talk about the missing women once it goes public. Scared clients are bad for business."

Thanatos's mouth curves downward. "Talk to Ezra, then, not to me."

Grinning, I clap my brother on the shoulder. "You're his right hand man. Make it happen for me."

The sun begins to set in the distance, casting long shadows all around us. Thanatos's gaze flickers to each of them as he mentally surveys the perimeter like a bad habit.

"We're on the estate, brother." I squeeze his shoulder. "Relax. This place is safer than anywhere else in the city."

Security on the main house quadrupled once our *pakhan* Andrei brought his wife Valentina home after their botched wedding. Rumor has it that he pulled our men from the city's perimeter and housed them here, and honestly, I don't blame him for it.

Nothing is more important than keeping your woman safe.

I picture Celia kneeling in our new cage, peering up at me with those big, round, doe-eyes. Her full breasts popping out of her bra and the swell of her stomach on full display, her soft hands reaching for my shaft as I feed it to her through the bars—

Drawing a breath, I hold it inside my chest and let the pressure ease the burn of my blood rushing between my thighs. As gorgeous and tempting every fantasy I've conjured of Celia in the cage is, its purpose isn't inherently sexual. I need to keep her off the streets and out of the public eye until we catch the bastard who dared threaten her safety. If I let her wander freely through the city, she'll gain attention on account of who she is and how well she carries herself. Both stranger and acquaintance can't help but watch her every time she walks by— she's fucking mesmerizing.

And our killer knows it.

Thanatos frowns again, the lines around his mouth deepening. I'm not sure that he's happy to be back in the city, but it can't have been sunshine and rainbows outside of it, either. We haven't kept in contact during the years he was away—keeping track of him was difficult when he was constantly on the move, and it's not like he kept up with a burner phone or wrote home the old fashioned way. He's the oldest of my brothers—older than me, even—and has always looked out for us, going so far as to defect from the bratva once our father cut and run to escape trial. Thanatos's selfless nature hasn't changed in all the years that have passed since we were kids.

He's always trying to keep us safe, even from ourselves.

"She isn't good for you," he says finally, breaching the topic of conversation we've been skirting around. He crosses his arms over his chest. "Let her go, Rage."

I shake my head. "I can't do that." I made a promise to my woman, and I'm going to keep it no matter what.

He knows where I'm going with this. "Break your promise, then. I'd rather you compromise your code of ethics than be tied to someone who doesn't deserve you. She's not pregnant. You can still end this before it's too late."

My fists clench. "She *will* be. I'm not abandoning the mother of my children."

Thanatos sighs. "You could pick anyone, Rage."

I know. "It has to be Celia."

Although my attraction to Celia started the moment I laid eyes on her at the Baranova wedding, our connection goes beyond that now. She's wrapped my brothers around her finger—no easy feat—and despite her claims otherwise, she's just as drawn to us as we are to her. I see it. I *feel* it. We are meant to be together, all four of us, now into eternity.

"Keep her safe," I tell Thanatos, meeting his eyes. "If not for her, then for me."

If there's one way to get through to him, it's by reminding him that it's not just Celia he will be protecting—but all of us, too. If she goes down, we all do.

A beat of silence passes before he nods, albeit reluctantly. "Fine. But only until you let her go, Rage."

That won't happen, but it's pointless to argue. He's just as convinced as I am about Celia, only on opposing sides of the argument.

We walk together in silence to the main house to give our separate reports for the day. Once we're standing before our *pakhan* and his two top *vors*, one of which being Celia's brother Mikhail Monrovia, I bring up another order of business.

Bringing Thanatos home where he belongs.

It takes some convincing, but we work together to negotiate a way for my brother to reorganize his current commitments to join our security detail at the club. Andrei isn't thrilled about letting his wife's new favorite bodyguard go, but he understands the importance of keeping both family and business assets safe, so he relinquishes his queen's hold over my brother as her personal bodyguard to give him back to us.

Once Thanatos and I are getting into a car to head back to the club, he turns to face me. "I'm not sleeping in your apartment." His nose crinkles, like he's picturing the rest of us jerking off to our woman—or *on* her, which sounds fucking fantastic to me.

I relent, however, seeing as how he agreed to stay with us in the first place. "You can have the other wing, then. It's unfurnished if you don't count the gym equipment, but it's spacious. You'll have multiple rooms to fuck around in."

We make the rest of the drive in silence until the club comes into view. My body thrums with renewed energy at the prospect of seeing Celia again—and even better, *touching* her. Tasting her. Fucking her.

A sharp ache seizes inside my chest as I remember the last time I opened up to her and how poorly *that* ended. I press a fist to my sternum to quell the feeling. The truth is, when Celia handcuffed me to my car and left me to rot, she hurt me. Not physically—but the aftershocks of the betrayal still run deep, constantly reminding me that although she initially chose me, although she let me plant my hopes to start a family deep inside her womb, although we made promises to each other and made fucking *love* to keep them...

I wasn't enough for her to stay.

Who I am might even be the reason she left.

Thanatos, the sharp motherfucker that he is, notices my discomfort and gives me a pitying look. "The people we love are the ones who hurt us the most."

Sadly, that's the lesson we keep learning over and over and over again, the spiral of agony continuing until we're addicted not only to the pleasure, but also the pain.

Celia ignores me when I return to the apartment, choosing to stare at the ceiling rather than watch me cross the room into the kitchen. She's lying on her back on the padded bench I provided, with her knees drawn up and her arms crossed over her stomach. I can't see much of her on account of the blanket covering damn near her entire body, but the clothes she wore earlier today are still in a pile on the floor. At least she knows not to push her boundaries *too* much.

Ignoring me, however, will not go uncorrected. We haven't set any rules for her behavior while she's on a tight leash, but that changes tonight. She isn't going to sit there looking pretty all damn day and night.

She's going to learn how to greet—and serve—her future husband.

While I roll up my shirtsleeves and wash my hands in the kitchen sink, there's a knock on the door, signaling the arrival of dinner. "Rebel," I call out, "get that." I glance over my shoulder to gauge Celia's interest in either my arrival or the mystery knock, but she doesn't so much as look in either direction.

I suppose exchanging pleasantries would be too normal for people like us.

Rebel's the one who breaks the relative silence in the room, padding to the door and swinging it open for Dmitri, the club's head chef, to deliver our meals. He pushes the cart through the door but doesn't step inside the apartment.

No one enters except for us.

Dmitri, having been on our payroll for over a decade, knows better than to ask questions. He merely glances between Celia's cage, Rebel's total nudity, and my casual monitoring of it all with a nod of his head before turning on his heel and retreating to the back elevator to return downstairs.

"Thank God," Rebel moans, lifting a gleaming silver cloche to reveal a thick ribeye cooked to perfection. "I'm fucking *starving*." He grabs the plate and abandons the cart, stumbling to one of the bar stools and plopping down with enough force to rock the chair. Grabbing the steak with his bare hands, he tears into it with his teeth and swallows a bite whole. Blood drips down his fingers and wrists as he devours another bite and groans. "That's the fucking spot."

I'd normally tear my brother a new one for sitting on the furniture naked, but every lick of his lips piques Celia's interest. She watches the occasional drip from Rebel's steak land on his chest and trail down his abs.

If I listen closely enough, I can hear her stomach growl.

I hand Rebel a spoon for the mashed potatoes and leave him to scarf down his meal. There are three remaining steak dinners, a basket of fresh bread, and a chilled bottle of champagne sitting in an ice bucket waiting for me. I help myself to one of the dinner plates and stand across the island from Rebel so that I can keep an eye on Celia.

Will she beg for her meal?

The stench of alcohol cuts through the pleasant aroma of bread and charred meat, the offense wafting off of Rebel like he's bathed in vodka all afternoon. "Have you been drinking?" I clench my jaw tightly. He was supposed to watch Celia while I was gone—not get shit-faced for the hell of it. Not to mention, he has clients tonight, and they won't tip nearly as well if he reeks of booze and his performance suffers because of it. "Your shift starts in an hour. Go wash it off."

With a sarcastic salute, he takes a huge, messy bite of uncut steak, slips off the stool, and starts walking back toward his room, still chewing loudly enough to grate on my nerves. When he walks past Celia, he pauses to look at her.

She ignores him, which shouldn't be nearly as satis-fying as it is.

At least she's being a bitch to *all* of us.

Rebel scowls, taking another monstrous bite as soon as he's swallowed the first.

Celia's stomach suddenly growls, and I catch Rebel smirking at the sound. The steak melts in your mouth, so pulling a piece off to dangle it in front of her is easy. "Want some meat, baby?" His dick twitches close to her face, doubling in size in record time as he gets a half-chub.

I watch the display with curiosity. Rebel excels in choosing unorthodox methods just to fuck with people. He likes chaos, feeding off of it like a leech while the rest of us suffer.

Whatever he's doing works, getting our girl's attention more than ignoring her has. Celia sits up on the bench and swings her legs around, straddling the seat to face Rebel. She stares curiously at his dick for a moment before lifting her gaze to his face. "If that's supposed to tempt me, you're going to have to try harder." Lifting her hand, she pretends to measure his dick with her forefinger and thumb. "Seems a little small."

The smirk on Rebel's face freezes. "You won't think it's small the next time you're choking on it."

She lifts an eyebrow. "What makes you think there will be a next time?"

"There's *always* a next time."

She rolls her eyes and crosses her arms over her chest, pushing her tits up beautifully. "Be a good boy and listen to your big brother. You smell like a cheap bar."

Rebel, undeterred, bites back. "Wonder whose fault that is."

"I didn't hand you the bottle, Rebel."

He tosses the strip of steak pinched between his fingers through the side of the cage, glaring as it lands on her cleavage. It *plops*, leaving a bloody smear.

Fucking *children*.

With a growl, I slam my palms down on the countertop. "*Rebel,* get the fuck in the shower. *Now.*"

For once, he listens, retreating into his bedroom and slamming his bathroom door shut. I wait until I hear the shower start before wetting a clean cloth under the faucet and bringing it to Celia. We stare at each other for a tense moment before I break the silence. "Press your chest against the bars."

She plucks the piece of meat from her chest and tosses it across the room. Ignoring my order, she meets my eyes. "I'm not letting you touch my tits."

The corner of my eye twitches. "Come here, Celia."

She reaches for the cloth, but I pull it away before her fingertips slip through the bars. Exhaling hotly, she wipes the juices from her skin with the corner of a bedsheet. "There. Happy now?"

No, I'm *pissed.*

I swallow as much rage as I can and reach into my pocket for the key to her cage. "You will follow my orders when I give them. The *first* time, not the second." I walk to the other side of the cage and unlock the door. Cracking it open, I gesture for her to come through. "Come here." She hesitates, and I snap my fingers, pointing to the ground at my feet. "*Now.*"

Fire flashes in her eyes. "I'm not your fucking pet!"

"You will listen to me," I hiss, grabbing the cage door and ripping it open, "because I am the only one taking care of you!" Throwing my hand toward Rebel's bedroom doorway, I continue, "do you think *he* would have fed you, Celia?" Clicking my tongue, I jerk my chin toward the staircase leading up to Ruin's loft. "What about him? Would he have provided blankets and a place to sleep, or would he have left you on the floor to shiver to death?"

She stares wide-eyed at me. "You've got to be kidding me. You aren't *seriously* suggesting that what you're doing is for *my* benefit?"

"Of course it is!" I lunge for her, wrapping my fist

around her wrist and dragging her from the cage. She gasps, struggling to crawl without being dragged, and my heart twinges in my chest. I beat back the flicker of remorse by reminding myself why all of this is even necessary.

Everything I'm doing is for her own good. "You were in a goddamn *shack*, Celia. Rolling around in the dirt, ignoring the cockroaches breeding in the corner and the cracked back window. A *child* could have broken into that place." I picture a full-blooded adult high on whatever street drug he could get his grimy hands on, breaking into the house and finding Celia inside. She was vulnerable every single second she spent in that place. "You were *not* safe there, no matter how much you've convinced yourself otherwise." I bare my teeth as we come to a stop by the dinner cart and plant her ass on top of my shoes. Her body weight grounds me, the chilled skin in my hands reminding me that I need to be gentle.

She *can* break, and it's my responsibility to ensure that doesn't happen.

Reaching for the bottle of champagne on the cart, I pop open the top and revel in the way she flinches. Foam pours from the tip, dousing my hand and wrist and dripping all over Celia's body. It fizzles against her skin as it settles, its crisp taste bubbling on my tongue when I take a swallow straight from the bottle.

She gazes up at me, the fire in her eyes burning brighter than the sun. "You're fucking crazy."

Crazy for you, Mama.

"Open your fucking mouth."

Pressing her lips tightly together, she silently refuses.

Cradling her throat in my palm, I tilt her head back as far as it will go, palming the delicate curve between my thumb and forefinger. Pressing up and applying pressure, I cut off her windpipe. Most people don't realize how easy it is to restrict someone's air flow, but there are a thousand ways to take control—to grab the delicate life thread keeping a person conscious and rip it from their grasp. I hold on tightly, ignoring Celia's attempts to pry my hand loose. Her nails scratch my skin, creating shallow cuts that send sparks down my spine.

When I drop the bottle and hold my other hand over her mouth and nose, completely cutting off her oxygen supply, she digs painful grooves into my wrists and kicks her feet, uselessly banging her heels against the floor. Her eyes water, but not a single tear falls free.

I press an upside-down kiss to her forehead, then spread twin kisses across each of her cheekbones. "Stubborn girl."

She can't take much more without passing out, but I hold on, knowing that she'll cave. They always do, preferring to gasp for the life I graciously give them than to succumb to the unknown shadows that wait beyond the grave.

Seconds tick by. I count every single one, my frustration growing as we get closer and closer to the fifteen-second mark when most people pass out. I let up a little of the pressure on her neck so that she can snag some air, but her chest doesn't expand, and her lips don't move behind my palm in an effort to breathe.

I remove my hand from her face, expecting her to take a breath once she's free.

She glares up at me until the last second, her face flushed bright pink until the moment her eyes roll back and she faints, collapsing against my legs.

I cradle her head in my hands and lower myself to the floor, pulling her into my lap to check her pulse. It's slow, as expected after falling unconscious, and I take deep breaths to calm down.

No one *ever* chooses to willingly suffocate until they pass out. No one except for...

Me.

And now, my future wife, too.

I run my fingers through Celia's hair as I remember what it felt like to be at her mercy. The power she possessed. The determination. The thrill of being so important that she had to cut me out of her life or risk falling for me. I'm sure that she doesn't see it that way, but I know the truth she keeps denying.

We're meant to be together, and what happened here tonight proves it.

She's too scared to let herself have a good thing.

Rebel appears from his bedroom a few moments later, an unwelcome visitor to this monumental miscalculation. His gaze pings to Celia instantly, his eyes widening at the new bruising around her neck. "What the *fuck,* Rage." He rushes toward us and drops to his knees in front of her, holding his hands out like he wants to touch her but isn't sure where to land. Water drips from his hair onto her skin while he gingerly prods the bruises with his fingertips. Hissing, he snaps the collar from around her neck and tosses it to the floor. A heart-shaped print is embedded into her skin. "*This* is why she won't trust us. You're fucking everything up! Shit, man."

"She was supposed to concede," I growl, hugging her body to my chest. She remains limp, and although I know I haven't caused any permanent damage, Rebel might be right.

This will be another grievance that she holds against me.

"There's—" Rebel's eyes lock onto Celia's throat. "There's a heart." He traces the shape with his fingertip before leaning in and kissing it. His lips linger against her throat, likely without him intending it, and I wrestle with the knowledge that despite our fucked-up displays of affection, the three of us really *do* care for her.

Rebel rakes a hand through his messy wet hair and pulls his snakebite into his mouth. Groaning, he leans back on his haunches and shuts his eyes. "What are we doing, Rage? We can't—we don't—" He huffs and adjusts his sitting position until his legs are sprawled out in front of him, the tears in his dark jeans threatening to rip. "I don't like being this person." Rubbing his chest, he sighs.

I cage off my heart, knowing that if any of us softens, all of our plans will fall apart. "She deserves this." I brush my fingertips against her arm. "She deserves *us*. If we let her run off and do whatever she damn well pleases, she'll make a mistake. She'll choose wrong, just like she did before." I shake my head as I think of her idiot ex-husband, *Ted*, who doesn't deserve the air Celia fucking breathes. "I'm not letting her make those mistakes again. We're going to keep her safe and satisfied, like she deserves. We'll be the family she's always wanted."

She will learn to be grateful when she understands why this—the cage, the rules, the punishments and pleasures—is necessary.

Rebel's eyebrows pinch together. "She deserves *this*?" He stares at the bruising around her neck, the mottled purples and reds bleeding into the shapes of my fingers. "I'm pissed at her too, but I'll get over it. I think. Maybe." Standing, he brushes off his jeans and looks down at the two of us, a frown etched across his face. "Don't mistake your revenge as kindness, man. It's not pretty. And it won't—" He draws a breath—"it won't make her love you."

After my brother leaves to get ready for another night of counting cards for rich old men, I sit with my woman cradled in my arms for far longer than I should, indulging in her presence. I run my fingers through her silky hair, brush my lips across her temple, and whisper promises into her ear.

She may not ever choose to love me, but that doesn't mean I'll stop loving her.

I can't.

I *won't.*

If there's one good thing I can do in this life, it'll be for her.

Everything will be for her.

CHAPTER 4

CELIA

THE HEAVY *BANG* from a door slamming shut jolts me awake. My tongue feels like sandpaper, my throat hoarse and raw, my eyes glued shut. Prying them open takes a million years, then it takes a million more to sit up.

A tendril of smoke curls in the air a few feet away, the tip of a cigarette glowing as its owner inhales. Then Rebel's rings *click* as he wraps his fingers around the cage door and draws a breath. The room is pitch black, but I can make out his eyes and lips when he takes another pull from his cigarette.

Exhaustion stares back at me before the room goes dark. I smell the smoke as he breathes in my direction.

"Take a break, Ruin," Rebel mumbles, the sound of keys jingling making the hairs on my neck rise. "I've got her."

I squint in the darkness and look around for Ruin, but I never sense where he is. How long has he been watching over me? Have I been asleep the entire time?

My stomach cramps from hunger, and I choke on my next breath. *That* hurts, too, the sudden ache in my neck making it difficult to swallow. I think back to what happened before I fell asleep, and I remember Rage coming home, Rebel gnawing on a slab of steak, and then...

Swallowing painfully, I touch my throat and prod the tender spots with my fingertips. Then, I wrap my hand around my neck, and a violent shiver tumbles down my spine as a memory flickers. But my hand isn't large enough to match the bruises—someone else touched me here. Someone whose hands are warm and calloused and rough, just as dangerous as the rest of him.

Rage must have squeezed so hard that I passed out. Vaguely, I remember him covering not only my neck, but my face as well, cutting off my ability to breathe. It would be one thing if this were a game, some kind of kink in action, but I know that he didn't suffocate me to get his rocks off.

He did it to teach me a lesson.

One that I refused to learn.

Wincing, I remove my hand from my throat and take a shallow breath as I replay the scene in my head. I could have taken a breath before I passed out. Rage stopped covering my nose and mouth, perhaps expecting me to gasp for air, but I didn't.

I let the sweet relief that comes from unconsciousness pull me under, and I feel damn good about denying Rage the one thing he wants: obedience. If he wants a wife, he's going to have to learn that he can't force me into anything. I'll either go willingly, or not at all.

Even if it kills me.

Shadows suddenly shift in my field of vision, but by the time I realize what's happening, it's too late. I'm no longer alone inside my cage.

Fingertips ghost across my cheek, then a rumble of muted laughter follows. "Shhh, baby, or you'll wake the big bad wolf." Rebel chuckles again, and I can taste the alcohol and cigarettes on his breath. My stomach knots, fighting a wave of nausea and failing miserably.

Is this what my life has become? A series of assaults disguised as flirtation?

Rebel crouches in the cramped space while I sit up straighter, our legs touching through the quilt. Blessed warmth bleeds from his body into mine, and I resist the urge to crawl into his lap and hold him. He might get the wrong idea. No, he *would*. This is survival now, not desire, and I doubt he understands the difference between the two. "What are you doing here, Rebel?"

He plucks at the quilt wrapped around my thighs. "I live here."

Rolling my tired eyes, I wrap my arms around my stomach. "No, I mean, what are you doing *here*? In my —" I refuse to call this *my* cage—"bed?"

He hums to himself, playing with the blankets that make up my so-called bed. Ignoring my question, he instead asks, "wanna get out of here?"

My heart skips. Is he letting me go?

"What?"

Leaning closer, he slides his palm over my hip and sighs into my hair. "Do you," he whispers, "want to," his arm curls around my waist, "get out of here?"

The suggestion in his voice ignites desire deep in my body, and I choke on a response. My mind may understand the need for survival, but my heart clearly doesn't. I've always been attracted to Rebel, and this is the purest possible proof.

Some part of me still wants him, despite how fucked up my current situation is.

My mind races as I consider what he's asking. What will happen if I leave with him? Where will we go? What will we *do*? As Rebel's hand slips inside the blanket and wanders up my back, I nearly moan at how gentle his touch is—and how *warm*. If I were a cat, I bet I'd be purring, and that's *not* a good sign.

Rebel is just as much at fault—and as much of an asshole—as his brothers. He isn't off the hook just because, despite all sense, I still like him.

Clearing my throat, I finally manage to summon my voice. "What's the catch?"

He chuckles as he traces tiny circles into my lower back. "No catch, only..." His voice hums in my ear, sensual and alluring. "We can't get caught."

Anxiety flutters inside my chest. "Won't Rage find out?" I glance toward his where his bedroom door should be, but it's closed, the man himself supposedly sleeping just out of sight.

"Not if you can keep a secret."

This is a bad idea. A very, very bad idea that could

backfire any moment. But if I have any chance at a life outside of these gold bars, it's by winning these men over again... starting with the easiest target. I bite my bottom lip and make a hasty decision, praying that I won't regret it. "I can keep a secret."

He kisses my cheek, the hint of a smile on his lips. "I know you can, baby. Let's go."

We move quickly from the cage to his bedroom, Rebel leading the way through the relative darkness. Using only the blue LED backlight to see by, he tosses me one of his band t-shirts from his closet, then a black leather jacket and a pair of sweatpants. "Put those on." While I'm getting dressed, my stomach growls loud enough that I freeze, my eyes pinging to the wall separating Rebel's room from Rage's.

A muscle in Rebel's jaw tics as he stares at my stomach. "He didn't feed you?"

My face flushes. "I think, ah, I've been out cold all evening."

"Fucking bastard," he murmurs, running a hand down his face. "I thought he would—" Cutting himself off, he growls. "Piece of shit."

I throw on the t-shirt, admiring how soft the fabric is. It must be one of Rebel's favorites. I try not to smile as I put on the rest of his clothes. They look casual, but the material has that soft yet durable texture that means not only are the comfortable, but they're premium quality. Someone has expensive tastes. I glance up at Rebel to find him staring at me, another soft smile playing on his lips as I shrug on the leather jacket next. It feels like a dream—like we're stepping back into our lives from a week ago—and I try not to let it get to me. I really do, but... the jacket smells just like him, and I find myself smiling as I wrap it tighter around my body. Rebel's always had a charm to him, and even though we're not on good terms right now, I can still feel it—that magnetism between us. I catch him staring at me, and he doesn't look away until I do.

Yeah, he might be feeling it, too.

Clearing his throat, he gestures toward the door. "After you."

I hold my breath as we exit Rebel's bedroom and sneak through the apartment. It's only once we're in the hallway that I can breathe again, relief that we made it out alive washing over me. An unexpected twinge of regret makes me glance back at the door, though. If Rage were in a better mood—

Shaking my head, I stop that line of thinking before it has time to take root. He's more than just an asshole; he's a terrible person, and I can't forget all of the horrible things he's done just because I'm having a moment of weakness...

...or because some part of me still craves that gentler side of him—the one that's capable of love.

Rebel, unaware of my emotional problems, continues our mission by gesturing for me to walk in front of him. "There's a stairwell over here on the right. We're going up."

"Up?" We're already on the second floor. "How tall is this building?"

"Three stories, but the third is only Ruin's loft and an attic. The rest is rooftop."

"So we're going to... an attic?"

Rebel places his hand on the small of my back to guide me forward. "Don't chicken out now."

When we reach the top of the stairs, I'm expecting dust and decay as Rebel pushes open the door, but instead, a gust of cold winter air greets us. We emerge onto a rooftop patio, complete with a bar, a simple metal patio table with three chairs, and a sun lounger forgotten in the corner. A small set of stairs leads to a walkway that disappears over the ledge, likely for a fire escape, and the sprawling city looms all around us. Lights of all shapes and colors dot the streets below, the most prominent being the diner across the street—aptly named *The Diner* —and a tattoo shop a block over. Both businesses scream OPEN in bright pink and blue displays.

"Where are we?" I don't recognize this part of the city. Despite being at the club several times now, I've never been allowed to see anything outside of my blindfold during transit. I glance over the ledge and find a red carpet rolled out below, a line of guests waiting to enter the building. "The club actually runs?"

"Like normal," Rebel answers from a distance, "yeah. We can't keep this place running on kinky sex nights alone. She has to earn her keep like the rest of us."

I glance over my shoulder to find him at the bar. My stomach drops while he rummages through rows of bottles. "Haven't you had enough tonight?" I step up to the bar and lean across it to snag his chosen bottle from his hand. The glass is freezing cold, but I don't dare let go. "Your liver's already swimming, Rebel. Give it a break."

He scoffs, pulling back empty-handed. "Didn't realize you cared." He shoves his hands in his jacket pockets—a leather one that matches mine—and glares at the vodka in my hand. "But fine, drop it and we'll go." Once I've set the bottle onto the bar, he leads me to the ledge of the rooftop, takes the three steps up to the walkway I noticed earlier, and spins around to wait for me. As soon as he's confident that I'm following him down the fire escape, he continues down the half-flights of stairs, only pausing to make sure I'm still behind him.

The back of my neck prickles as we reach the bottom. I look over my shoulder, expecting to see Rage come tumbling down the stairs after us. If he follows us outside, would we see him or hear him first?

"Chill out," Rebel grumbles, taking my hand and leading me down the last flight of stairs. "You're ruining the fun." We cross the street in silence, the bright, neon sign signaling *The Diner* lighting our path. The bell over the door chimes as we enter, and Rebel lifts a hand toward one of the wait staff before leading me down the long row of booths lining the front windows and picking our table. It's the one at the very end of the row, nestled into the corner of the restaurant.

Once I'm settled onto the seat, he slides in beside me, then drapes his arm over the back of our booth.

"What are you doing?" I look between him and the

perfectly-empty other side. "There's plenty of room over there."

"Let's get one thing straight." Gripping my chin, he turns my face toward his. "Just because we're fighting right now, doesn't mean that you are any less *mine*." He brushes his thumb across my bottom lip, his dark eyes swirling with emotion. "But I'm not kissing you, no matter how fucking tempting it is, because I *am* mad."

Our server arrives and Rebel orders a double cheeseburger with fries and a Coke, and I order the same in my rush to pick something. Rebel smirks, his fingertips brushing the tips of my left shoulder. "Rage is *so* going to flip his shit when he finds out I'm feeding you greasy burgers and fries."

I'm mesmerized by the stubble on his chin, the easygoing manner in which he makes everything feel so effortless, the way he touches me so gently even when he says he won't. It takes me a moment to gather my thoughts, and Rebel spends the time staring right back at me, the slow curve to his lips delicious and sinful. "I thought he wasn't supposed to find out?"

"Oh, he will. This whole area?" Rebel twirls his finger in a circle. "We own it. Well, technically your brother does since his name's on all the legal docs, but *we* run this part of town. Rage focuses on the club more than anything, but I pay regular visits to the other fine establishments on the strip. The diner, the tattoo shop, the vape store—there's even a valet for the club, so we run the lot, too, and everything in between." Winking at me, he smiles. "How do you think I got so sexy, baby? All my tats and piercings come from right here." He raps his knuckles on the table. "On home turf."

I glance at the other customers drinking coffee or scarfing down waffles, then I watch the staff as they move around the room and crack jokes with each other. Everything looks so... normal. "You're saying that the bratva owns this? They run this place?"

Rebel nods. "And all the others. We're not all heartless murderers and depraved criminals, you know." He takes a slow sip of his soda. "Sallie-Mae over there is working doubles to take care of her little brother since her parents are sacks of shit, and George on the grill has two little girls at home. But he's got a hell of a right hook, so he's run security for us a few times. We keep him out of the most dangerous runs, though, on account of his wife and kid. Then, see that couple over there?" He nods toward two teenagers out past their curfew. "That's Rina and Neve Ruskov. They're step-siblings, but you wouldn't know it, lookin' at 'em."

The teenagers are, in fact, sitting *really* close to each other. Neve, the boy, leans over to whisper something in Rina's ear, and her face flames bright red. They throw cash on the table and leave in record time, following each other closely to their car.

I bite my lip. "Shouldn't we tell their parents?"

Rebel laughs, his shoulders bouncing, while Sallie-Mae slides our burgers in front of us. As he shakes a ketchup bottle, he says, "trust me, they already know." He digs into his food, groaning as the first meaty, cheesy bite hits his tongue.

My stomach growls loudly, so I pick up a thin fry, dip it into Rebel's ketchup, and take a bite. Salt explodes on my tongue, the cool ketchup soothing the bite. I lick my lips and a wave of nostalgia washes over me.

I haven't eaten French fries in *years*.

Rebel pinches a handful of fries between his fingers and pops them into his mouth while I go slow and steady, savoring every bite. The Coke is sticky sweet and bubbly, and I suck it down greedily. Once Rebel notices, he replaces my empty glass with his half-full one until Sallie-Mae refreshes them. She smiles prettily at us, her eyes a gorgeous blue and her blonde hair pulled back into a neat ponytail. "Good to see you again, Rebel," she says warmly, still smiling. "Been busy lately? We've missed you on Friday nights."

He takes a sip of his drink before nodding. "You know how it is, Mae. Winter keeps those stiff-fucks indoors, and that's where I shine best." There's a bite of sarcasm in his voice, but neither of them comment on it. Instead, he closes his hand over my shoulder and squeezes. "This is my girl, Celia. Anytime you see her on the street, you say hello, okay?"

Sallie-Mae turns her bright smile onto me. "Of course! Any friend of Rebel's is a friend of mine. He's helped me out more than I can ever say. So anything you want, darlin', you just holler."

Lifting a finger, Rebel clicks his tongue. "Celia's not my *friend*, Mae, she's my *girlfriend*." To emphasize his point, he presses a tender kiss to my cheek. "Make sure everyone knows it."

She clears her throat, careful to keep her smile in place. "Of course. I'll spread the word."

Once Sallie-Mae has slipped into the back, Rebel relaxes.

My stomach churns all of a sudden, and I push my plate away. Sallie-Mae is friendly enough that Rebel feels the need to stake his claim over me, and something about it rubs me the wrong way. Clearing my throat, I try to keep my voice from shaking. "Have you fucked her?" I ask, keeping my voice down.

Rebel freezes, his drink halfway to his lips.

"I mean, it's okay if you have." My face heats. God, I've never had to have a conversation like this before, and it makes me feel really juvenile. Finding out that your husband is having an affair? Gut-wrenching. Asking your sometimes-boyfriend if he's had sex with another woman? Somehow, it feels like a precursor to bad news. I die a little inside as new, post-divorce insecurities rear their ugly heads. I never used to question my partner's loyalty, but now I feel like it's as inevitable as breathing. I shouldn't have even asked, but now that the genie is out of the bottle, I can't shove it back inside. Rebel is staring at me with this bewildered look on his face, like he can't believe what he's hearing as much as I can't believe I'm still talking about it.

"It's not like I have ownership over you. And you clearly have a life I know nothing about. It's just that I —" Flustered, I fidget with a paper napkin and tear it into strips. "I need to know, so that I don't feel like an idiot when she smiles at me like that."

Like she knows what it means to be Rebel's special girl.

"I know that it's none of my business—"

Rebel abruptly grabs my face in his hands and slams his mouth over mine, and suddenly, the booth isn't big enough for the two of us. He pins me to the seat, bumping the table across the booth as he presses his body as close as humanly possible to mine, suffocating any hope I had for space from his hot-and-cold attitude. I'm getting whiplash...

...until he kisses me like *that*.

His lips are a salty mess, but they slide against mine with a fervor that leaves no room for imagination. He might be angry with me for running away, but that hasn't changed a damn thing about how he feels about *us*.

Heat sizzles between us, and I grab the edges of his jacket to pull him closer. There's nothing nice about this kiss—it's hot and fast and damn delicious, setting my body on fire and making my heart skip three beats. He pulls back just enough to smirk against my lips. "Jealousy tastes so fucking good on you, baby."

His smirk still in place, he plops back down on the bench and chuckles as he fishes a handful of bills from his wallet. Tossing them onto the table, he slides from the booth and pinches his snakebite between his teeth while he waits for me to stand.

I stand as fast as I can, ignoring Sallie-Mae's cheerful goodbye as I rush out of the diner and onto the cold street. I shiver immediately, the high from

Rebel's kiss making the crash of reality that much harder.

He never answered my question. I take that as a *yes*, he's fucked Sallie-Mae, probably more than once. I'm so stupid for feeling jealous about it, but I can't help it. What if it's like Rebel said? He frequents all of the businesses on the strip. He could have slept with *anyone*. What if that's his thing? Is he well-known and well-liked because of how well-fucked he is? Is that why I find him so charming? He's practiced?

Rebel doesn't miss a beat, grabbing my hand and pulling me to a stop. The smile on his face disappears instantly. "Hey, talk to me, don't run away."

I laugh, the sound falling past my lips like dominos crashing. "What are we doing?" Shaking my head, I try to reign in my bitterness at how fucked-up our relationship is. "You say you won't kiss me, but then you call me your girlfriend and practically shove your tongue down my throat. Now we're just gonna go back to, *what*, locking me up in a cage while you drown yourself in alcohol? How is that okay?"

Late-night mist fogs the air and clings to our skin, blurring the lights from the diner and making the streetlights glow in an orange haze. Rebel holds onto my hand, refusing to let me go. "We're figuring this out, Celia. You *are* my girlfriend, at least I *think* so. Fuck, baby, I don't know what to call it, but does it matter? You're mine just as much as you are Rage's, and if I have to put you in that goddamn cage to keep you from running from me again, I fucking will." He drags me into his chest and slips his hand into my hair, tilting my head back to peer into my eyes. The orange light reflects like copper in his eyes, warm and melted like caramel. The mist clings to his hair, sparkling as he moves, making him even more beautiful than he already is.

It's hard to stay angry when he looks at me like he's falling in love.

"I've never done this before, so I'm going to fuck up sometimes," he murmurs, sweeping his thumb across my damp cheekbone. "But that doesn't make this any less real, okay? I want you, Celia. I want you more than I want air." He presses our foreheads together and sighs. "I know I can be a dick about it, so just... give me time... to figure this all out."

I lean into his warmth and try to process what he's saying. It feels like I'm the one falling—faster than I can see, the earth sliding out from under my feet, without any idea of which way is *up* anymore. I wrap my arms around his body and he melts into me, damn near purring like a cat. "Okay," I breathe, pressing my face into his neck, "let's figure this out. Together."

He presses a quick kiss to the top of my head. "You got it, *mama.*"

Snorting, I roll my eyes. "Please don't call me that." My heart jumps at the implication, both fearful and hopeful at the same time. How can something that's supposed to be beautiful and radiant feel so complicated?

Rebel pulls away and fondles the collar at my throat, the heart pendant as warm as his fingers. I'd forgotten I had it on.

"Why not? Are you saving it for Rage?"

"No." I scrunch my nose. "He's the last person who deserves it."

Especially if he *forces* a baby on me. There is no going back from that.

Biting his bottom lip, Rebel gets this goofy look on his face. It's quickly replaced by the usual suave smirk and glittering mischief, but I saw it—for one brief moment, Rebel looked like the most ridiculous, love-struck idiot on the planet.

I have no idea what he was thinking, and it's over so fast that I can't ask. In an instant, he's gone back to being completely composed, oozing sex appeal as though it comes as natural to him as breathing. "Can I..." He slips his fingers into the waistband of my sweatpants and teases my hip. "Can I show you something?"

"It's not your dick, is it?"

He throws his head back and laughs. "No, baby, not this time." Squeezing my hip, he spins me around and gently pushes me down the sidewalk. "It's just over here. It'll be a quick detour, and then we'll get you back to your cage, I promise." Although he winks like he's joking, I know that it's only a matter of time before I'm locked away again.

"Fine," I agree, walking into the unknown with Rebel at my heels. "One detour." He whoops loudly, making me laugh right along with him.

Figuring things out between us might take time, but for tonight, I'm okay just going along for the ride.

CHAPTER 5

CELIA

As we walk a few blocks down the sidewalk, I'm grateful for Rebel's leather jacket. The winter chill has set in for the season, which would normally bring a new wave of products into my boutique. Pashmina scarves, knit hats, and woolen gloves, either displayed to match or paired in various color-combinations, all designed to entice the eye in addition to keeping its owner warm. My soul mourns the fact that I'm wearing my worn leather boots and Rebel's baggy sweatpants instead of a soft cashmere ensemble, awash with gentle cremes and beiges that provide a delicate, fresh look for any woman—and for me especially. White is my signature color, and I always look forward to the first winter frost to show off my latest look.

Rebel's clothes, consisting of a smattering of dark grays and blacks, faded band logos and soft beanies, is the opposite of everything I stand for. But matching outfits with him as we wander the late night streets in the hazy glow of cold moonlight makes me feel more at ease by his side. We blend in with the night—and with each other.

A few minutes after leaving the diner, we approach a gated lot filled with cars of all shapes and sizes, nearly all of them gleaming to perfection. Sports cars catch my eye first, each one of them beckoning me closer. My ex-husband used to own a sleek black convertible, and when we were at our happiest, he would take me for joyrides all over the city just to see me smile.

I'm sure he took his secretary too.

Thinking of Ted's affair sours the memories of zipping past streetlights with the wind roaring in my ears, but only for a moment. Rebel works as an easy distraction as he approaches the guard shack at the front of the lot and greets the two security officers with a friendly smile and smack to their shoulders. While he makes small talk, I check out our location. The lot is well-maintained like the rest of the street, the four-story parking garage pristine and damn near shining, even in the middle of a misty night. Not only is every square inch of the property well-lit and covered in cameras, but each parking space is numbered with bright white paint and every car hosts a valet ticket on its dashboard.

When I start to wander too far, Rebel beckons me back to him and immediately drapes his arm over my shoulder. "Boys, meet Celia Monrovia. She's priority number one, got it? If the lot's on fire and you can only save one thing, you save her, got it?"

That's ridiculous. We're standing next to a Ferrari. A very expensive, twin-engine Ferrari that likely carries more horsepower than I'll ever experience in my life. If that beauty goes down in a fire, its owner is going to be furious that I was spared in place of their precious baby.

But maybe to Rebel, I'm just as important as that Ferrari is to its owner.

Rebel presses a kiss to the top of my head and leads us inside the guard shack. It's simply-decorated but oozing money, with plush leather couches, an expensive espresso machine, and a state of the art security system with twelve monitors that seem to cover the entire lot. Rebel gestures to the key rack along the far wall, dozens of key rings and car fobs hanging before our eyes. "Pick a ride, baby. Anything you like." He kisses my cheek. "But if you choose a four-seater, I'm overruling you. Gotta pick something with *style*."

Adrenaline rushes through my veins as I stare at the endless rows of keys, each one sporting a numbered tag. I know exactly which car I want without having to browse the rest of the lot. The chance to test drive a dream car makes me giddy with excitement, and I bounce over to the wall to make my selection. Rebel smiles as he watches me scan the numbers for the one I want. It doesn't take long until I've found it.

Number twelve: the cherry red Ferrari I spotted just outside.

"Good choice," Rebel muses, watching me snatch the keys as quickly as I can. I'm vibrating as I lead the way to spot twelve. Sliding into the front seat feels smooth as silk, the interior polished to perfection and wicked soft.

Once I push to start, I run my hands over the steering wheel as I listen to her purr.

"Never took you for a car girl." Rebel props his foot on the dashboard as soon as he's seated, his lips curving into a smirk. He watches me fondle the stitched leather seat. "It's hot."

I don't advertise my affection for fast cars. It's not a dainty little hobby for bratva girls to love. "My ex-husband drove a fast car," I explain, biting my bottom lip. "He's the one who introduced me to them."

And took them away when we were trying to conceive. All for the safety of the baby he gave his secretary instead of me.

My heart pangs in my chest, but I beat back the pain with a grin that's real enough. A silver fox pendant glints beneath the rearview mirror, the only personal item in the cab. "Whose car is this?"

Rebel shrugs. "Don't know, don't care. Push the gas, baby; let's get out of here."

He doesn't have to tell me twice.

As soon as we pass the gate and hit the street, I slam down the gas and we go flying. Rebel holds onto the roof of the car and grins, his bright smile warming my heart. "Turn here, baby," he directs, taking us down a long stretch of road, "and floor it!"

The car punches forward, both of us cackling as we zip across double lines and ignore every local traffic law. We weave in and out of cars, ignore speed limits, and can't keep our eyes off of each other for a damn minute.

It's dangerous. It's reckless. But *holy shit*, is it fun.

"Damn, girl." Rebel flicks his gaze from the street-lights back to me, his eyes sparkling with every neon light we fly past. "Who knew you could *drive*." He licks his lips and unabashedly palms his crotch, the thick outline of his dick making me do a double-take. "You're hot as hell, baby."

I shake my head with a tiny laugh. "Who knew you could get me into a car like *this*." I spread my palm across the dash, appreciating her beauty. "I might've sucked your dick for a ride like this." My face flushes bright crimson at the confession, and although I'm not sure if I really mean it, Rebel latches onto my words in an heartbeat.

"Yeah?" He bites his lip, sucking his snakebite into his mouth. "We've still got time, if you're interested." Flexing his hips, he stretches out as much as possible, giving me a generous eyeful of his abs and the tuft of hair disappearing behind the waistband of his skinny jeans.

It takes effort, *so much effort*, to keep us from swerving. Giggling and feeling ridiculous about it, I turn on a familiar road that leads up to a hilltop overlooking this part of the city. It's known as North Side's Makeout Point, and although I've lived in Harlin Heights my entire life, I've never actually brought anyone up here—or been invited. Courtesy of being a mafia daughter with a protective twin brother—the boys stayed away all through high school, and I never went to college. The most I've learned about running a business came from online courses on Youtube and whatever snippets I've gleaned from conversation with my brother. Not foolproof, but good enough with the right amount of money to throw at things.

My lack of dating experience means, however, that aside from my ex-husband, I haven't really been with anyone long enough for something as cheeky as a trip to Makeout Point.

We park at the midway point, as far away from the other cars idling along the ridge as possible. There are only a few hanging around, but two of them are fogged up on the inside and one is rocking. I'd rather pretend they don't exist than admit that whatever they're doing might actually be something I'm curious to try.

Good girls don't fantasize about having sex inside a Ferrari.

Rebel stretches lazily once we're parked and settles into his seat. "Never took you for a Makeout Point girl, either," he muses, a smirk on his lips. He reclines the seat and pats his lap. "Climb on over, beautiful. I want to feel you."

Okay, maybe *this* good girl indulges the fantasy a little.

My body is on fire before he even touches me. Somehow, I manage to swing my body over the console and settle onto his lap, straddling his waist while leaning across his chest. He hums happily and plants his hands on my hips, grinning up at me with boyish charm. He flicks the hair from his eyes and rubs his palms up and down my waist, slipping his hands inside my shirt to touch my skin. His fingers are cold, making me shiver as goosebumps trail down my arms. Kissing my wrist, he pins me with a heated stare.

"You're beautiful, Celia."

I bite my bottom lip, my nerves ratcheting higher. "Tell me something else." I've always been known within the bratva as *the pretty one*, and I'm starting to think that beauty isn't all it's cracked up to be. It makes it easier to run a fashion business when people want to look like me, and it makes it easier to attract men like Rebel when I doll myself up in kitten heels and a little black dress, but tonight, I don't want to be pretty.

I want to feel *real.*

Rebel studies me for a moment, suddenly cupping my ass. "You're a know-it-all."

Gasping, I smack his chest. "What! I am not!"

"You *are!*" He grins. "You always think you know everything, and I get it. You're used to calling the shots, or whatever. You wanna be Miss Independent." He slides one of his hands up my waist until he reaches my chest, gently tapping the space over my heart. "I know your ex hurt you, but I'm not—*we're* not him. None of us want to control you, baby; we just want what's best for all of us."

The electric buzz in the air fizzles out, my happiness fading fast. I sit up, rocking back on Rebel's obvious erection with the movement, and force myself not to focus on how hot and hard he is beneath me. I cross my arms over my chest, forcing Rebel's hand away. "How is locking me in a cage not about being in control? How is forcing me to my knees in front of a crowd of people not about control?" I shake my head. "You say one thing, but then you guys do the opposite. You only want me if it fits inside your perfect parameters."

Rebel raises an eyebrow. "Sounds pretty fucking familiar."

Warmth blooms across my cheeks as I blush at being called out so easily. "That's not true."

Except... Aren't I the one pushing them out of my life because I don't think they fit within it?

I cringe, pursing my lips. "Okay, maybe it's a little true, but—"

"No buts. Celia, baby, if we're going to make this work between us, between *all* of us, you're gonna have to relax those boundaries and let us in. All this fighting? It's only gonna hurt. That's all Rage wants, you know, for you to accept him. Every time you tell him no, he's gonna hold on tighter and tighter until one of you breaks."

Rebel sits up and wraps his arms around my waist, tilting his head back to gaze up at me. His eyes reflect the glowing city behind me, burning with warmth that burrows deep in my chest and wraps around my pounding heart. "I don't wanna have to put you back together. I want to keep you just as you are, whole and healthy and full of life. Because you *are* beautiful, and not just for that ass." He squeezes my butt and grins wickedly. "You're beautiful because you're so fucking stubborn and headstrong and out of my goddamn league. I could throw my whole life away just to see where your light shines next." Nuzzling my jaw, he skims his lips over mine. "You're dynamite, girl, and you blow me the fuck away."

Tears pool in the corners of my eyes, my heart swelling with emotion I don't dare name. Falling for Rebel is bad news. I'm supposed to be running away right now, not straddling his lap in a Ferrari!

It's like he reads my mind. "You wanna run away and start a new life?" He smacks my ass. "Start the engine, baby, and let's roll." Rolling his hips for effect, he moans unabashedly, shuddering as he drags in a lungful of air. "But if you want to stay and build a life here—with us— it won't be easy, and we're all gonna have to learn to give a little on these boundary things, but it'll be so goddamn worth it." The conviction in his voice settles into my bones, giving me strength I hadn't known I needed.

Could we actually make this work?

"So *please*." He lifts my t-shirt shirt and bends to press a gentle kiss to my chest, directly over my heart. "Stop running. Let us love you—let *me* love you."

My heart hammers loudly, willing me to fall. To let go. To say, *fuck it*, and give him what he wants.

Because in the end, I might want it, too. More than I've wanted to admit.

With Rebel, I can picture the future I've always imagined.

Cupping his face in my hands, I let myself fall— leaping headfirst alongside the lightning beat of his heart, against the hard lines of his body, and into whatever comes next. Our lips crash together, and the groan rever- berating inside Rebel's chest leaves me buzzing from the sound. "Do that again," I rasp, my eyes fluttering shut as his teeth skim my jaw.

He chuckles. "Oh, did you like tha—*oh, fuuuuck.*"

As I grind down on top of his iron-hard length, he moans loudly, flopping back onto the seat to gaze up at me through half-lidded eyes. Biting his bottom lip, he thrusts up, smirking when I gasp. "That's it, baby, take what you want. I need you to feel good." Cupping my breasts, he squeezes, massaging them and pinching my nipples between his knuckles. The thin red lace bra doesn't hide anything, and within seconds, he's rolling my nipples into hard peaks. I keen as pleasure ripples through me, soaking my panties and making me writhe that much harder on top of him.

Rebel curses under his breath, both of us panting. "*Fuck*, baby, *fuck.*"

Slipping off the leather jacket and pulling my t-shirt over my head, I gasp as he suddenly tears the lace down to free my tits. Massaging them in his warm palm, he moans again, lifting his hips as he chases his high. When I reach down to undo his belt, he bucks up into me, hissing as my nails scratch his abdomen. "That's right, pull me out, baby, feel how hard I am for you." Lifting my hips, I shove his jeans down as much as I can, finding him bare underneath. His cock springs free, just as hard as promised, hot and silky-smooth when I grab the shaft. Twin piercings, two silver balls just beneath the head, gleam in the lowlight, and I gently brush my thumb over them.

He gasps, tossing his head back as I stroke him hard.

"*Fuck.*" Pre-cum leaks from the tip, and I smear it across his slit, making him pant harder. "Don't tease me, just— just let me feel you, baby." He reaches for my waistband, but I smack his hand away. Eyes wide, he watches as I spit on his dick and continue stroking, his body twitching every time I pull his skin over the head and rub directly over his piercing. "F-fuck," he stutters, biting his lip. "You're driving me crazy, Celia, baby, *please.* Fuck, don't tease me."

My body is on fire, but Rebel looks like he's about to combust. Sweat breaks out across his forehead and chest, a flush trailing down his neck and across his tattoos. Their colors are muddied in the yellowed streetlight, but the flex of his muscles beneath the skin is clear as day. He thrusts in time with my hand, puffing hot air every time he exhales. "C-Celia," he moans, biting his lip. "Baby, you're gonna make me—" His breath catches as more pre-cum spills from the tip of his cock. "So close. Please. Let me—*ah!*"

I reach between us and cup his balls, massaging them while I stroke his shaft. My back and shoulders scream at me to switch positions, but I don't dare, not when Rebel's clawing at the car door and writhing in the leather seat.

Whoever said that men can't come from hand jobs was fucking *lying.*

Rebel comes hard, a whine tearing through his throat as his hips jerk up into my palm, thick ropes of his cum splashing against his abs. I stroke him through it gently, saying the first, unfiltered thing that comes to mind—

"Good boy."

He shudders at the praise, moaning as another spurt of cum coats my fingers. Still panting, he reaches for my free hand and squeezes tightly.

I bring his hand to my lips and kiss his knuckles. "Such a good boy, coming for me," I continue, enjoying the way his cheeks flush. "Do you feel good, baby?" I squeeze his cock, enjoying its twitch in my palm.

He bites his plush bottom lip and swallows. "Y-yes."

I smile brightly, elated that I can elicit such a strong response from him. "Me too." I cup his jaw and lean in to kiss the wide-eyed look off his face. We melt into each other, humming with each press of our lips. Rebel runs his fingers through my hair and deepens the kiss, using his other hand to drag my hips higher, trapping his slick cock beneath me. It's already growing in size, thickening with each flick of our tongues.

As much as I'd love to have sex right now, I don't know how to handle the backlash if Rage finds out, and that uncertainty is enough for me to break away.

The soft, dazed look on Rebel's face makes it hard to sit up. "We should head back," I murmur, pressing a quick kiss to his forehead. "Thanks for the ride."

He sobers up fast, huffing loudly as he runs a hand through his sweat-slicked hair. "Not fair. Let me get you off. I bet you're *soaked.*" His eyes travel my body from my tits to my hips. "I can feel how hot you are down there. Scorching." With a slow thrust, he presses his cock against my core, making me shiver with heat. He tugs at my sweatpants, pulling them down an inch. "C'mon, take these off. Let's go for a *real* ride."

I bite my lip, the temptation tipping the scales in Rebel's favor. "Won't he find out?"

"He? Who—*Rage?*" Rebel blinks, stunned into silence for a split second, before surging up to kiss me hard, his tongue and teeth working together to make me whine with need. When he pulls back, his eyes are steely. "You're thinking about *my brother* right now, when I'm trying to fuck you?" Thrusting his hips into mine, he hisses, "*fuck that.* Sit on my cock, baby, and I'll show you how a *real* man fucks."

I hesitate, knowing that it's a bad idea, but also knowing that my body is begging for release, wound tight from all the kissing and grinding. "Won't I be fucking you since I'm on top?"

Rebel flashes me a cocky grin. "Time to fuck around and find out."

Chapter 6

——

Rebel

Fuck.

This girl will be the death of me, wringing every last drop of pleasure from my body with the tiniest flutter of her eyelashes and the simplest of phrases on her lips—

Good boy.

I shiver in anticipation as she splays her palm flat on my chest and lifts her hips, both of us working together to rid her of those pesky sweatpants. Having her wear my clothes is hot, but it's even hotter when she takes them off. Her creamy thighs are a gift from Heaven, soft to the touch and warm—so goddamn warm—as they wrap around my hips.

Fuck.

She settles into my lap slowly, her bottom lip wedged between her teeth and tresses of long, luxurious hair spilling across her shoulders. She looks like a fucking goddess—a *fucking* goddess, if things go according to plan—and my cock twitches to life, aching and full and so goddamn ready to plunge inside of her.

I've been waiting far too long for this.

Rage had his turn and fucked that shit up so bad that she ran—now, it's my turn to fix things. I don't know if a woman can fall in love from receiving S-tier dick, but I'm sure as hell gonna try.

But *damn*, am I in danger of falling for her first.

It doesn't matter that I'm supposed to be angry with her. When we're together, none of the bullshit makes sense anymore, and I find myself forgetting to care about anything but the woman right in front of me.

Celia blushes, her face as warm as her thighs. I cup her rosy cheeks and pull her down on top of me for an earth-shattering kiss, groaning into her mouth when she lets me in. *She lets me in.* Fuck, I never thought kissing Celia could get any better, but this moment proves me wrong.

Everything about the way I'm feeling proves the rest of the goddamn world wrong—having a girlfriend cradle your fucking ballsack and praise you for the mega load you're about to deliver is so delicious, I might never go back to whatever I was doing before, because clearly, I was living life with my glass half empty. Now, all I wanna do is ensure that no matter what, I fill that bad boy up until it overflows.

Starting with the gorgeous woman in front of me..

I gasp for air when she goes for my throat, nipping my Adam's apple and giggling, still too in her head, still a little shy, uncertain about what to do with her hands or how to be the one in charge.

"Have you ever done this before? On top?"

She stills, her heart beating like a drum, loud enough that I can hear it. "Once." Sighing into my ear, she presses her tits against my chest, the lace of her bra catching on my skin, on all the scars she has yet to ask about.

When she does, I'll tell her how hot the fire burned, but the flames of Hell don't compare to how hot she makes me.

Yeah, that's a dumb line.

But when she's like this, with all her delicate skin on display, trembling with every touch of my hands on her body, I don't care how stupid it sounds.

Everything she makes me feel is real, from the frustration that boils in my gut to the visceral agony tearing its way through my flesh, down to the harsh sinew of my bones, the jagged cut of my teeth and the burning fire in my blood, all the way back up to the heavy pump of my heart, covering my soul in her softness, her glow. All the rough parts of me turn gentle in her hands, and she doesn't even realize it.

Sometimes, she makes me believe that if the fire had never happened and I was a regular guy with a regular job, I could have made her happy in the kind of way she always wanted. We would have fit together without friction, without all the tension and bickering and uncertainty, because we both would know that *this feels right* from the start.

Neither of us would run. Or fight. Or bleed. We'd have this seamless connection right from the start.

I bury my hand in her hair and press my nose against her temple, breathing in the delicate scent of her soap mingling with the tang of her sweat. I don't like to think of her screwing other men, but I have to ask, "Was he good to you?" I pray that she says no, that I'll get the chance to be her first good thing in this position. A memory she'll hold onto forever.

Her throat clicks on a swallow. "Um... I think so. Sort of."

That's not *nearly* good enough. My heart soars as the possibility of being her first good lay like this materializes before my eyes. I can taste it, like honey mixed with wildfire. "What do you mean?"

"I came," she admits softly, "but it wasn't really..." Her lips twist against my skin. "Like I imagined it would be."

I dig my fingertips into her hips to keep myself from moving too fast, because fuck, do I wanna move fast. But this feels important, and the confident woman who called me her *good boy* isn't here right now. "Tell me how you imagined it." I scratch her scalp, and she relaxes, melting on top of me.

Better.

She exhales slowly. "I don't know, I thought I would feel powerful, I guess."

"Why didn't you?" There's no reason she shouldn't have been in charge while on top. Unless the guy was an asshole—or trying to come really fast—but the two aren't mutually exclusive. I mean, even if I *do* fuck her from the bottom, she's gonna have me begging for her to sink that slick pussy down over me harder, faster—

"He doesn't really give me room to breathe."

Present tense, not past, like the man in question is still around.

Blood pumps heavy as iron through my veins as I piece together the only possible man that could be—my piece of shit older brother. The fucking cunt, ruining everything. Destroying my girl's confidence. Did he put her on top only to shove his dick inside of her too fast? For fuck's sake.

In the end, what he did or didn't do with her doesn't matter, because I'm going to fix it.

Tilting Celia's head back, I meet her eyes. "You don't have to feel that way with me." I press my palm against her chest and take a deep breath, grateful that she mirrors the movement. "Just breathe, baby. You can trust me."

God, I hope that's true.

She bites her lip again, and I steal a gentle kiss, pressing of those perfect lips to mine and licking into her mouth when she sighs, loosening up even more for me. Once I'm confident that she's ready, I lay back and lift my arms over my head. Gripping the headrest tightly, I commit not to touch her unless she asks for it. I nod. "Go for it, baby. Ride me. Do whatever makes you feel good."

It takes her a minute to get comfortable. First, she pulls my pants down until she can sit on my thighs without touching the zipper, then she takes off her bra so that her mouth-watering tits spill free, and finally, she pulls one of her legs out from her red lace panties, leaving them wrapped around her other knee.

Fuck me.

My cock twitches, aching and impatient. We never cleaned up the cum from the hand job, so it's smeared across my stomach and all over my cock. I can see it glistening on Celia's knuckles. *God*, she touched herself with that hand while removing her clothes. My cum is probably all over her skin, marking every inch of her as mine.

She pulls my t-shirt over my head, trapping it across the top of my shoulders. My leather jacket's lost in the floorboard, long forgotten, and I suddenly wish she were wearing it. As beautiful as she is naked, she'd be downright *stunning* with my leather slapping her tits as she bounces up and down on my cock.

I swallow hard. "Ready when you are, beautiful."

She surprises me with a kiss, dragging my bottom lip between her teeth and pulling a groan from my chest. She flicks her tongue against my snakebite, playing with it before slipping her tongue inside my mouth. The heat from her body spreads like a fever, overtaking me in one quick rush that leaves me trembling. She fists my hair and tugs, shooting both pain and pleasure down my spine, where it settles between my thighs. I flex my hips and plant my feet on the dashboard, determined to let her lead.

I'm so glad that I came once already, because as soon as her slick pussy touches my cock, I'm a fucking goner.

Groaning, I throw my head back while she grinds on

my shaft, rocking her hips back and forth in a slow, delicious torture that makes my balls tingle. I know I'm hitting her clit. My dick piercing doubles as a clit-magnet, an extra pressure point that drives women wild on top. I bite my lip and watch my woman unravel, a beautiful queen claiming her king for the first time. She's taking these little gasps of air every time she surges forward, her hands pushing my shoulders down, keeping me still as she takes her pleasure.

A shadow crosses in front of the windshield, and in the next instant, the driver's side door unlocks with a *click*. It pops open and a man steps inside, the crisp lines of his suit making me roll my eyes. As soon as my older brother comes into full view, the vein in his neck throbbing as much as my goddamn cock, I curse his fucking name. "Goddamn it, Rage, get the hell out!"

He must have followed us. Woken up and stepped outside his bedroom to find Celia and me both gone, went ballistic, and tracked us down. I glance at the heart-shaped collar on Celia's neck and grit my teeth. I bet the fucker put a tracker inside. Part of me respects it, but the other part is fucking annoyed. This is supposed to be *my* time with Celia, and he *has* to show up and ruin it. Fucking typical.

Rage tosses the spare car keys onto the dash without looking, staring intently at Celia instead, keeping his composure as long as we don't count how hard he white-knuckles the steering wheel. When Celia freezes in place, he bares his teeth like a wolf. "Keep going."

She cups her tits in her hands and shakes her head. "Get out!"

Rage grinds his teeth. "No."

They glare at each other, and once again, it's up to me to fix this shit. "Baby, look at me." I thrust my hips, loving the way her eyelashes flutter as I press my cock between her swollen lips. I rock forward, bumping her clit with the tip of my dick, and her mouth parts in a pretty *O*. "That's it, pretty girl. Feel how wet you are. Touch yourself. Doesn't that feel good?"

Biting her lip, she gives Rage a cursory glance before reaching between her thighs and pressing her fingertips to her clit, shuddering as I punch my hips forward again. We both lose ourselves in these little thrusts, our soft breaths mingling in the air as she swirls her fingertips around her clit and I brush the tip of my cock against them. Her rosy nipples darken, begging to be plucked. I glance over at Rage, who hasn't moved a fucking inch. "Can he touch your tits, baby?"

Her gorgeous hazel eyes flick toward Rage. She grinds down harder, slipping an inch of my cock inside her slick heat. I clench my entire body for ever-loving Heaven and Hell. If she's going to wage war against Rage with my body as a weapon, *holy fucking shit*, I might be the luckiest man alive.

"No," she sighs, lifting her hips so that we can all see my cock glistening from her desire. "He can watch."

She sinks down and makes this high-pitched little *ah!* sound when she bottoms out, her thighs quivering as she feels how deep I am, how *fucking gone* I am, already twitching like crazy inside of her. My muscles convulse from the strain of tensing them for so long, and I cry out when she rocks her hips, sucking my cock deeper. Slowly, she rides me, puffing warm breaths over the top of my head and using my shoulders as an anchor point to keep herself steady. I moan for her every time she grinds her hips, and she drinks in the sound of my voice like an addict, her eyes sparkling like fucking diamonds.

It doesn't take long for her to pick up the pace. Our bodies fit together perfectly, the wet glide of her pussy fucking *Heaven*, and as the sun rises over the city, a pink halo of light surrounds her body in ethereal beauty. As the seconds tick by and the strawberry sunrise bleeds through the fogged windows, I can count the freckles dotting her shoulders, taste the desire on her tongue when she devours my lips, and catch the glint of gold from the heart tag kissing her throat. She leans back and moans so loudly that it reverberates in the air. Two pumps—*up and down*—and I'm busting my nut. "F-fuck," I pant, jerking my hips up. Her body invites me inside, warm and wet and so goddamn perfect.

Celia grinds down *hard*, clawing my knees as she takes my load as deep as she can. Then she lifts her hips and rubs my dick against the front walls of her pussy, bouncing with reckless abandon as she chases her release, a chorus of moans and *yesyesyes* spilling past her lips. She holds her breath as she comes, her face burning bright red and her thighs quivering.

I spill another rope of cum inside of her, moaning loud enough to get Rage's attention. I finally spare my brother a glance, and he's wound up tight. Somehow, he's spread his thighs wide enough to lay his knee on top of the middle console, his thick cock in his hand as he chokes it to death. His eyes are pitch black, their pupils so blown that he looks like a demon ready to devour its chosen victim.

To my surprise, even as Celia is lost to her pleasure and unable to fight back, he doesn't touch her. Doesn't even try. Teeth clenched, he grabs his cock and jerks it in short, rough strokes that would make me cringe if I weren't buried inside our woman. My body and soul are in pure bliss, and even Rage's flaring temper and stupid games won't bring me down.

He doesn't come, growling with frustration as he witnesses how beautiful our girl is when she wants to be touched—to be *loved*—by *me*, not by him.

I bury my grin in Celia's hair as she crashes against my chest. Her body is hot to the touch, and I crave every inch of her warm skin against mine. I wrap my arms around her and hold her close, reveling in the frantic drum of her heartbeat and the way her soft lips feel on my neck. I don't want to ruin the moment, but *holy fucking shit*, this was worth the goddamn wait. I can't stop smiling like some lucky idiot, and I close my eyes to revel in this perfect moment.

"Thank you," Celia murmurs, wrapping her arms around my neck, "for everything. Tonight's been..." Her lips curve into a small smile. "Good for me."

The driver's side door snaps open and slams back shut, my brother having seen enough.

And, honestly?

After all the bullshit he's put Celia through, he can go jerk off his pathetic rage-boner over the side of a cliff.

Right now, in this perfect moment, Celia's all mine.

I'm not wasting a damn second.

Chapter 7

RUIN

RAGE KEEPS his emotions locked inside of an impenetrable box. Its lid is strong, made from layer upon layer of fury and frustration that he condenses down to its most dense form, which then slides securely over the rim and keeps every other human emotion locked up tight. It's why I was surprised that he formed an attachment to Celia so quickly after finding her, but that involved strategy, not just emotion.

Claiming Celia for himself isn't only because he likes her. It's because he knows that Rebel and I will like her, too—and finding someone who can tolerate the three of us isn't something you simply *do*. It's an act of divine intervention having thrown her in our path.

When she ran away the first time, it was mostly anger that slipped free.

Now that she's disappeared from under his nose for a second time, it isn't just anger rising up—it's pain.

Because despite all of his best efforts, he has to come to terms with the fact that some things are out of his control.

Celia may be one of those.

"This is not your fault." I stare at the empty cage in our living room, my arms crossed over my chest. She didn't break out—our brother Rebel let her out. "He broke the rules."

Rage is barely listening, too focused on his phone to hear me. He grunts in response, glaring at the screen. "I shouldn't have given him a key."

Of course, he'll continue to find ways to blame himself.

He pours over security feed, tracking their descent from the roof to the diner across the street, until finally they end up in one of the cars from the club's valet lot. "They went for a little joyride," he growls, shoving his phone into his pocket. After running a hand through his hair and tucking in his shirt, he shrugs on his suit jacket and grabs the keys to his SUV.

I finger the knife strapped to my hip, slipping it in and out of its holster. "Where are they now?"

"Not far. Let's go."

Pinpointing Celia's location is easy with the GPS tracker inside her collar. We stop by the valet office for a spare key before following the map to one of the most popular hills in the city and silently scanning each car idling on the cliffside overlook. Most of them are your typical suburban outfit, but one stands out—the bright red Ferrari. In typical Rebel style, he chose the most inconspicuous joyride possible.

Not only that, but it's *rocking*.

We pull up beside them and Rage jumps out of our car before we've even stopped. I slide the gear shift into *park* while he interrupts our brother's fun.

I wasn't invited to watch, but I slip out of the passenger seat and make my way to the front of their car to peer through the window. It's too fogged inside for me to make out more than shadows, but with Rage sitting in the driver's seat, it's easy to picture Celia and Rebel on the passenger side. Is she the one rocking in his lap, or is he crammed against the dash while ramming inside of her? Are their bodies woven tightly together, blurring the lines between where she starts and he ends, or are they barely touching one another?

I wonder what it's like to be wrapped up inside of her. To be consumed in her presence, unable to see anything outside of her light and warmth. I picture Celia kissing each of my brothers and wonder what it is about her lips that they enjoy. If *I* kiss her, will I taste a kaleidoscope on her tongue?

That could be why Rage and Rebel are so obsessed. Not to her, but to the waves of color she radiates. The taste and touch of a blushing rose, or the radiant gold of honey laced with a sugar so sweet, we're doomed to gorge ourselves to death.

I can hear them moaning, their voices neither clashing nor melodic. Merely the sounds of two people falling apart. Within seconds after the crescendo, Rage reappears, snapping the driver's door shut and storming off into the distance. I keep my hands in my pockets and watch him until he disappears up the long stretch of road toward the hilltop. He'll be back once he cools off.

Someone inside the car suddenly presses their hand against the windshield, smearing the condensation and allowing me to peer inside. Celia is wrangling her body back inside her clothes as quickly as possible, clumsily bumping into both the window and the ceiling of the car, until finally she tumbles out of the side door.

Her hair is a wild tangle of warm auburn locks framing her face in a fiery halo from the pink sunrise. She looks up and around quickly, her eyes wide and sweatpants on backwards. "Where did he go?" she asks, still looking around while fidgeting with the ends of her t-shirt.

I nod toward the slope extending up the hill. "He'll be back."

She curses under her breath and rakes her fingers through her hair. "He just—he just sat there."

Rebel emerges from the car a second later, his skin flushed and his hair as wild as hers. "Baby, don't worry about him. He just needs to walk it off." He slips Celia's arms into a leather jacket and zips it up halfway, then does the same for his own.

Touching her throat, Celia prods the fresh bruises peeking out from around her leather collar. "He's going to be angry. I wasn't in the cage like I was supposed to be." She looks over at me like I hold the secrets to solving her problems with Rage. All I can do is stare right back. There's a layer of sweat at her hairline, little wisps curling and sticking to her skin.

While Rebel tries to soothe her, I commit Celia's current appearance to memory. Not only is she flushed from what I assume is sex with Rebel, but she's also distressed, a worry line creasing on her forehead. She looks at me without truly seeing me, lost to the turmoil inside her head.

"He's always angry. That's his thing." Rebel pulls her into his arms and murmurs something in her ear, leaving me out of the conversation. He kisses her cheek, then tilts her head up to kiss her lips. It's a tender moment, made even softer by the way she looks at him once they pull apart.

Like he's holding her heart in his hands.

Unlike Rage, it doesn't bother me that Rebel and Celia are getting closer. It was bound to happen the moment I carried her back into our lives. "He's upset that you chose Rebel," I interject, "before him."

Celia turns her frown onto me. "Why the hell would I choose to be with the maniac who'd rather choke me out than be nice to me?"

It doesn't have to make sense. It's just what Rage wanted.

"Don't worry," Rebel says, pressing another kiss to Celia's lips, "he won't take it out on you. I promise." Releasing her, he gives me a quick look before heading up the road. "I'll go talk to him. Stay here with Ruin."

"Are you crazy?" She looks between the two of us

before following Rebel up the slope toward the top of the hill. "You just said he needs to walk it off!"

"It'll go faster if he has a punching bag."

"You've got to be fucking kidding me!"

I follow the two of them on foot, keeping watch of our surroundings. All three of them are so wound up in each other that they're forgetting who and where we are. Bratva families will keep their distance if they recognize us, but we're on North Side. Many civilians live here, and their daily commute is about to start. We'll be a walking spectacle within minutes.

As the sun rises, the sky turns a deeper shade of pink, bleeding all around us. Only when we reach the top of the hill does the sun break over the horizon. A crown of gold shoots into the heavens, and standing at the hilltop overlooking the city is my oldest brother Rage. His fists are clenched tightly by his sides, his gaze absorbed in the waking city below.

"Brother," Rebel calls out, jogging toward him. "Listen—"

Rage spins, throwing his body weight into a punch that lands square on Rebel's jaw. Their weight classes are different, and Rebel can't take hits like that without consequences. He tips backward and stumbles, gravel spraying around his feet as he catches himself. Straightening, he throws his arms out and spits blood onto the ground. "Come on, you call that a hit?"

I grab Celia as she lunges toward them. "Don't," I warn, "or it will be your blood on the ground instead of his." She struggles in my arms, and I lock her in a loose chokehold to keep her from squirming hard enough to actually get loose. I can't let her throw herself into the fight. I doubt they would intentionally hurt her, but if Rage throws a punch and she jumps in the way, even if he pulls back, she won't get out unscathed.

Rebel can take a hit without passing out, but I'm not sure about Celia. If she gets injured, things are only going to get worse for all of us.

Rage lunges. Rebel deftly dodges to the side, using his speed to his advantage. It's been years since they've gone at each other and longer still since they've honed their distinct fighting styles, but their best techniques fly out the window as they slip back into old habits. It's like I'm watching a replay from fifteen years ago when Rebel got his ass handed to him for coming home drunk after a high school party. Only this time, he's drunk off of a woman instead of liquor.

Still, he's grinning even when Rage's fist connects with his ribs. He groans, then quickly kicks out at Rage's shin and covers his pants in dust. "You mad, bro? What, because I fucked your girl?" Shaking his head, he laughs again. "Or is it because I broke your precious rules?"

"I locked her in there for a reason!" Rage shoves Rebel back a few steps. "You can't take her out whenever you damn well please!"

"She was starving!" Rebel's smile hardens and he jabs Rage in the throat without doing enough damage to repel him. They grapple each other and tumble to the ground, Rebel landing on top. "You didn't fucking feed her! You lock her up, knock her the fuck out, and then you don't actually take care of her! You should have stayed with her until she woke up! Made sure she was okay! Called the fucking doctor!" He punches Rage's face, growling, "how can you say you want a child if you can't even take care of its mother? You'll kill any kid you have!"

Grabbing Rebel's hand mid-punch, Rage squeezes until Rebel yelps. "Because *fucking her* is so much better, huh?" He rolls them over and pins Rebel to the ground with a knee on his chest. "You couldn't wait to get your dick wet, so you bribed her with dinner to win her over. Father of the fucking year, right here."

"I'm not the one trying to knock her up!"

"You will, though!" Rage slams Rebel's shoulders into the ground. "She's ovulating, you piece of shit!"

Celia stops breathing. I unwind my arms from her neck and spin her around, grabbing her face to keep her eyes on me. "*Krosotka.* Breathe."

She tries to shake her head. "Let me go. I need—I need air."

"No. You breathe here, with me." There are too many layers between us for me to feel her body heat, but I can feel the flush of her cheeks in my palms. I squeeze her face until I feel the cut of her teeth. "You are safe, *krosotka,* I promise." She can't open her mouth to argue because of how I'm holding her, so I drag her toward the overlook facing the sunrise. "Look." I slide my hands up into her hair and tilt her face toward the sun. Clouds cover its face, but the light remains warm and bright, shining like a beacon. "That glow is you. All the red around it, the parts that bleed, those are us. You cut through the red, *krosotka*. Watch."

Slowly, the sky starts to transform as dawn breaks. The streaks of gold from the sun blend into their harsh surroundings, muting the reds and turning them orange, then peach, then lavender. As the sun rises, the landscape around us changes, too. The shadows lurking beneath trees and cars disappear as night shifts to day and the entire world awakens.

Celia's like that, too. She wakes up our world.

I press my chest to her back, wanting to feel what it's like to be as close to her as my brothers are. "You make our shadows disappear," I tell her, hoping that she understands. We're flawed men. We won't get everything right. We'll try to be better, but when we've cut our teeth on bullets and bone our entire lives, it's hard to remember how to be soft.

But Celia makes me want to remember.

She reaches up to touch my face, her fingertips ghosting across my mask. When they reach the edge, she hooks them underneath, tugging gently to pry it off.

I stop her before she succeeds. Grabbing her hand, I pull it away from my face and hold it by my side.

Her voice is as soft as her skin. "I deserve to know what kind of shadows I'm dealing with, Ruin."

My scars itch, the worst ones begging to be peeled off and left bloody. I don't reply, because what can I say?

I don't want her to shine her light so close that there's nothing of me left.

Rage and Rebel, on the other hand, crave it. They

want her to obliterate every dark thing inside themselves and replace it with something worth holding onto—a future born of love instead of bloodshed. *A family* and all the unconditional love it provides.

But I can't live in that world, and pretending otherwise is dangerous.

I think she understands that danger. It's why she has always resisted living within the bratva and being tied to men like us. Danger lives *within* us.

If she carries my brother's child, that danger will live inside of her, too. It will change her, just like it's changed him, and their child will be no different than either of its parents.

She wraps her arms around her body and slumps against me. "I can't get pregnant," she whispers, shivering. "Not like this. Not when I'm—" Her voice cracks, and she doesn't finish her thought.

I think I understand that, too.

When we stole Celia from her normal life, her entire world shifted. She could no longer see the future she wanted because we were standing in the way. But it's in those moments—the ones where we feel stuck in uncertainty—that carving a path ahead becomes as important as breathing. She can either keep banging her fists against our bodies to try and force her way to the future she's always wanted, or she can take our outstretched hands and let us lead her to the future she's always *needed*.

Because the two paths don't have to divide. They can merge somewhere in the middle to create something even better than she ever imaged… and better than we ever dreamed.

I press my palm to her stomach and wonder what it'll look like—her golds mixed with my reds, or Rebel's blues, or Rage's greens. Will it be as beautiful as she is? Or even brighter?

My brothers limp over and stand next to us, the two of them leaning on each other. Rebel has a black eye and split lip, while Rage has scratches from Rebel's rings on his cheeks and rips in his suit. Rebel grins at Celia, his teeth bloodied from the fight. "Careful, baby. You two look good together. I might get jealous."

She stares between the two of them, then cranes her neck to look up at me. "If we're going to make this work," she says slowly, "we need some ground rules." Clutching my hand over her stomach, she takes a deep breath. "I can't have a baby in a cage."

Rage grumbles under his breath. "You'd be out of the cage by then."

Jabbing his elbow into Rage's side, Rebel hisses, "*dude*, not helping."

"I don't want to be in a cage at all!" Celia's eyes flash with anger. "So get rid of it!"

"I am *not* getting rid of the cage." Rage drops Rebel's weight and steps in front of Celia, leaving our brother to grumble and groan as he drops onto the guardrail. Her eyes meet his and sparks fly between them, intense enough that I can feel her trembling in my arms. "*Until* you're pregnant, I'm not letting you out of our sight.

And even then—" his nostrils flare—"I need you safe. That's what the cage is for. Safety."

She crinkles her nose. "It's a prison."

"It serves a purpose." Rage won't budge, but I never expected him to. He grips her chin and presses the pad of his thumb against her lips. "Once you show me that you can behave like a wife instead of a runaway, I'll reconsider."

Rebel rolls his eyes behind Rage's back but doesn't verbally disagree. It's only a matter of time before he lets Celia out again... or I do. My heart thrums with energy, the possibility of learning new things about Celia swirling in my head. What would she do if I was the one to sneak her outside? Would she happily follow me like she did with Rebel, or would she insist on staying locked away until someone else came for her?

Could I drag her out?

Would she scream?

I clutch Celia's stomach tighter, feeling her flesh give beneath my fingers. When Rebel grabbed her hips earlier, did he leave marks like the ones Rage left on her neck? If I remove her collar, I bet I can count the fingerprints on her skin. One-two-three-four—

She takes a shaky breath and clutches my hand tighter, derailing my thoughts until the only thing that's left is the pressure of her fingers sliding through mine.

"What if I'm already pregnant?"

"Impossible," Rebel calls out, a cocky grin plastered on his face. "I know I'm skilled, but even my swimmers need time to cross the finish line."

Shaking her head, Celia meets Rage's eyes and repeats her question. "What if I'm already pregnant?"

They stare at each other in silence until finally, Rage releases the iron grip on his emotions. The impassible stone in his eyes crumbles, and he presses the palm of his hand directly beneath mine and Celia's to touch her abdomen. "Impossible," he breathes, repeating Rebel's turn of phrase. "That's impossible, Celia. You—" He slams his jaw shut, forcing his next words through clenched teeth. "You took the pill. I saw it. Rebel saw it. The box was empty, and there wasn't a single pill in your trash or anywhere on the bathroom floor. I checked. I checked *five times.* You swallowed it. You must have." He wraps his hand around her throat and squeezes. "Tell me that you swallowed that pill."

I hear Celia's throat click on a timely swallow.

"I swallowed it."

Rage sneers. "I fucking knew it—"

Celia flinches at the venom in his voice. "And then I threw it back up."

"*Liar.*" Rage squeezes tighter, and I grab his wrist to keep him from suffocating her. He snarls, turning his glare onto me, and pushes off of her neck to pace in front of the guardrail. "You just want out of the cage." He laughs bitterly and kicks a rock off the cliff's edge. When that doesn't satisfy him, he grabs a fallen branch and hurls it over with a yell that echoes all around us. "You can't be pregnant. You *can't.* Because that would mean—"

"—that you've been hurting the mother of your

child? That you *suffocated* me when I didn't deserve it?" Celia pulls free from my arms and jabs Rage in the chest with her fist. "I took the pill, yes, but I couldn't hold it. Not when I—" She takes a shaky breath. "When all I really want is a baby."

Rage freezes in his tracks, his eyes pinging all over her body, like he's looking for the truth to her claims. "You're lying."

"Call my bluff, then." Grabbing hold of his shirt, she pulls him down to her level and brushes her lips across his. "Or are you scared to find out how shitty of a dad you are?"

Rebel and I lunge for Rage at the same time, both of us latching onto his arms to keep him from touching her. He snarls, anger rolling off of him in waves as he fights our grasp. When it's clear he isn't going anywhere, he laughs, the sound hollow.

It sounds just like our father did right before he used to beat the shit out of one of us. Rage doesn't realize it, but the more bitterness he lets in, the more like the monster he becomes.

"Alright, mama. You win. We'll get you tested."

Celia's shoulders relax.

"But when the test comes back negative—" Rage smiles, the sharp curve of his teeth transforming him from the overprotective lover back into the bratva enforcer that makes grown men beg for mercy—"it's back to the cage until I fuck that baby you want so badly into your womb."

Lifting her chin, Celia keeps her composure well

enough to fool Rage, maybe even to fool Rebel, as she nods in agreement. But I can see the truth in her muddied eyes. She's scared, and she should be, because Rage doesn't make idle threats.

If he isn't a father yet, he will be soon.

Then we'll finally learn if he can overcome the man who raised us to be monsters, or if he's doomed to succumb to the violent call of our bloodline.

Chapter 8

Celia

After years of OBGYN visits, I thought I had become immune to the waiting game. Sitting in the lobby. Hovering inside the exam room. Waiting for the doctor to arrive.

But I never anticipated how the waiting game changes once you have three muscled mafiosos in tow, two of which are sporting cuts and bruises on their faces and hands, while the third is wearing a faceless mask. People staring, I'm used to. But people whispering behind my back, I'm not.

Rage scowls at every person in the office, including the front desk staff who are simply trying to do their jobs. Rebel flirts with one of the women in scrubs, trying to convince her to speed things along for us. And Ruin...

Well, he stands at the side of the room next to a potted tree, looking about as obtuse as a beached whale.

Either by the grace of God or the Monrovia name earning me some points, we file out of the waiting area within twenty minutes, and I breathe a sigh of relief as the nurses take my vitals and bring us to a private room. The door closes behind us, and all of a sudden, I'm brought right back to the last time I was sitting in this very room, waiting for pregnancy results on my own. My ex-husband was at work as usual, and I hadn't told my mother or brother about my latest attempt to fall pregnant, so I went to the appointment alone.

I didn't cry about the negative test results until I made it home that evening, which was longer than I had lasted before then. Still, the memory stings, and I try to focus on the three large, tattooed differences between that appointment and this one.

They won't stop staring at me.

I fidget on the examination chair, the crinkle of the sterile paper under my butt loud enough to make me wince. All three of my men are standing in different corners of the room pretending to mind their own business, but every few seconds, I catch them all staring at me, like they're waiting for the baby to pop out *today*. Rebel actively plays with the medical supplies stored in little glass jars on the counter, Ruin stands directly beside the door ready to pounce at the first sign of danger, and Rage is... well, overbearing as usual.

"Could you give me some space?" I rub my temples and pretend that the warmth on my back isn't Rage's hand—it's the sun, or a heating pad, or a fluffy white cat curled up into the cutest little ball of fur. But every time he rubs up and down my spine in these slow, torturous strokes, I'm reminded of how he touched me last night.

I swallow hard and pray that Dr. Sakovia doesn't ask about the collar or the bruises underneath.

"Why don't you let Rebel wrap your knuckles?" I ask, nodding toward the man pulling strips of gauze into teeny-tiny pieces. They fall like snow on the formica counter, a steady pile growing with each passing minute. Rebel pulls a face that says *gross*, while Rage takes my hand and engulfs my knuckles with his own. The bruises and broken skin don't faze him, but I'm already nauseous, and the metallic tang of blood in the air isn't helping.

"I'd rather you help me," he murmurs, lacing our fingers together.

I stare at our entwined hands before tugging mine free. "No thanks."

The smile freezes on his face. "No thanks?"

"You heard me." Clearing my throat, I pat the crinkle paper behind my back. "Rebel, bring the gauze and antibacterial creme over here and I'll clean your cuts."

Rage tilts my chin up. "What are you doing, *krosotka*?"

"I don't know what you mean."

Rebel, however, cuts right through the bullshit. "Holding her hand isn't gonna make her forgive you," he says, reaching into the cabinet to grab a fresh box of gauze and tape. He tosses them at Rage's chest. "Stop trying to force it."

I take the supplies from Rage's hands and busy myself with preparing strips of gauze and tape. He glares at his bruised knuckles, then at his younger brother, brooding expertly as he clenches and unclenches his fists.

He doesn't like to lose, and right now, he's losing *big time.*

"I won't apologize for loving you, Celia."

My heart races at his sudden admission. Flicking my gaze to his, I try not to shrink from the intensity in his eyes. "What did you say?"

Rage places his hand on my thigh and leans in close enough that I can smell what little remains of his cologne. Brushing his lips across my temple, he smirks against my skin. "You heard me." As Rebel wanders over with the brightest little smile on his face, Rage presses a chaste kiss to my forehead and steps back to make room. Although I turn my attention to cleaning the cuts on Rebel's hands and trying to salvage his split lip, I can feel Rage's eyes on me.

He won't apologize for anything, because he doesn't think that he's done anything wrong.

I use too much force to close Rebel's lip and tear some of the skin off with the tape. The cut splits back open, dripping blood. He winces but still manages to smile. "Don't worry, I've healed from way worse than this. I'll be back to kissing you in no time. Unless—" His ebony eyes spark with mischief—"you wanna get a little dirty with it."

I dodge a messy kiss attempt while Rage growls from across the room. "Don't you *dare* get blood on her."

Rebel whines. "You're no fun. She might like it!" He winks at me, and I can't help but laugh as I wrap gauze around his knuckles and tape it into place. I can't ever see myself wanting blood with my kisses, but I guess if the mood is right and it's only a *little*—

"Blood washes off," Ruin murmurs from across the room. I finish taping Rebel's hands and look over to find him staring as usual, but there's a tension in his shoulders that wasn't there earlier.

Rage throws *him* a death glare this time, but I'm more careful with my approach. I may not know enough about Ruin yet, but that doesn't mean I'm going to shoot down his attempts at conversation, no matter how unorthodox. "Yeah, you're right. Blood does wash off."

The doctor arrives then, announcing himself at the door. "Celia Monrovia," Dr. Sakovia greets, a friendly smile on his face as he reads my chart. "It's been a while since I last saw you. What brings you to—" He looks up and notices all three brothers staring at him intently. "Gentleman." Closing and locking the door behind him, he rolls up his white coat sleeves. "I didn't realize you were affiliated with Miss Monrovia."

"Damn right we're affiliated," Rebel says with a bright smile. "She's my girl, Doc." He throws his arm around my shoulder.

"She's *ours*," Rage attempts to clarify, the sour look on his face pinching as he squares up to the doctor. "So anything related to her care, we are your first call, got it?"

I'm sure that intimidation tactics usually work for Rage, but Dr. Sakovia is experienced with unruly men. He ignores Rage and looks directly at me. "It's your call,

Celia. We can add them to your HIPPA authorization before you leave today... *if* that's what you want."

I set the medical supplies down and lace my fingers together in my lap. "I know how this works, doctor." They could get my records even without my consent, so it's a matter of policy. I'd never want to hurt Dr. Sakovia's reputation—he's one of the most reliable doctors in the city, known for his discretion with bratva matters. "I'll sign the forms."

Doctor Sakovia isn't much older than I suspect Rage is, but he's had silver hair for as long as I can remember. A *silver fox*, as the ladies in my neighborhood HOA used to call him. Despite working in medicine and keeping bratva clients out of his records for years, he doesn't look a day older than thirty at most. It's what makes it easy to be around him—he's calm and collected and sitting on the right side of gorgeous.

He smiles kindly and washes his hands in the sink, humming to himself while Rage hovers way too closely to be comfortable. Any other man might be unnerved.

Wren Sakovia looks right at home with thugs and criminals.

"Alright, then. Your intake forms say you might be pregnant?" After drying off, he snaps on a pair of latex gloves and wheels over the phlebotomy kit a nurse brought in earlier. "How are you feeling?"

I swallow. "Um. A little nervous." I bite my lip and avoid looking at the three men whose sole focus is suddenly back to me. My face heats, and I wring my hands together. "You know how hard it's been for me to... conceive."

Wren isn't a gynecologist or obstetrician by trade, but I've met with him for checkups over the years, so he knows my history better than most. He always agrees to meet with me when I call.

"I want this to be a healthy pregnancy," I continue, "and I'd like to go back on my fertility supplements if possible."

"Let's see if you're pregnant first, and then we can prescribe as needed." As Wren fills two vials with my blood, all three of my men watch in earnest.

It's Rebel who speaks first. "How soon until we find out the results?"

"A few days. We'll call with the results and update Celia's chart on her patient portal."

"And paternity?" Rage's jaw looks glued shut from how hard he's clenching. It's a miracle he can speak at all. "How do we know who's the father?"

I shake my head while Wren wraps my forearm in a bright pink bandage. "I don't want to know. Finding out during pregnancy can risk the baby's safety if we're not careful."

"It's a little more nuanced than that," Wren interjects, "but you can talk amongst yourselves and come to a decision closer to then. We won't be able to test for paternity for a few more weeks, and we have non-invasive procedures that are safe for both the baby and the mother."

"She must get pregnant first," Ruin mumbles, his

voice obscured by his mask. I look up to find him staring intently at my stomach, like he's picturing a baby inside of me right now. Although I wouldn't call his gaze soft, especially considering the expressionless mask on his face, his energy isn't nearly as dark and mysterious as normal. If anything, he seems... curious.

"A few days," Rebel repeats, a tiny smile pulling on his lips. "Say, Doc, tell me more about this whole *ovulation* thing. That's when she's fertile, right? How do we know when that is?"

Rage grunts. "I'm tracking her cycle. I'll know when it is."

My face flames. "Excuse me?" Since when has he been doing that? And why? I know he *said* I was ovulating this morning, but I thought he was bullshitting us in the heat of the moment—not *actually* tracking my cycle.

Pulling out his phone, Rage proceeds to show Rebel the period tracker app on his phone, complete with notes about when we've had sex. "Each little heart in the corner means we've filled her up that day, and this flower here means that she's ovulating. The best days for sex are these."

Rebel's face brightens. "That's my heart from today?"

"Don't get your hopes up. *I'm* going to be the father." Rage takes my hand and squeezes, meeting my eyes. "I made a promise that I intend to keep."

My breath catches as I'm transported back to the safe house, Rage and I wrapped in each other's arms as we whisper promises to each other about the future. My heart swells with emotion, caught up in the intensity of Rage's smoldering gaze.

Although my ex-husband made a similar promise, it felt nothing like this.

I have no doubt that Rage intends to keep his promise.

"What if I wanna be the one to knock her up?" Rebel takes my face in his hands and plants a kiss on my lips, tasting of copper and smoke. When he pulls away, he's grinning. A smear of blood coats his lips. "See, I've marked her. She's mine."

I touch my fingertips to my lips and pull them away to find blood.

Dr. Sakovia clears his throat. "Gentleman—"

Grabbing my hand, Ruin smears my fingertips across my cheek, leaving a wet streak. His voice rumbles low, muttering something in Russian, as he leans in and prods my bottom lip with his gloved finger. He slips it inside my mouth, prodding my tongue with the leather and forcing me to swallow what little remains of Rebel's blood. "Good girl," he purrs, removing his finger to grab my chin and rub his thumb back and forth across my lips, caressing the seam.

Heat blossoms deep in my core, making it impossible not to kiss Ruin's gloved finger. We stare at each other until Wren clears his throat again, breaking the moment.

"Do you need anything else, Miss Monrovia?"

I look between all three brothers, from Ruin's strange fascination to Rebel's mischievous smirk and

Rage's brooding stare. These men are wild, but I'm starting to believe that they're mine. "I think I'm good, thank you."

"We'll take care of her, Doc," Rebel assures him, turning to slap Wren's shoulder. "But if you have any pamphlets on pregnancy and ovulation, I'll take three."

"Four," Rage interjects. "Thanatos is staying at the house, and he'll need to watch for any signs of distress in case there's an emergency."

My chest seizes at Thanatos's name. "H-he is?" The last man I want around my child is the one who said such horrible things to me. My ears ring, and I take quick, shallow breaths to fight off rising panic. "Why?"

"He's family." Rage searches my eyes, frowning. "And he's the best at security within the bratva."

"She doesn't like him." Ruin glances up at Rage. "He said mean things to her."

"I was there. I already told him to cool the fuck off."

"No, you weren't." My heart beats in overtime, making my hands shake. "When he brought me back to the club, he gave me a parting gift." A laugh bubbles up in my throat, sounding as unhinged as I feel. *Of course* the verbally abusive asshole would move in after claiming he wanted nothing to do with me. He probably gets off on making girls cry. "He told me that I'd be a horrible mother."

"That the baby would be better off dead," Ruin corrects, his tone as icy as the memory. "He made her cry."

Rage's hands clench into tight fists. "He *what?*"

I stand from the chair and blink away tears threatening to rise. "Don't make me live with him, Rage." Pressing the flat of my palm to Rage's chest, I lift up onto my tiptoes and press a quick kiss to his lips. I know we're not on good terms and that kissing him is a cheap shot, but I need for this to work.

I can't live with Thanatos.

"It won't be good for the baby," I murmur against his jaw.

Rage wraps his arms around my waist and holds me tight. I can feel him shaking as he slips his hands beneath my waistband to hold my hips. Taking a deep breath, he releases some of his anger on the exhale. "Don't worry, mama." He presses a kiss to my hair. "I'll take care of you and our baby."

I ignore the thread of anxiety tying knots in my stomach as we leave the clinic. As long as they think I'm pregnant, I'm safe. I won't be put back in the cage for them to fuck every waking moment of the day.

But a familiar wave of hope, intoxicating and bubbly and bright, is what makes it hard to breathe.

I clutch the pregnancy pamphlets to my chest, praying to whichever god is listening that they be kind and gentle this time—that they give me a beautiful, healthy baby... and a father who wants them.

CHAPTER 9

REBEL

AFTER CELIA'S unexpected pregnancy test at the doctor's office, I flip through the pamphlets as Ruin drives us home. I've read a few paragraphs aloud about how the body changes since I know he's listening. He might be more interested in Celia's body than the baby itself, but he doesn't have to be a father figure since the baby will have me.

And, I guess, it'll have Rage too. The fucker is determined to knock Celia up first, but according to his phone app, she's ovulating *now,* not when they had sex a week or two ago. My chances of being *daddy* are stronger than ever, and they'll be even better once I nut inside of her again.

"It's pure Heaven, man," I muse, tossing the pamphlets into the backseat of the SUV. Rage insisted on driving Celia home in the Ferrari himself, citing that *he can't trust me* not to take a detour.

He's right, but he doesn't have to be such a dick about it.

"She feels like the finest silk wrapped around your cock. Tight and soft and so goddamn *warm*." I smack Ruin's shoulder. "You ever had a girl like that?" To be honest, I'm not sure if he's ever gotten his dick wet in his life. It's not exactly a conversation we've had, despite living together for over twenty years now. Our youngest brother isn't exactly a talker, and if he's gotten pussy outside of the house, he hasn't fessed up to it.

Ruin grunts, pulling to a stop at a red light. "She is soft on the inside." He flexes his fingers over the steering wheel, like he's remembering how it feels to touch her.

So damn good.

I shake my head, smiling. "Yeah, man, she is. But you should stick something other than your fingers inside her. Not a knife," I clarify, tapping the handle of the nine-incher he keeps strapped to his hip, "but your dick, bro."

He's silent for a moment. "She would scream."

"Hell yeah, she'd scream. Creaming all over your cock, tits bouncing as you pound into her." I lick my lips at the memory of those very tits, round and soft and so goddamn perfect. I need to suck her nipples next time. Soon. No, tonight. Fuck, as soon as we get back. She's still fertile, so my chances of knocking her up will double if I come inside of her again. I may not know how the all the biology works, but that math should check out.

Ruin's phone suddenly rings, vibrating inside the

cupholder. He pays it no attention, like always, meaning that I have to be the one to answer. "Go for Rebel."

Static crackles across the line. "Rebel? Hey, put Ruin on."

"He's driving." I kick my foot up on the dash. "What's up?"

"Turn on the Bluetooth, motherfucker!"

Rolling my eyes, I hang up to connect the Bluetooth, then call back. The name *Zane* lights up Ruin's phone screen. I've nicknamed him and his brother Kane *The Brothers Grimm* on account of how fucking macabre they are. Killing for sport and using the victims as inspiration for their next series of paintings is a bit too rich for my blood, but Ruin and them go way back, all the way to grade school. They may have learned how to carve up bodies so well together, for all I know.

Masters in the art of killing, all of them. No pun intended.

"Ruin," Zane says urgently, "there's a body drop in The Backyard. Before you ask, it's not one of ours. I know you've been keeping this shit out of the news, but the cops are sniffing around on account of a drug bust a few houses down. We'll move her if you want—"

"You'll owe us," Kane interrupts, sounding as arrogant as I remember. "But we'll do it for you."

"Move the body," Ruin says simply, "and send location." He turns on our blinker and takes a sudden right, heading towards the district that the bratva affectionately calls The Backyard, a seedy shit hole with more problems than the city's police force can keep up with. If you want drugs or sex, you're guaranteed a hit in The Backyard. Whether or not it's a *good* hit is up for debate.

"Stay with the body until we arrive."

Kane hisses, "we don't have time for—"

"We will *make* time. Mercy isn't going anywhere that we won't know about." There's a scuffle across the line, then Zane sighs. "Sorry, he's on edge since we found our next target. Impatient, you know?"

I don't know and don't care. Hanging up, I run a hand through my hair. I'd *kill* for a shower, a double shot of vodka, and a handful of painkillers. Rage did a number on my body during our brawl, not to mention the hangover pounding inside my skull. I roll down my window to try not to hurl.

"Call Rage," Ruin orders, adjusting his rearview mirror to check for the red Ferrari tailing us. They're a few cars down, Rage likely too distracted by Celia's tits stretching my t-shirt to follow closely. Sighing dramatically, I pull up his number in my contacts, but his name pops up on the screen before I can hit the call button. The fucker is always on top of this kind of shit.

"There's been a body drop," he announces, "I'm sending you the coordinates."

"We already got 'em." It feels good to be one step ahead of Rage. "Race ya there."

Celia mutters something in the background.

"What's that, baby?" I ask, smiling as I picture her sitting in the very seat we fucked in earlier. I bet she's soaking her panties, remembering how good it felt to ride me.

"I said," she huffs, "we'll never make it with *grandpa* driving, over here!"

"I'm keeping you *safe*—"

She growls in frustration. "This car isn't meant to be safe! It's meant to *drive!*"

"I am not risking your life—"

"Let me drive!"

"No."

Celia chuffs loudly. "This is exactly why Rebel gets laid before you."

I cackle with glee at their banter, doubly satisfied when Ruin chuckles, too. "Don't worry, baby, you can take me for a ride anytime."

The call ends abruptly as they hang up, no doubt on account of Rage throwing a fit. I whistle as we drive down the city streets, feeling better than I have all week. Things aren't perfect, but damn, they're sure shaping up to be entertaining.

CHAPTER 10

THANATOS

MY JOINTS SCREAM in protest as I haul my aching body up a fourth flight of stairs. This janky apartment complex has seen better days; dirt and rust seem to flurry in the open-air breezeways, mingling with the sound of aluminum cans shifting in the wind. This part of town is the worst—which means that it's the one that gets the most criminal activity. Although our bratva isn't directly affiliated with the police, we keep unofficial tabs on each other. My police scanner hasn't picked up this particular incident yet, meaning that we have time to absorb the impact before it lands.

If news about a serial killer targeting the city's prettiest women gets out, it will go one of two ways: the fat, balding men hoarding trophy wives will shell out *big* and make a public show of finding the killer—or, more likely, every father who gives a damn about his family will lock up their households tight and hire the city's underbelly to sniff out the knife-happy rat gutting their wives and burning their daughters.

It wouldn't be a problem if we didn't have competition on the streets, but like all cities, if there's a king ruling with an iron fist... then there's an underground resistance movement scurrying through the shadows.

The movement isn't large—it's mostly comprised of people who are still miffed about how Valentina's grandmother Katya Dolohov and all the other "old blood" leaders suddenly disappeared after their attempted coup —but it's steady enough that when civilians go looking for help with our serial killer problem, they'll end up paying the wrong side... which means that I'll have to deal with any clean-up that follows a job done wrong— and *all* amateur hit men leave tracks.

I don't have time for that, so it's best we tackle the murderer before he goes public.

Another body drop out in the open, however, means that he isn't trying to hide his kills. He's trying to send a message. And for some inexplicable reason, that message brings everything back to Celia fucking Monrovia. The disaster my brothers can't seem to shake. Over the past week, I've poured over all public and private records about her life that I can get my hands on. Marriage and birth certificates, bank notes, doctor's appointments, medical records—countless documents, spanning nearly three decades with her upcoming thirtieth birthday. Trying to figure out what makes her so fucking special is driving me insane.

I hear her voice in my sleep, from the champagne bubble of her laughter from the wedding video I downloaded to my phone to the sobbing wreck of a woman crying her eyes out in therapy after her ex-husband had an affair. Her therapist prescribed her sleeping pills and antidepressants, but Celia never refilled either, so I'm not sure if she took them in the first place. Piecing together Celia's life and motivations should be easy—every piece of information that I've found has been straightforward. There are innumerable facts about her upbringing and early adult life that I have committed to memory.

But none of it explains why my brothers chose *her*.

The bratva bitch with baggage.

Any other woman would be crawling into their laps to bounce on their dicks and call them daddy, but not her, not Celia. *Of course,* the prettiest one would be the most broken. I've stared at her photographs for hours, trying to find the cracks. The pieces I can chip away to reveal the bitch underneath, the part my brothers refuse to see.

Now, I'm not only hearing her voice in my sleep, but she's right there with me in my dreams, her wide, doe-eyes shining with tears as we lie next to each other in bed —*my* bed, the one she and Rage fucked in—naked and trembling and so goddamn beautiful that it *hurts*.

In my dreams, the conversation she had with her therapist is directed at me instead.

I tried my best. I really did. She sniffles as we lie in bed beside each other, bringing the crisp white bedsheet up to her chin. It falls over her waist and hips like satin, showing her delicate curves and transforming into a silken wedding dress. She's warm to the touch as my palm glides up her waist and across her collarbone. A tear slips past her chin, and it catches on my fingertip. Her voice floats between us despite her lips not moving. *I loved him as best I knew how. I did everything to make him love me. How am I still not enough?*

The image shifts, and suddenly she's straddling my lap, the white slip draped across her body bunching up over her hips to reveal gorgeous, tanned thighs, and between them, a tuft of soft curls and glistening lips as she sinks down onto my shaft, making my balls ache and my teeth clench.

More tears fall as she rides me, her voice a scratch inside my skull. *If we just had a baby*—her breath hitches—*everything would be perfect.*

I slam my fist on the drywall inside the stairwell, banishing the fucked-up nightmares, daydreams, *wet dreams*—

Hissing through my teeth, I tear open the door to the fifth floor and fight the pounding ache in my skull.

Everything would be fine if it weren't for Celia. The serial killer is only here because of some freaky obsession with her. My brothers are only ignoring their bratva duties because of her presence in their lives. No one can see reason because she's a poison in our veins, taking over our lives without us realizing the danger until it's too late. She's a sickness, a plague, a—

Fucking bombshell.

My gaze snaps directly to her the moment I step into

the empty apartment. Teeth still clenched, I take in her appearance from head to toe. I've never seen her like this —not in any of her records and definitely not in person. Her pouty lips are swollen and pink, the tip of her nose and tops of her cheeks matching in color from the cold winter air. Her hair is a wave tumbling down her shoulders, caressing the swell of her breasts hidden beneath a *Pierce the Veil* t-shirt that undoubtably belongs to Rebel, the leather jacket slung across her torso looking sinfully sexy despite the sweatpants doing absolutely nothing for her figure.

Our eyes meet, and an electric rush sparks like lightning in my veins.

What *is* it with this woman?

Rebel claps me on the shoulder while Ruin closes the door behind me. "Than!" he cheers, grinning. "Glad you could join us. The body's over here." Leading me into the adjoining bedroom, I find Rage kneeling alongside Zane, one of the men we contract out for odds and ends relating to corpse removal. He and his brother are some of the best at hiding evidence, so it makes sense that they're here.

Banishing thoughts of Celia from my mind becomes impossible once I crouch beside them.

The victim looks damn near like her.

"Does she know?" I ask, rubbing the backs of my eyelids. Surely, they've at least told Celia that she might be in danger. It's not just one victim anymore—it's four in the span of a few weeks. The killer is ramping up, growing more impatient as he grabs the next best thing he can rip apart. There's no telling when he'll finally go after Celia.

Rage grunts, which isn't really an answer. But the tension in his shoulders and the vein throbbing in his neck tell me that *no,* he hasn't said anything to her about the murders.

Because admitting that your father might be out to kill your girl—well, I don't envy him or the others for that truth bomb.

Not one fucking bit.

Not even when Rebel hooks his arm around her waist and presses tender kisses to her neck, or when Ruin loops his fingers through hers, or when Rage reenters the room and crashes into her like a tidal wave, kissing her with such force that they tumble into the wall. She makes these little gasping sounds, like his fingers on her skin feels as electric as her voice does on mine, each willowy sound setting my nerves on fire more than seeing him devour her does.

They break away and he's breathless, lost in the warmth of her doe-eyes, when he finally speaks.

"I need to tell you something, and you can't freak out about it."

She bites her plush bottom lip, just like how she does in my dreams. "Why not?"

"Because if you freak out," Rage murmurs, thumbing a golden pendant dangling against her throat, "it could hurt the baby."

My ears ring loud enough to make me wince.

The baby? There's no way she's pregnant. It's too

soon. I just dropped her off a few days ago—there's *no* way—

Unless.

The image of Rage fucking Celia in my bed at the safe house flashes in my mind hotter than hellfire. I never saw them have sex, only walking in at the right moment to witness the aftermath, but I haven't been able to get the idea of it out of my head. Was he gentle? Slow? Furious while he pounded deep and flooded her womb? Or did she ride him like she rides me—full of sorrow and need and hurt—trying to fill the hole in her chest with the hole between her legs?

I've never had sex with Celia, but when I can't sleep and her voice is whispering in my head, I find myself wondering what it would be like—dreaming of the possibilities, of the taste of her skin and the soft, tender sound of her cries as she comes.

I take a deep breath to calm my raging heart, but it drops to my stomach like a rock. If there was ever any hope that my brothers would let her go, it's extinguished in this exact moment—in the way they hold her, touch her, taste her, each of them as gentle as the last, like they need her in one, solid piece for the news that comes next.

Rage breaks the news without warming up to it. "The man who broke into your house? He's killing people." He tenderly cups her cheek. "He's killing women who look just like you."

"He is practicing," Ruin rumbles nearby, "for his real target."

"Because she's perfect." Rebel's lips curl into a sneer.

I hadn't noticed when I first walked in, but he's got one hell of a shiner and a busted bottom lip. "If she's perfect for his sons, she's perfect for him too. God *dammit*."

Celia blinks and looks between the three of them. "I don't understand."

Sighing, I meet her bewildered gaze. Maybe if I'm the one to give her the bad news, she'll hate me for it, and I can finally get her out of my head. "Our father. He's here in the city. He's killing women to send us a message." I wasn't sure that it was him before, but he left a note tied to the victim's wrist this time, addressing it to all four of his sons.

this is all your fault
all of you
you let her die
you chose to save him
a DEVIL over your own mother
now its your turn
you cant save her

Our father was never what I'd call *sane*, but losing my step-mother was a tipping point that sent him careening off the side of a cliff. I nod toward Celia and finish giving the news. "He wants to kill you. He wants *revenge*."

Celia's mouth falls open. She looks at Rage, but he

doesn't console her or tell her that this is a joke. "I don't even know him!"

Ruin scratches the scars on his neck and makes a garbled mix of sounds, ending on a whine that seems more canine than human. He tears at his clothes, ripping the turtleneck from his body and chucking it to the floor. Burn scars cover his torso from top to bottom, his flesh marred even further by deep scratches carved into his skin. Years have passed since the fire burned down our family home and scarred my brothers, but you wouldn't know that by watching Ruin. It's like he's still breathing in the smoke, choking on the pain of his past. "He's here," Ruin whines, already scratching his chest and struggling to breathe. "It burns. Burns, burns, burns." As Ruin turns in place to try and reach his back, I recognize the criss-crossing scars rippling across his shoulders from when our father lashed him for being a devil.

Our father may have thought Ruin was evil, but the true devil was inside himself.

Rebel latches onto our youngest brother and bands his arms around Ruin's torso to keep him from hurting himself. "Easy, there, *easy*. It's okay. You're okay. Take a deep breath. There's no smoke here, alright? Fresh, clean air. That's it. Breathe."

Celia watches the display with wide eyes, her gaze glued to Ruin's body. "What—what happened?" she asks, her voice barely more than a whisper.

I close the distance between us, coming to a stop directly behind Rage. He's blocking me from reaching Celia, but I'm fine with that—I don't need to touch her when I can already feel her phantom caress in my dreams. I meet her gaze, and a thread of sorrow tightens between us. A part of her must understand, because there are tears in her eyes.

"Our father happened."

"He tried to kill Ruin," Rage swallows, "and ended up burning our mother alive instead."

"And all of you," Celia realizes, tracing a burn scar curving beneath the collar of Rage's shirt. "That's horrible."

My lips curve into a bitter grin. "That's our father. He's a sick fucking bastard."

Rage turns to face me, his eyes steely. "We're going to kill him."

It's not a question—it's a promise.

We're going to kill our father before he can touch what's ours ever again.

CHAPTER 11

RAGE

ALTHOUGH WE MAKE it back to the apartment without further incident, Ruin immediately locks himself in his bedroom. He won't return until he's blitzed out of his mind and keeping the flashbacks at bay. In the meantime, however, I make the executive decision to keep him and Celia together for the foreseeable future. If my dad is in town and going after Celia, he won't miss the opportunity to *also* take out Ruin. He blames my brother for everything wrong in his life, which is complete and utter bullshit, but the man has problems.

We all do because of him.

Celia, on the other hand, doesn't like my brilliant plan.

"I can't stay here until you catch him!" She crosses her arms over her chest, Rebel's hideous t-shirt riding up her stomach. "What the hell am I supposed to do, *clean?*" She makes a face like cleaning is the worst thing in the world. I find it therapeutic. "I have a job that I need to get back to, Rage. I have employees. I have a gala coming up!" Her voice ratchets higher with each responsibility she lists off. "I need to contact my clients and let them know that everything is still on track. They'll think I've ghosted them and stolen their deposits. I *can't* let you ruin my reputation."

Here we go again with her precious reputation. My eye twitches at the mention of it. A person's reputation shouldn't dictate their entire life. "You shouldn't care so much about your reputation," I grumble, "because it's not something you can control."

"Like hell it is. I've worked hard on it, Rage. For *years.*" Her eyes narrow and she juts out her hip. "People actually *like* me." She glares up at me, all two hundred pounds of her glowing as brightly as the goddamn sun, and all I can think about is how fucking gorgeous she is when she's like this—all fired up and ready to fight.

It makes me horny as hell.

My cock hardens within seconds, a swift reminder of how much I *need* to be inside of her. The thought of filling her up brings the afternoon's events to the forefront of my mind, the doctor's words echoing in my head.

A few days.

In a few days, I'll know whether or not I'm a father. My heart squeezes tightly, making it hard to breathe.

I can't lose Celia. I can't lose our *child.*

Keeping Celia on a tight leash will piss her off, but it's the only way I know how to keep her safe. Handcuffing her to my brothers will keep them all safer together than apart.

I'm not risking any of their lives for the sake of her fucking *reputation*.

"You're staying here. That's final." I place my hand on the cage in our living room and swing the door open. "If you keep arguing, I'll send you to bed before dinner." My cock twitches at the idea of Celia locked up tight, safe and warm and snug with my cum filling her to the brim. Just because she might be pregnant doesn't mean we should waste a good nut—and I've got one ready to go right now.

In fact, it might be clouding my judgement. Getting off would make the whole planning process a hell of a lot smoother. I crowd closer to Celia, and she continues glaring up at me.

But she doesn't back away. She meets me right where I am, letting me bend to brush my lips across her cheek. I inhale her sweet scent, my blood on fire with the need to taste her. *Fuck*, it's been way too long since I ate her out. I grab her around the waist and unceremoniously swing her body inside the cage, laying her flat on her back across the bench. I put this little leather seat in here intention-ally—it's a good bench for fucking—and it's about time we break it in.

Celia clings to my shoulders, her breaths punching out in panicked gasps. "Hey! You can't just—"

I drag the sweatpants down her legs and her scent washes over me. Rebel claimed her last, so I know he's in there, but *fuck*, I need to taste her. I tear her panties off her body, the *rip* of red lace music to my ears—but not nearly as satisfying as the shrill little cry she makes when I push her thighs apart and get on my knees for her.

"Wh—what are you doing?" Her honeyed eyes are wide and warm, just like her plush pussy lips, swollen and slick and so fucking *mine.* It's been hours since she fucked Rebel, but she's still glistening down here.

I take a deep breath, savoring the moment. "I'm licking your pussy clean, mama, before I give you another baby." Looking up at her flushed face, I press my palm to her stomach and imagine it growing, her belly rounding with my child inside.

My child.

Not my brothers'.

Mine.

There's only one way to ensure that happens—and it's going to be the highlight of my year until I get a ring on her finger and a baby in her belly. I shudder at the mental image of Celia wearing white lace, the fabric banded around our child as I rock inside of her gently, coaxing bliss from her body as I imprint on her soul. This woman is *mine,* and the world will see it on her body, but I want her to feel it down to the marrow of her bones and beyond.

Celia covers her blushing face with her hands. "Oh, God."

I hook her thighs over my shoulders and kiss her clit, playing with her sweet bundle of nerves with a flat swipe of my tongue. Groaning, I lick her again and again, remembering how sweet she is, her presence filling me up like sunlight.

A week apart is way too goddamn long.

She claws my scalp like she always does, only this time, she doesn't keep her moans to herself. There are no customers around to hear us, so she lets go, filling my ears with a symphony of pleasure that goes straight to my heart. My cock pulses in time with every beat of my aching heart, both of them beyond saving. I couldn't give a damn as long as she stays just like this—open and willing—for the rest of our lives.

I slip a finger inside her heat, finding her g-spot with ease, and coax her orgasm closer. *That's it.* Her thighs quiver and her breath catches.

"R-Rage," she whines, arching her back and grinding her pussy on my mouth. "This is—You're—*ohgod.*" Trembling, she gasps for air. "*Rage!*"

Music to my ears.

I devour every last drop of her release, craving this special piece of her that only I can provide. No one else can make her come like this. I'm the one who started eating her out when her pussy begged for more—and I'll be the one to drown in her desire before I let another man or woman take that from me. This pleasure is all mine.

Humming happily to myself, I pull my fingers from her sticky wet hole and undo my belt, shucking my pants and shirt in record time. Then, I pull her shirt over her head just as quickly. I want to feel every inch of her skin as I claim her body one mouthwatering inch at a time.

Crawling over Celia, I lock her throat beneath my palm and squeeze gently. "You want me." The bench isn't wide enough for me to lean on, so I straddle the seat and slide Celia's hips flush against mine. Lifting her up by her throat, I lean her against the cool metal bars and thrust my hips, sliding my cock through her soaking wet lips. The tip bumps her clit, making her gasp, and I swallow the sound with a bruising kiss.

She tastes like salt and smoke, no doubt remnants of my brother. I could tear his fucking tongue out for it.

But I won't.

Growling, I grab her hip and thrust again, this time notching my cock in the right place. Celia writhes against my chest, her pupils blown so wide that they match mine —as black as my soul. I grip her chin and seal her lips to mine, not ready to hear her protest. She *wants* this. She wants *me*. I know she does.

Hearing her lie one more time will fucking *wreck* me.

"Tell me you want me," I snarl, snapping my hips and sliding two thick inches inside. She cries out at the sudden pressure, her eyes fluttering shut. "*No*," I hiss, pulling back out. "Look at me, mama. Look into my eyes while I fuck my baby inside of you."

Her eyes snap open, that fire I love burning bright within. "You're crazy," she huffs, blowing a loose strand of hair from her eyes. "You're fucking crazy."

That's not what I want to hear.

My heart roars with the need to hear the truth from her lips. I'll fucking take it from her one orgasm at a time if I have to, but that's not what I want. I want her to say it. Out loud. No more barriers between us. "Tell me you want me!" My body coils tight like a cord about to snap. I'm either going to fuck my woman because she deserves the fucking of her life for being honest, or I'm going to pound the shit out of her pussy as punishment for lying. Either way, I'm filling her womb with *my* fucking seed, and she will get pregnant with *my* child.

A maniacal grin pulls at her lips. "Will you fuck me harder if I say no?"

Precum seeps from my cock. *Fuck*, she loves to test me.

"I'll fuck you however I want," I growl, grinding my shaft against her pussy, feeling her flutter and quiver with need. Every hot, little sound she makes spurs me on, her breath warm across my face. Our eyes meet as she rakes her fingers through my sweat-slicked hair, scratching my scalp with her sharp manicure. I groan and sink another inch inside her heat, panting into her open mouth. "Say it." I'm damn near begging, my voice close to cracking. "Say it, Celia."

Please.

She locks her arms around my neck and ghosts her lips over mine. "Put a baby inside me, Rage." She shivers, her nipples pebbling into tight peaks. "I know I made a mistake last time, and I'm so—" her voice breaks—"I'm *sorry.*" Tears pool in her gorgeous eyes, the green flecks in their depths swirling with emotion. "I shouldn't have— You just—I'm scared of you sometimes." A bright bubble of laughter bursts from her chest. "You're so powerful and overwhelming and I just—"

I thrust deeper, scraping my teeth across her cheek as I sink another inch inside. Her breath punches from her lungs and her eyes go glossy. *Fuck*, she's tight. Wet, tight, resisting. Always resisting. "Let me in, mama." Gritting my teeth, I slide back out and push back in slowly, so goddamn slowly that my whole body shakes. "Tell me that you want me inside you. Because once I'm there—once I'm inside your heart—you're not getting rid of me. *Ever*. This baby is only the beginning." I kiss the side of her neck, tasting her salt, and groan as I work my way inside.

Clutching me tight against her chest, she whimpers in my ear. "You're too much, Rage. You take up so much room, so much air, that there's none left for me."

Not fucking possible.

"Whatever is mine is yours, remember? You need air, you fucking take it. Take it from me. I don't need it. I don't *want* it. Everything I am is yours." Grabbing her hand, I press it to my chest so that she can feel the thundering of my heart—all the power she gives me without even realizing it. "You *own* me, mama. My body. My strength. My heart. My soul." I ghost my lips across hers, begging for her kiss but not letting myself have it. Not yet.

I need to hear her say that she wants me. I can give her every part of my black, twisted soul, and it won't mean a damn thing if she doesn't accept it.

If she doesn't accept *me*.

Celia takes the tiniest breath. "I want..." Her gaze wanders to my lips as she cups my cheek. "I want to *try*."

She brushes her thumb across the scar on my cheek. "Is that okay? To take things slow?"

Slow?

My dick is inside of her, and she wants to take things slow?

I laugh darkly, the sound rising from the depths of my soul. In business, I take things slow, planning my approach until I conquer my opponents. But in love?

No fucking chance.

"You will fall in love with me," I growl, grabbing her hip and punching forward. My cock slides inside easily, slotting itself in her heat and damn near blinding me with how fucking *perfect* her pussy feels. I drag in a breath and move, fucking her hard and deep. "Now, tomorrow, once our baby arrives—it *will* happen."

She shudders and slams her head back against the bars, her mouth parted in a beautiful, silent *O* that makes me hotter for her. I slam my hips up, sealing our bodies together with a low hiss. Her pussy clenches tightly around my shaft, her slick desire making the glide easy. Her body wants to move fast.

It's her mind that's slowing her down.

Being this close to her—touching her, fucking her— but not *having her* will drive a man crazy. I know she'll fall for Rebel faster than she'll fall for me, and watching it unfold will be the most bittersweet karma of my life. But if that's what it takes for her to fall in love with me, if she needs to fall for him first to realize that I'm right here waiting, like I always have been, then fuck it.

"Take all the time you need."

Relief washes over her face until I wrap my fist in her hair and grin down at her. "I'm still fucking my baby in you either way."

She moans as I drive deep, making good on my promise. I want her mouth, but I resist the urge and press hot, open-mouthed kisses along her jawline instead. Maybe if I keep the kissing to a minimum, she'll crave it. She'll want my kiss as much as she wants my brother's. Jealousy sears like a brand across my heart, and I grit my teeth against the sting. Sweat drips down my back, across my scars, and I almost laugh at how fucking absurd my devotion to her is.

I'm burning alive for this woman, and I'll turn to ash if it means she'll finally love me.

I'll do anything for her.

Grabbing one of the bars beside her head, I thrust hard enough that she screams, the sound echoing through the room. We removed all of the furniture, and the consequences come with heightened acoustics. I know that Rebel can hear us loud and clear from his bedroom. Hell, Ruin likely can too despite being one floor above us. I wouldn't be surprised if Thanatos was jerking off right outside the door, the repressed fucker.

But these screams were made for me.

"That's it," I groan, "*fuck*, that's it." My balls tighten with every delicious sound her body makes for me, from the wet heat between her thighs to the screams of pleasure she makes with each thrust of my hips. I pound into her relentlessly, fearlessly, knowing that her heart will be mine as soon as she lets herself fall.

Until then, I'll give her every last fucking drop of my battered soul and all the cum that comes with it.

Her muscles tighten all at once and she claws my shoulders hard enough to break the skin. The pain is what tips me over the edge, and we come side by side, both of our bodies shaking from the force of it. My cock twitches with each rope of cum filling up her tight channel, and I groan, thrusting as deep as I can. Stuffing her full. Cock. Cum. *Me.* There's no way she can wash my scent off her body now—I'm buried deep, deeper than even Rebel was, and that alone brings a satisfied smile to my lips.

I'm definitely going to be the father of our first baby.

Once Celia comes down from her orgasm, she takes quick breaths, her face flushed a pretty crimson. Pulling herself up by my shoulders, she stares into my eyes and her lips form a hard line. "You're a fucking asshole." It takes effort, but she detangles from my body and stumbles onto the pad of blankets and pillows on the floor.

I lift an eyebrow and swing my leg across the bench, my cock still glistening from her god-tier pussy. "For what? Doing exactly what you wanted me to?" I run a hand through my hair and grin down at her. "You told me to put a baby in you. I'm merely delivering on my promise. You can't be *that* mad."

The glare she throws my way is only half-hearted, which means that we're making progress.

"You wanted a hard fuck, and you know it," I continue. "Anytime that itch needs scratched, you know where to find me."

Celia crawls out from the cage, giving me a perfect view of not only her ass, but her leaking slit. *Damn,* I did a good job.

Once she's standing, she turns on her heel and glares at me. "I'll fuck your brother before I ever fuck you again!"

I can't help it. I smile.

That pisses her off even more.

"Go ahead. Fuck Rebel. Hell, fuck Ruin for all I care. If you want a *good* lay, the kind that makes your throat raw and your body so blissed out that you can't even stand—" I grin at the way her knees threaten to buckle— "I'll be waiting."

She doesn't bother covering herself up as she walks butt-ass naked into the half-bath, filled with cum and not an ounce of honest regret. It's not me she's mad at—not really. She's mad at herself for *liking* the sex... and for wanting me at all.

I may not have heard her say that she wants me, but I can *see* it, and that's damn close enough to make me happy until she comes crawling back for more.

Chapter 12

Ruin

I can hear them fighting.

Fucking.

Breathing in each other's pain and expelling it through their bodies, working together to wring each other out until there's nothing left but a tranquil state of peace.

Or so I used to think. Owning at a night club that doubles as an invite-only swingers club has proven that people usually pass out after having sex, or they're drunk on hormones and ecstasy and feeling good enough not to care what happens next. They could be fucking one minute and flatlined the next.

Sometimes, they are.

I don't always invite my targets to the club, but every once in a while I'll study them before killing them. How they move. How they speak. Who they choose as partners, if any at all, and what they value during their last night on earth.

Celia isn't a target. I'm not getting paid to kill her. No one has put a hit out for her, and I'm not obligated to study her.

But I do anyway.

While Rage slides his cock in and out of her body, I listen to the sounds she makes. The high-pitched little cries catching in her throat, the sopping wet squelch of her body as she accepts him over and over and over again. I stretch my fingers, remembering the heat of her pussy as I held her down on the mattress inside her master bedroom and made her come. So long ago, now, it feels like the ocean tide—receding, out of reach.

I take a heavy drag of my joint and let the THC fill my lungs. My body still itches all over, but I fight the urge to scratch and pick at my scars. Once the drug hits my system, I can relax one muscle at a time, working my way from top to bottom.

Rebel says that I should try something harder than marijuana, but I don't want to lose myself. I just want to peel back the harshest layers of light and turn the world down a few notches. Make things quieter. Smoother.

Then, I can breathe.

I hear them arguing. Raised voices. Rage's laugh, rough as a cliffside and dark as a starless sky. I walk down the stairs to the main level and watch Rage disappear into his bedroom, but Celia is missing from view. I scan the room once, twice, until finally, I hear the water running inside the guest bathroom. None of us use it, and we never have guests, so I doubt there's even soap in there. Once I've grabbed a bar from my bathroom and carried it downstairs, I tap the box against the guest bath door. The soap rattles inside the tiny box.

A few seconds pass before the running water stops and the door lock clicks. Slowly, Celia pries back the door to peer through the crack. "Ruin?" She opens the door wider, her eyes flicking from my mask to the soap in my hand. "What's that for?"

She's completely naked.

My gaze sweeps her body for bruises, my dick thickening at the sight of them. A few linger on her neck, the fingerprints still visible, and a few more dot her hips and waist. She bruises easily. Pinks and purples paint her skin, and I long to touch each and every rosy mark.

I pull the door open wider and place the box in her palm. "You."

Her lips twist in a half-smile. "Thank you." Placing the box on the vanity, she ruffles her hair and shuts her eyes. "How is it that you got all the nice genes in the family?"

I didn't.

Moving through the doorway, I shut and lock the door behind me. "Open the box."

Her eyes snap open and her chest expands on a breath. "What?"

"Open the box."

Carefully, she does as she's told and slips the bar of soap into her hands. The cardboard falls uselessly to the floor, and I kick it with my boot as I step closer, crowding Celia against the sink. This is almost like the night we met, only without the candles and the midnight chase.

But the earth-shattering orgasm—that remains to be seen.

My fingers twitch with the need to touch her. To see what my brothers have done. How she's changed. Are her pussy as lips swollen and red as her mouth, or can she take a beating from both above and below? I've seen her swallow my brother's cock, and now I've heard her take one, too.

I want to see more. Feel more. Taste more.

"Sit on the counter."

She hesitates, and I wait for her to follow instructions. Unlike my brothers, I can be patient. I can wait. She *will* do as I say—

Because she thinks I'm the nice brother.

My lips curve into a smile as she obeys, hopping up onto the vanity and dangling her legs over the edge. She reaches for the faucet and I grab her hand to stop her. "Hold still." Carefully, I brush the hair from her eyes and tuck it behind her ear, following the curve of her neck to her collar bone. My leather gloves make it hard to feel, so I pull them off, toss them to the floor, and repeat the pattern, trailing my fingertips from her cheek, to her ear, down the column of her throat and across every single bruise Rage put there, to the dip of her collarbone.

These are hard to break, but not impossible.

"What are you doing?" she asks, her throat clicking on a swallow.

I consider her question for a few silent seconds.

"Learning."

I press the flat of my palm to her chest and her heartbeat ticks up a notch. Leaning closer, I take in her cloyingly sweet scent, the hint of peaches in the waves of her hair, the smoke clinging to her skin, and the overpowering smell of sex radiating from between her legs. I lick my lips, wondering what she tastes like after my brothers have ruined her. How she will taste after *I* do.

When my palm slips lower, over the swell of her breast and its sensitive bud, she inhales sharply. I pause, staring at the flush of her cheeks and the subtle tremble of her bottom lip, before cupping her breast in my hand. She's warm, warmer than I remember, and a sound catches in my throat. A groan? A grunt?

I squeeze her supple flesh and she gasps, her back arching as my knuckles pinch her nipple. My gaze wanders from her face to that sensitive spot, its peak angling upward, knotted and dense and—

Celia gasps again and shoots out her hand, clutching my upper arm. "Ruin, that—it's really sensitive." Her lips part and she makes no move to close them, her body shivering. Goosebumps trail down her arms and across her chest, making her nipples even tighter.

"I noticed."

Grabbing the handle strapped to my belt, I whip out my favorite blade from its sheath. It glints in the light, its edge wicked sharp. I've carved up many people in my lifetime—those deserving of a face lift and sometimes those who didn't—peeling back thick layers of flesh until I find the bone underneath. Sometimes, I forget that no matter how deep I carve, I can't reveal the monster underneath.

Not really. But I know it's there—the essence of a soul, tainted and twisted and laughing, grinning just like me as we tear through muscle and sinew to dig deeper, to find the one thing that's missing—the one thing that's just out of reach—

I always find it in their eyes. The last breath, the final look, the moment a soul lifts to the surface and fades into oblivion. Gone as soon as it's found. I keep digging inside bodies in search of their echoes, but I never find them.

Pressing the flat edge of the blade to Celia's breast, I hum to myself at how pretty they look together.

Celia seems to disagree. She recoils back against the mirror, banging her elbows as she scrambles away from my knife. "What the hell, Ruin!"

I glance up at her eyes, and that's when I see it—a glimpse of her soul tucked safely underneath the flash of fear. My knife finds her flesh again, this time at the curve of her neck, and a bead of blood collects where they kiss. "Let me see."

Her body freezes, but her mind doesn't. She looks between the two of us with quick, analytical flicks of her eyes, checking for weak points in my stance, my posture, my body.

Little does she know, they don't exist.

"The fire," I begin calmly, grabbing my shirt and tugging. I lift the fabric over my stomach so that she can see the mottled flesh underneath. "The fire took pieces of me, *krosotka,* pieces I haven't been able to find. Look all you want, but you won't find them, either."

Her eyes scour the contours of my abdomen, across every inch of skin and hidden muscle. "Find what?"

"An opening."

I keep the blade to her neck while I touch her body, ignoring her breast for her ribs. I run my fingers along the ladder, feeling the dip of each and how much give there is between them. Most are hidden—it's not like Celia is malnourished—so I press harder to find them. They would be easier to see if I could just—

Slowly, I slide my knife down her flesh, careful not to cut open her skin any more. My brothers won't be happy if I leave too many marks. Not yet. Not until they've had their fill. Then I'll have mine. Always taking turns, the clock ticking, the world spinning.

Celia remains still while I continue my tour of her body, the knife mirroring my hand, both of them teasing her waist, her hips, digging into her thighs. Her breath catches when I prod open her legs, spreading her wide.

This is what I want to see more than anything.

How pretty she is down here. Soft, pink, swollen, warm.

Hot, actually. Her thighs were warm but her slit—it's like nothing I've ever seen.

She twitches, her muscles likely burning, and I click my tongue. "Still, *krostoka,* be still for us."

I pull her lips apart to find her glistening and slick. "Which part is you," I murmur, "and which parts are them?" Keeping my fingers and her pussy spread, I prod her hole with the handle of my blade.

"Oh, God," Celia gasps, her muscles going rigid. "Ruin, please, *please* don't—"

A half inch disappears inside, then an inch, and I find myself *fascinated* by how quickly her body reacts. Her thighs quiver, her eyes clench tightly shut, and she makes those sounds—the tiny whimpers I've heard her make with my brothers.

Licking my lips, I tip my knife in and out and play with her opening, watching it expand to fit the handle, then feeling it try to take even more from me.

Was her body made for this, too?

I'd nearly forgotten about my cock, but it roars to life now, pulsing in time with Celia's own heartbeat. If I press my fingertip to her clit, I can feel it—the heavy beat of her heart pumping blood throughout her body, all the way down to *this* sensitive spot.

But that's not my focus for this evening. It's the way that Celia's pussy begs for more of my knife that captivates me. Most people think that the blade and its unforgiving edge are the most important part of a knife, but they'd be wrong. It's the handle, the part you hold, that matters most. Our connection is intimate, the two of us working in tandem to achieve our goals, to take life and, sometimes, keep our own intact.

It's a sacred bond that I'm sharing with Celia now.

Her body understands.

"Ruin," Celia moans, her hand gripping my arm tight enough that *she* might leave a mark, "you're—you're bleeding!"

Oh.

I spare a moment to check my palm, but all I see is the gush of red from my grip around the blade... and how it drips onto Celia's body. Her stomach. Her thighs. Her pussy. Painting her crimson with *my* blood.

My cock leaks from the tip, and I pull the knife away before I stumble and shove it deeper. I bet she could handle it, but *I* can't.

"*F—fuck*," I groan, my knife clattering into the sink basin while my cock jerks inside my pants. Hissing, I grab Celia's thigh with my bloodied hand, finally feeling a lick of pain in my palm while my cock spills, the heady mixture of pleasure and pain making me dizzy. I lean over Celia and drag in lungfuls of air, my body suddenly too hot, too tight. The mask covering my face feels like a prison, locking me away from *more*.

More air. More light. More *feeling*.

More of *her*.

Celia's warm little hands wrap around my shoulders, and she holds me close while my body shakes. "Easy there, easy," she coos, hugging me tight. Her body heat is lost on my chest and back, but her thighs blaze against mine, reminding me how sticky sweet red she is—now *mine* as much as my brothers'.

I reach between us and cup her pussy with my uninjured hand, rubbing my blood into those soft curls and the hot flesh tucked beneath, dipping my fingers inside of her to paint her with *my* essence.

She cries out at the sudden intrusion, but I'm not going to fuck her. I merely slip my bloodied fingers inside her sex and leave remnants of myself there.

If I have a soul, I want it to nestle next to hers.

"Stay still," I remind her as I pull away. Her eyes are wide, open windows, and I glimpse the bright light of her soul tangling with the shadows of mine. Satisfaction rolls through me, and for the first time in years, it's like I have control of my entire body instead of the mangled pieces left after the fire.

I pick up my knife from the sink and the bar of soap beside it. The knife slides into its sheath while the soap slips into Celia's palm. I curl her fingers around the bar and squeeze until I know she won't drop it. "Clean up. Go on."

"But your hand—"

Holding my palm up to the light, I inspect the straight-lined cut jutting across the center. It's deeper than I'd like, but I'll be fine. "Flesh will mend," I remind her, squeezing my hand into a fist to stop the bleeding. I'm not concerned about it in the slightest, but Celia's eying my closed fist skeptically. Taking a breath and scenting the metallic tang of my blood in the air, I remember the last time Celia patched up my arm, and my lips curve up. If I asked, she'd help me this time, too, I'm sure.

But I won't ask any more of her tonight.

"Clean yourself up," I say again, retreating to the door. The turn lock is slick in my hands, and I frown at all the blood I'm dripping. Rage will be angry at the mess. "The bathroom, too."

He'll also be angry if he finds out that I pulled out my knife and touched Celia with it, but some rewards are worth the risk.

I give Celia one last, long look before retreating upstairs to clean and cover my open wound, my mouth curving into a smile as I replay the last thirty minutes over and over and over again in my head.

The temptation has never been sweeter, and the fruit never wetter.

Chapter 13

Celia

For the first time since returning to the boys' lives, I'm finally alone.

Once Ruin disappears and leaves me to tend to the bloody aftermath of his—what the hell do I even call it? —*visit*, I finally decide, I stare at my reflection in the mirror. I've done this a thousand times. Not just in my lifetime, but since my divorce. Staring at the girl in the mirror, wondering where she came from. How she got here. And most importantly, where she's going.

If you asked my reflection a year ago, she wouldn't have had any idea. Drifting along the river of time, merely treading water, trying not to drown, was a full time job. Once the current of grief settled and I could look myself in the eye without flinching, I began to float.

The river twisted and bent and somehow, I ended up here. With three men vying for my attention, my body, and quite possibly, my heart.

I clutch my chest, expecting to the feel sharp, stabbing pain that's accompanied me for so long now. A broken heart can't beat without it, and mine's been broken for so long, that I've forgotten what life feels like without the pain.

My heart beats, and for once, everything feels...

Calm.

The bathroom looks like a crime scene with my body as its victim, and yet, *I'm okay.*

I'm breathing.

I'm in one piece.

And despite how unorthodox Rage, Rebel, and Ruin are with how they show affection, I know they're trying. That has to count for something, right?

I draw my gaze to my navel, tracking the bloody handprint on my hips, the crimson drops on my thighs, down to the apex between them, my curls more red than black. I'm a sticky mess. My pussy throbs from the battering it's received from two dicks and the tip of a knife handle, with the latter being, surprisingly, the most gentle of the three. With a hiss, I run soapy fingers through my folds and try to clean up the mess. Without a towel or toilet paper or *anything* to catch the suds, pink bubbles slip down my legs and pool onto the tile floor. A real shower, with a generous stream of steaming hot water and enough soap to sustain an army, would work wonders.

But leaving this room means I might run into any one of the brothers, and I'm not sure how to handle them after today.

Turning off the faucet, I shake off as much water

from my hands as I can. The soap cleaned up as much of the blood from my body as it could without a cloth, but the bathroom is still a hot mess. I pull my hair back and knot it in a loose bun at the base of my neck, wrapping a strand of hair around it as a makeshift tie and tucking the end inside. The bun is loose, but it holds well enough for my hair to be out of the way.

I guess I'm cleaning, after all.

Unlocking the bathroom door takes an enormous amount of willpower, and opening it is like ripping off a band-aid. It has to be done. I shiver in the cool air as I peer out into the living room.

Empty.

The brothers are nowhere to be seen.

Walking into the room without one of them watching feels strange. Stranger still is walking past the cage without being thrown inside. I hover at its gleaming golden door, wondering if I'm expected to crawl back inside. Would that make Rage happy?

The bench he fucked me on waits inside, its dark leather smeared with streaks of white. Stains across the surface—likely sweat or oils from our skin—makes the top hazy rather than shiny smooth. The blankets and pillows lining the bottom of the cage are in a disarray, tumbled into a messy heap. Rage's clothes are gone, as are the sweatpants and t-shirt Rebel loaned me.

I lock the cage from the outside, feeling satisfied once it clicks into place.

Then, I move on.

Rebel's bedroom door is nonexistent, so breaking

into his room is easy. Dirty t-shirts and skinny jeans litter the floor around his bed, like he couldn't care less to clean up after himself, with the only tidy space in the room being a simple metal desk with playing cards stacked neatly to the side. A poker chip stand sits in the corner, with a deep red velvet overlay taking up most of the desk top.

Does Rebel play cards?

I think back to all of our conversations in the *before*, when I was a regular working woman coming home to dinner and a kiss every evening. Rebel never mentioned that he gambled. In fact, any conversation surrounding his work gently slipped away without any real focus on an alternative topic.

The man is a master of redirection... with his favorite tactic being backing me up against a wall and expertly kissing away any thought that didn't involve his mouth on mine.

I bite my bottom lip and brush my fingertips over the playing mat. I really don't know much about him at all—or about any of them.

It's about time I learn more.

But first, a shower.

Rebel's bathroom mirrors Rage's, the exception being how many hair and tattoo creams Rebel owns. Spare piercings lying on the counter catch my eye, and I look at the handful of silver rings and balls with interest. Which ones are for his lip and which ones are for his... dick?

My cheeks flush and I quickly move on, grabbing

what looks like the cleanest towel in the room and turning on the shower. I jump in before the water has had a chance to warm, moaning as I scrub the cum, sweat, and blood from my body. I stand in the spray for as long as humanly possible, scrubbing my body from head to toe multiple times, combing my fingers through the knots in my hair, rubbing the kinks in my shoulders and back. When I finally step out of the steam and wrap the towel around my body, I expect to find one of them standing there. Rage, leaning against the counter, a gleam in his eye as he eye-fucks me from across the room. Or Rebel, sitting on the counter with his lip pinched between his teeth as he rubs his dick through his jeans. And finally, I picture Ruin standing there, a quiet enigma with more trauma than I know how to unpack.

While I dig through the bathroom drawers for a hairbrush, I think about Ruin the most.

He fucked me with a knife handle.

A shiver runs down my spine. While he was enraptured with the hilt sliding in and out of my pussy, I couldn't stop staring at his eyes. Glittering onyx, focused and intent on their target.

Is that what I am to him? A target? A plaything to use when the mood strikes?

At least with Rebel and Rage, I have an idea of where I stand. For better or worse, Rebel's my boyfriend in the loosest sense of the word, and Rage is...

Let me fuck a baby inside you.

I press my palm to my lower abdomen as a familiar thread of hope curls around my heart.

Rage is the father of my child.

Emotions tumble like gemstones inside my chest, each one rough and chaotic as they clash. I have mixed feelings about Rage more than the other two, but he's the one trying the hardest to give me what I want.

I'm sure he thinks I should be grateful, and on some level, I am. He clearly cares about my happiness as long as it aligns with what he thinks is in his best interest... but therein lies the problem. His best interests and mine don't always coincide.

It's this thought that keeps me moving. If I've learned anything over the past few years, it's that the only person I can rely on is myself. Husbands don't always keep their promises, and I doubt that Rage, Rebel, and Ruin will be an exception to that, no matter how our relationship unfolds and no matter how much Rage may claim otherwise.

I throw on clothes from Rebel's dresser, pass through his bedroom doorframe, find my discarded boots near the entrance to their apartment, and quickly open the door to reenter the real world. If I can swing by the boutique before anyone catches me, I can check on Sara *and* our inventory, grab a handful of invoices and color swatches from my desk, finally place uninterrupted calls to my clients—

The door clicks shut behind me and a low, throaty *growl* fills the air.

Thanatos looks up from his cell phone, clutching the device so tightly that I swear, I hear the screen crack. He doesn't push off from the wall he's leaning on, choosing instead to glare at me as I hover in the hallway. If he weren't already imposing with the armor plating strapped to his chest and the Glock hanging from his belt, his bulging biceps and triceps would do the trick. Pair the muscles with the salt and pepper stubble coloring his high cheekbones and streaking through his hair, he quickly becomes any good girl's wet dream.

Mine included.

"Where do you think you're going?" His voice is raspy and deep, and my overstimulated body responds accordingly: my knees buckle and I drop.

With alarming speed, Thanatos lunges and catches me before I hit the floor. He holds me against his chest and exhales hotly into my hair, his body going completely rigid as he keeps me steady and on my feet.

I push away from him as hard as I can as my adrenaline kicks into overdrive. This is the man who hates my guts. The one who hog-tied me and spat in my face, calling me a terrible mother, saying that my baby would be better off—I gasp as pain lances through my chest, the memory hurting more than I can bear. "Let me go," I cry, trembling. *Shit.* I can't cry. Not here. Not now. *Not with him.*

"What's wrong?" He searches my eyes, and I spot the familial resemblance immediately. Although his brothers' eyes are all variants of black, Thanatos's are a deep, charcoal gray with flecks of green making them appear lighter. I wonder what he sees when he looks at me—the desperate woman taking advantage of his brothers, or the fragile girl in the mirror I thought I'd left behind?

"Get off of me!"

A muscle in his jaw tics. "Tell me what's wrong, Celia."

"I didn't—" I take a shallow breath. "I didn't know you'd be here!" Just like with his brothers, he's too strong for me to escape by strength alone. I dig the heel of my palm into a gap in his armor, hoping to find flesh beneath but hitting a bulletproof vest instead. "What the hell are you wearing?" I ask, exasperated and growing more tired by the second. I didn't get enough sleep before Rebel dragged me out of the apartment last night, and after all the emotions from learning I might be— could be—hopefully am—pregnant, and how bone-tired I am from all the sexual stimulation today, I'm running on pure willpower and a sense of responsibility that's fading extraordinarily fast.

Thanatos pulls me to my feet. He tries to let me go, but when he does I fall back toward the wall and he's forced to grab me again. With another growl, he curses under his breath. "So much fucking trouble," he grumbles, gripping my arms tight. "Shouldn't you be in bed?"

I blink up at him, and he sighs.

"You're pregnant," he clarifies, taking a step back to hold me at arm's length. He probably thinks the baby is a disease or a menace or, I don't know, something inherently *bad*. He's said it before, and I'm bracing myself for him to say it again when his gaze drifts down to my belly. "You need to be more careful," he murmurs, quickly looking away and clearing his throat. "That's all."

My mouth falls open. That's *not* what I expected him to say at all.

"I can take care of myself," I remind him. "I was doing fine before you kidnapped me, remember?"

He scoffs. "You were rolling around in a dump like a stray dog."

I shove his chest as my anger flares. "*Excuse me?*"

"I grabbed you within sixty seconds, if even that." He checks my body from head to toe, clearly displeased with what he sees. "Your gun wasn't even within arm's reach, and you didn't have an alarm system or a dog to warn you of any security threats. It was sloppy work, which created a bad outcome for you, and an easy pickup for me. It's like you *wanted* us to catch you."

My anger flares even hotter, burning in the back of my throat like lava. "I would have been fine against anyone *normal!*" I wriggle out of his grasp. The only reason I slip away is because he *lets* me, and it pisses me off even more. He's right. I was sloppy with security, and even now, I stepped into the hall without a weapon. I didn't even look for one before leaving.

"You have a murderer following you," Thanatos continues, crossing his arms over his broad chest. "You can't afford to be careless, or it's light's out, Princess."

This again. Gritting my teeth, I mirror his posture and cross my arms. "Good thing I have three overbearing men to protect me, then. If I fail—" I barely contain a wince, but I manage—"they'll keep me safe. Problem solved."

He swallows, but it looks like he's downing a bucket

full of nails. His mouth pinches at the edges, the creases around his eyes giving away his age. Older than Rage, but by how much? Five years? Ten?

"Four," he grunts.

I blink. How did he read my mind?

"You have *four* men now, Princess."

Oh, *fuck* no.

I open my mouth to protest, but he clamps his hand over my lips.

Grimacing, he shuts his eyes and takes a deep breath. "Look, we don't have to get along. You don't have to *like* me. But until my dad is out of the picture, you need all the protection you can get. He won't spare your life just because of that baby in your belly. Do you understand?"

I wrap my arms around my middle and fight the panic rising like a tide. Silently, I nod, unable to speak. If I thought having Rage as a father was bad, having his dad as a grandfather is undoubtedly worse. I chew on the inside of my cheeks while Thanatos and I stare at each other, the seconds ticking past. Finally, he removes his hand from my face and looks away. "Good. That's settled, then."

An idea forms slowly as my emotions settle, a few of the tumbling stones inside my chest polished enough for me to grasp. I pluck out the most refined for the moment, the one that makes the most sense, and take a deep breath. "Teach me, then."

Thanatos visibly flinches, a flush creeping across his neck. "What?"

I clear my throat, trying not to get embarrassed and

utterly failing. Clearly, he doesn't want to spend any more time with me than he already has to. I'm about to ask him to sacrifice his time—hell, a good part of his life, probably—for *my* sake.

And he *hates* me.

"Please... teach me. I need to know what to do if someone comes after me. I—" I bite my lip—"I know I'm a bratva daughter, but my father didn't believe in girls having guns, and I was happy enough to ignore the need for most of my life. The gun you saw when you kidnapped me isn't even mine. It's my brother's. I've never used it. I don't even know how to load it or clean it or—"

Thanatos curses in heavy Russian, suddenly walking down the hallway. He runs his hands through his hair, stops about twenty feet away, then turns on his heel and stares at me.

My heart thunders in my chest. I take a few steps closer to him, knowing that even if he hates me, he loves his brothers. He loves his family. And like it or not, we're going to be family if this pregnancy is real and I'm carrying his brother's child.

"Please," I murmur, clenching my hands by my sides. I can't read his expression. I don't know what he's thinking. I don't know if he'll say yes or insult me some more or—

"*Fine,*" he grumbles, holding out his hand. When I don't take it, he reaches for my hand and shakes it stiffly. "We start tomorrow. *After* you get a full night's sleep. I'll tell Dmitri that you need a real meal—not that shit Rebel eats—and you'll eat every bite he puts in front of you. I won't have you passing out because you haven't had enough calories."

I'm so stunned that all I can do is grab his entire arm in earnest. "Thank you," I breathe, overwhelmed with relief. "Thank you so much." He falls forward as I shake his arm, caught off guard by my enthusiasm, and tumbles forward. Before he crashes into me, he slams his hand on the wall beside my head and steadies himself.

We stand in suspended silence as he studies my face, his gaze flicking from my eyes down to my lips. His warm breath ghosts across my cheeks as he exhales. "Be ready at eight A.M. sharp, Princess." He pushes himself off the wall and opens the apartment door for me. "Now get back inside before Rage finds out you tried to leave."

I don't move, and he scowls. "What is it now?"

"I have things I need to do out here."

"Like *what?*"

"I have a business to run, thank you very much!" I roll my eyes. "I'm not just a baby factory, you know! How many times do I have to tell you guys? I have responsibilities!"

Thanatos clenches his jaw. "What do you need to do your job from here?"

I purse my lips. "I can't do my job from here."

"You managed just fine for the week you stayed in your little hideaway," he snaps, glaring at me.

So much for progress.

"I need things from my office. And a cell phone. And to check on my employees and my shop." I count on my fingers as I list items off. "But it would be much easier if I could get everything myself—

"No."

I throw my hands up. "You won't know what you're looking for if you go without me!"

"I'll manage."

"No, you won't!" I jab his chest with my finger. "I need my things, and I need my tasks done properly. No one can do this but me."

Thanatos doesn't look moved by my plight. "Give up the business, then. It's not like clothes are as important as, oh, I don't know, *your life.*" He glares right back at me. "If I take you outside of this building, Rage will blow a fucking gasket. Not to mention, I'll have to work double-time to watch your ass, because your situational awareness is some of the worst I've ever seen."

My body shakes with fury. "You don't know what I've put into this business. None of you know. It means a lot to me, and I—"

He lifts an eyebrow and cuts me off. "You sure about that?" Gesturing broadly all around us, he scoffs. "Have you forgotten where we are? Who runs this place? Who *owns* it?" Shaking his head, he smacks the heavy metal door to his brothers' apartment. "If anyone will understand, it's that man you fight with so goddamn much. Talk to Rage about your business, and he just might help you keep it." He nods toward the apartment, and my gaze lands on the golden cage gleaming within.

Fucking *Rage.*

"He won't listen," I protest.

"Then you have to make him listen." Thanatos plants his hand on my lower back and shoves me through the open doorway. "Make him listen or lose everything you've worked for in your life. Your choice."

The door slams shut behind me, and I turn around and kick it, screaming. "You've got to be fucking *kidding* me!"

I hear Thanatos's laughter louder than any *fuck you* I've ever gotten in my life. The man might be willing to teach me self-defense and basic weapons handling, but beyond that?

He isn't interested in helping me at all.

CHAPTER 14

REBEL

WHEN I PULL into the garage after a long night of schmoozing rich fucks in expensive suits and their dick-starved, whoring wives, the club is in full swing. Music thrums through the walls and the floor vibrates with the club's erratic heartbeat. Mikhail Monrovia insists that he had the "best of the best" architects build the place, but after a few years of excessive partying day in and day out, the cracks are starting to show. He wouldn't admit it, but I see it.

I live here, for fuck's sake.

It's not my job to maintain a fucking building. We pay people for that shit. Still...

I glance up at the ceiling, knowing that somewhere up there, Celia is waiting. Likely brooding, much like Rage does, that little furrow between her eyebrows begging for me to smooth it over with a kiss. For an independent woman, she worries a lot. About her boutique. About her family. And now, about the baby.

As I toss my keys onto a workbench, I wonder what it will be like to have a baby around. Can you raise a baby over a club? What kind of life will the kid have if sex swings and strobe lights become the normal? Not that *my* upbringing was any more normal than its will be—but at least it won't suffer abuse at the hands of its father.

Fathers. With an S.

I scratch the back of my neck as I ignore the party and trod upstairs to the second floor. If the baby is Rage's, will he share responsibilities? Or will he expect Celia to do all the work while I sit around with my thumb up my ass? Shaking my head, I quickly decide that no matter what, Celia won't be raising her baby alone. She deserves better than that. How shitty would it be to finally become a mother but have zero support?

Not that Rage wouldn't support her, but the man is busier than he lets on. The club doesn't actually run itself, and to top it off, we're still at Ezra's beck-and-call twenty-four seven. Our boss has cooled off since he got with the *pakhan*'s girl Valentina, thank Christ, but it's only a matter of time before the honeymoon phase ends and I'm smashing kneecaps with a baseball bat again.

I don't particularly miss that part of my job.

It's strange how much a single person can change everything.

It's strange how much I *like* it.

As soon as I step inside our apartment, I strip down to my birthday suit, tossing my clothes wherever the fuck they land. I have no patience for stuffy colognes and cloyingly sweet perfumes, preferring a natural, clean scent, yet every time I come back from one of our gambling halls, I reek of them. Downing an entire water bottle and grabbing a second for the bedroom, I spare a moment to check on Celia inside her cage. She's awfully quiet for a woman who hates the damn thing—

I squint in the darkness, expecting to find her hiding beneath a mountain of blankets, only to notice that she's missing.

My first guess is that she's in Rage's room, the fucking *hog*. The bastard's probably got her wrapped up in his arms again, or cuffed to his headboard, or sucking his cock—

I step into my bedroom and jump out of my goddamn skin. "Jesus, dude, what the fuck!"

Ruin is standing silently over my bed, staring into the darkness.

"What, did they fuck on my bed?" I give him a once-over, checking where his head's at. Sometimes it's hard to read him, but lately what's been throwing me off is how often he's been around. Ezra hasn't been giving him targets, and the idle time could be fucking with his mental state. He's usually best with a knife in his hand and a target to hunt. Everything seems normal, except— "What happened to you?" His gloves are suspiciously missing, and a bandage covers his right hand. "Did someone actually stab you back?"

He grunts.

Sighing, I shoulder past him and head for the bathroom. "Yeah, well, don't let them get too close, alright? Do you have a new target, or something?"

"There is only one target."

Ah, right. Dad.

I leave the bathroom door open and turn on the shower. "How's that going?"

Silence. But I never expect too much with conversation from Ruin. I rinse all of the perfumes and colognes from my hair and soap up my entire body, ready to crawl into bed and pass the fuck out. Taking Celia to the diner and then the car lot last night was worth it—a thousand fucking times worth it—but staying out all night takes its toll. Not to mention the fifty ounces of vodka I drank twenty-four hours ago.

My stomach churns and I quickly switch to other thoughts. Like how happy Celia looked at the doctor's office—no, not quite happy, maybe like... hopeful. She clearly knew Wren and they have rapport with each other, which is a good thing, because if she stays with us, he'll be her primary and secondary doctor. Really, he'll be her only one, more than likely, just like he is for the rest of us.

I wonder what it'll be like, living with Celia full time.

Visiting her at home was fun and all, but it'll be even better to keep her in *my* bed and show her what *my* life is all about. The diner was only the beginning—I can't wait to show her all the other secrets the strip has in store.

I smile as I imagine her in the tattoo shop with me, a baby on her hip while I get new ink. Something significant. Maybe her initials—or the baby's.

Who's gonna name it once it's born?

When I stumble back into my bedroom, I'm not

surprised to find Ruin still standing there in the dark, but I *am* surprised once I realize what he's staring at... or who.

I run my hand down my face, figuring she's a figment of my sleep-deprived imagination. But no, Celia is wrapped up in my bedsheets, wearing *my* shirt—fuck yeah. Eyes closed, lips parted, body warm and waiting for me to slide up behind. I glance up at my younger brother. "You could have gotten in, dude," I remind him, throwing my towel to the floor. "C'mon, I'll slide up behind her, and you can take the front, or whatever, just get in with me. But take off your fucking clothes." I wrinkle my nose. "Maybe take a shower first. Could you do that?"

Ruin's gaze flicks up from Celia's sleeping form. He nods. "Okay."

Whoaaa, progress.

I find him a towel and wait until he's in the shower before returning to my sleeping beauty. Ruin is a man of function—he won't spend an hour wasting hot water—so I've only got a few seconds alone with her before he reappears. I slide between the sheets and *shit,* she's a fucking furnace. A chill races down my spine, but I fucking love it. Wrapping one arm around her waist, I pull her against my chest and sigh into her hair. She smells like... is that...

A chuckle rumbles in my chest. She used my shampoo. Sandalwood and Madagascar Vanilla, or some shit. I'm told the ladies love it. Maybe Celia does, too. Warmth blossoms in my chest, seeping into my bones everywhere we touch. I press a kiss to her forehead and brush my fingertips across her cheek.

She felt safe enough to come to my bed, and somehow, that feels like the biggest win in the world.

As predicted, Ruin appears within seconds. He hasn't bothered drying off, but at least he hasn't put his clothes back on. I glance up at him and nod for him to join us. "C'mon, I left room for you." Behind her instead of in front, but whatever. I'm prettier to look at. Besides, I wanted to see her sleeping face and kiss her sweet lips. Speaking of—I lean in and press my lips to hers gently while Ruin climbs in behind her.

It's selfish to continue kissing her with Ruin watching, but fuck it, we're in *my* bed. I sigh against her mouth and drag her body closer, cocooning my body in her warmth, because damn, is she *warm*. I used to slip my hands in her pockets any time we were in her freezer box of a house, so this is reminiscent of those early days. It's kind of nice.

She stirs, slowly waking. It takes her a moment to adjust, but in that moment, she snuggles against my chest and takes my breath away.

"Hey, beautiful," I murmur with a smile, "careful, or you'll spoil me. I might need this to survive."

Her voice is scratchy when she speaks. "Need what?"

I tilt her chin up and capture her lips in another kiss, loving the way she melts into me. *This* is what I've missed. These little moments when it's just the two of us without all the bullshit in the way. She moans, and the sound goes straight to my cock. *Fuck.* Pushing her onto her back, I slide my knee between her thighs and crawl on top of her.

She looks up at me with those warm, brown eyes, and my heart does this stupid little flip inside my chest.

My answer comes easy. "You, baby, just like this." I tug on her shirt, reconsidering. "Maybe naked next time."

At first, she smiles back at me, her deliciously warm hands wandering across my torso, touching me for no other reason than she *wants* to. Once she realizes Ruin is beside us, however, she jumps out of fright. "Ruin! What —what are you doing here?"

Oh, yeah. I guess he is here.

Her cheeks flush as I look between the two of them. Hm. "Did something happen while I was gone?" I ask, slipping Celia's fingers through mine. I pin her hand beside her head, and *fuck*, she's gorgeous. She's so fucking gorgeous like this. Thick waves of chestnut spiral out on the pillow behind her head, then she licks her perfect, pouty lips, and her body—she takes a quick little breath as our chests touch, tempting me to slip my hand up her shirt and caress that soft, caramel skin of hers. I *was* going to go to sleep, but now...

"Nothing happened," Celia says quickly, squeezing my hand.

Ruin stares at our joined hands and lifts his own, carefully grabbing Celia's right hand and lifting it beside her head. He wraps his fingers around hers and pins them down to the mattress.

She wiggles beneath me, giving my dick all kinds of ideas. "What are you two doing?"

"Don't know," I answer honestly, grinning. "But I wanna find out." I glance over at my brother. "Hey, if I eat her out, you wanna kiss her? She'll love it."

I don't actually think my brother's ever kissed anyone. If he has, he's kept that secret on lockdown, but I can't imagine him removing his mask for anyone other than himself. Sometimes he'll take it off when we're home, but I know it makes him uncomfortable.

Unlike Rage and me, the fire really fucked him up, and he never really came to terms with the damage.

He's silent for a long moment, and surprisingly, so is Celia. She's staring at him like a curious little kitten, and hopefully, they'll both agree. It would be good for them to become more familiar with each other—more physically intimate.

Hell, *I* want to see that shit.

"No," he says finally, clutching her hand tighter.

Damn.

"Fair enough," I sigh, a little more than disappointed. *Crushed* might be too strong, but still. The rejection stings. I thought it was a pretty good idea.

Celia feels the sting, too, by the looks of her. She struggles to free her hand from his, but he doesn't take the cue to let her go. "Hey, hey," I murmur, cupping her cheek. "Don't worry, baby, he'll come around. Won't you, Ruin? You'll let Celia see your face. You'll kiss her too, won't you? Like this. Watch." I lean in and steal another kiss, this time slipping my tongue past her lips.

She's stiff and unresponsive at first, but I'm quickly becoming an expert in what she likes. I start gentle and slow, tasting her lips with reverence and teasing her tongue with mine, until she's moaning and kissing me back, her body shaking, her breaths shallow and soft.

"See," I murmur, breaking away. Her eyes are glossy, and it fills me with pride to see her wanting.

I did that.

Ruin tilts her chin toward him to get a better look, and her gaze wanders his naked chest. It's too dark to see much, but it's enough to pique her curiosity. While they stare at each other, I slowly let go of her hand and slide off of her. I'd much rather feel her body beneath mine, but I can't be all over Rage's ass about sharing and not do the same.

She reaches up and touches his chest, trailing her fingers across long stretches of scars. He doesn't have many tattoos despite having an S-tier pain tolerance, because he doesn't like people seeing what's hidden beneath his clothes. Still, the same way Celia tracks the ink on my chest, she tracks the scars on his.

He remains perfectly still while she touches him.

"Does it hurt?" she asks, pushing up on her elbow to caress his neck. Her hair cascades down her back, and I greedily slide up behind her and bury my face in the soft strands. I slide my hand over her hip and kiss the sensitive spot behind her ear, unable to keep my hands off of her while she's like this—not just in my bed, but opening up to Ruin.

And he's *letting* her.

He swallows, and her fingertips brush across his Adam's apple as it bobs. Then he reaches out and touches a spot on her neck, a cut I hadn't noticed, and a sound catches in his throat. "Does it hurt?" he parrots back, thumbing the spot.

"No, it doesn't," she murmurs.

I kiss the tiny cut and she shivers. It wasn't there when I left this afternoon, and I know damn well Rage wouldn't make her bleed. Ruin got a hold of her after we explicitly told him *not* to use his knife. And yet, here she is, not freaking out about it.

She really is perfect.

Not just for me, but for all of us.

And I think, after today, she just might be starting to accept it.

CHAPTER 15

CELIA

AFTER DETANGLING from Rebel's koala grip and rushing to the bathroom to pee in the morning, the three of us emerge from Rebel's bedroom to find a full breakfast spread sitting on the kitchen island while Rage pours fresh coffee into three mugs. When I reach for one, he moves it out of range. "No caffeine," he says, leaning in to press a quick kiss to my forehead. Then he nods to the smallest and healthiest portion of food: a bowl of oatmeal with a handful of berries on the side. "That one's yours."

"Great," I murmur, plopping down onto the nearest bar stool. But my heart isn't in the grumbled complaint, because on the other side, hope stretches its wings and flutters like a hummingbird against my ribs.

There's a reason I'm being fed non-greasy, non-fat foods, and it has everything to do with the life I might be carrying.

That makes the sacrifice worth it.

I grab a spoon and dunk it into my oatmeal, making a mental note to thank Dmitri—if I ever meet him—for the conscientiousness displayed while choosing my breakfast. Then I wonder if Thanatos told him what to make for me or if he left the chef to his own devices. Do either of them know what to feed a pregnant woman, or did they make their best guess?

Either way, I'm grateful for the effort being put into keeping me and the baby healthy.

It's more consideration than a certain *someone* has shown the entire time I've known him. I glance up at Rage when he's not looking and wonder what he's thinking. After our little spat inside the cage yesterday, he disappeared as usual, taking all of the testosterone and frustration hanging in the air with him. It's like he materializes from the shadows every sunlit morning to torment me, then fades out of existence any time I might actually need him for something.

Thanatos' voice echoes in my head.

Talk to Rage about your business, and he just might help you keep it.

My stomach knots at the mere idea of asking Rage for anything, let alone for help with my boutique. I have to force myself to swallow another spoonful of oatmeal. Is Rage really the one running the club, or does he employ a full staff? No, of course he has a full staff—but how does he manage them? Who coordinates the secret invitations to *Midnight*, and who transforms the club from its normal nightlife functions into the debaucherous, clandestine invite-only events?

He can't do everything himself. I've seen what he can do with his fists—those aren't negotiation tools for business, they're weapons for eradicating threats to the bratva. Someone else has to be running the club—with Rage as the face, or maybe even as the money, if he's the one making deals in back rooms. I wouldn't be surprised if the club is a money laundering scheme masquerading as city nightlife. In fact, I should expect it. I may not be the most prominent figure within our bratva by choice, but I do know that no matter which family name runs the outfit, *all* bratvas have dipped their fingers into dark deals and illicit affairs. It's how the bratva business has continued running for centuries. One main family spearheads the traditions and values held by the many, with all family units—cousins, uncles, second aunts, longtime loyal friends and confidants—focused on protecting what's theirs. Money, property, reputation, family.

Children.

I press my hand to my stomach and take a deep breath. Despite any misgivings I have about the bratva, it produces strong individuals and even stronger families. What happened to my father—the way he died so suddenly—was an anomaly that proves that...

I swallow hard. I've always believed that my father was a good man at heart and that the life of a criminal didn't suit him. That despite being Russian, despite being a member of one of the most respected bratvas in the country, he never quite fit in. This, I've reasoned, is why he died. He was a criminal living a dangerous life, and that lifestyle is what snuffed him out.

But then I look at men like Rage, Rebel, or Ruin—the kind of men who seem to thrive in the chaos—and wonder if being labeled a criminal is what really killed my father... or if he died from something worse.

Like being *weak*.

Good, strong men don't leave home without kissing their daughters goodbye. He doesn't keep a secret safe house from his wife, or stash thousands of dollars in the walls of their family home, or pack a single suitcase and buy a one-way plane ticket out of the country for just himself.

His *pakhan* doesn't erase his name from bratva record or refuse to bury his body in the Monrovia family crypt. Good, loyal men and women are dressed in satin and gold when they're laid to rest.

After he died, my father never had a funeral. I don't know what happened to his body or if there were any pieces left to bury at all.

I watch Rage fiddle with each of his brothers' plates and note the care he takes to ensure that they both receive not only a full meal, but the shiniest silverware, perfectly-folded cloth napkins, a full, steaming mug of hot coffee, and for Ruin in particular, a mysterious paper to-go bag that the youngest brother immediately carts upstairs along with his meal. Then Rage pours me a glass of spring water, folds my napkin into a perfect square, and slides it over toward me with a tiny packet of organic brown sugar on top.

The scars on his knuckles shine in the bright kitchen

light. For such a violent man, he's precise with his movements. Deliberate. Like he... cares.

I bite the inside of my cheek as warmth spreads across my face. A good father takes care of and supports his family. Maybe it's the baby fever talking or my hormones going crazy from all the sex I've been having lately, but for the first time since I met Rage, he doesn't look like a bruiser raring for a fight.

He looks like a head of household—like a leader.

Like a *father*.

And it's *doing things* to my insides.

As I take the sugar packet, our fingers brush and fiery sparks spread from that tiny point of contact all the way up my arm, burrowing deep in my chest. I bite the inside of my cheek and quickly tear into the packet, spraying sugar all over the island. Rage's lips twitch as he grabs a second packet and pours it directly into my oatmeal. "Someone's jittery this morning."

As Rebel slides onto the bar stool beside me, he presses a quick kiss to my cheek and hums in the back of his throat. "Sugary sweet," he rumbles, his voice still deep and raspy from sleep. He flicks his tongue across my cheek and hums deeper, like he's licking sticky sweet sugar from my skin and *really* enjoying it.

Rage's eyes narrow and a muscle in his jaw jumps. "Eat your breakfast."

"This is better." Rebel practically purrs as he pulls me into a slow, sensual kiss that melts every lingering hint of tension in my body. This kiss is over as soon as it's begun, but the after-effects linger. My heart flutters and my body warms from the inside-out, creating a flush that curves down my neck. I'm dazed, blinking at Rebel's poorly hidden smirk and Rage's clenched fists on the bar's edge.

Just like that, the peaceful start to the morning snaps into razor-sharp pieces.

"I'm told you have training today," Rage says abruptly, "with Thanatos." Our eyes meet, and the blush across my chest blooms brighter at the flash of jealousy in his eyes.

I clear my throat and ignore my body's reaction to both of them as much as possible. Focusing on the task ahead helps tremendously. "That's correct."

Rebel flicks the hair from his eyes. "Why? I thought you hated him."

"He's—" I frown and try to avoid calling their half-brother *a necessary evil*. "He's offered to help, and I see no reason not to take him up on it. I need to be able to defend myself."

"From what?"

"From *whom*."

Both brothers stare at each other for a half-second before Rage scoffs aloud and crosses his arms over his broad chest. "You're safe as long as you're here."

"With us," Rebel amends, wrapping an arm around my waist. "Anywhere we are, baby, you don't have to worry about a thing."

"You can't be with me twenty-four seven, and there's only so much you can do from behind a screen if I get attacked." I push my half-empty bowl away and slip out of Rebel's grasp to stand. "I'm not too proud to admit that I have weak spots. I need to know what they are so I can work around them. Thanatos made it very clear with my kidnapping that I have more of them than I realized. Out of the four of you, he has the most experience with spotting them, and—" I side-step away from Rebel's wandering hands, ignoring the *adorable* pout on his lips —"he's the only one who won't try to get in my pants. He'll be focused on our goal the entire time, unlike the rest of you."

"I can focus," Rebel protests, swirling his bar stool around to face me. Licking his lips, he slips from his seat and slinks closer. "Especially when it's on you."

I jump back and put distance between us. If he gets his hands on me, I'll be late to training. A quick glance at the clock shows that I have less than twenty minutes before eight o'clock. Am I meeting Thanatos somewhere or is he picking me up? Are we going to a public gym, or does he have some kind of private facility for this kind of thing? Nerves trickle down my spine as I realize just how little I know about today's plans. We never discussed any details. He just told me *eight o'clock,* like that's all the info I need.

"What are you wearing?" Rage lifts a single eyebrow and interrupts my thoughts.

I glance down at my dirty t-shirt and sweatpants, hand-me-downs from Rebel. It's not like I have many options, and there's no way in hell I'm wearing lingerie. "This is all I have."

Rage sets his coffee mug down with a bang. "Come

with me." He heads to his bedroom, slams his palm on the scanner to unlock the door, and swings it open wide. I follow with Rebel close on my heels, both of us staring inside Rage's room from the safety of the doorway.

"Come *here*," Rage huffs, grabbing my hand and pulling me inside. Keeping my hand in his, he opens his closet door and reveals an expensive rack of clothing with a dozen shoeboxes lined up in two neat rows beneath. It may not be a walk-in closet like I have at home, but it's spacious enough for a full seasonal wardrobe, complete with warm sweaters, hats, and scarves that are *clearly* not the man's size. The size of his forearm alone would tear these shirts at the seams, not to mention the fabric—

I gasp and grab a delicate cashmere sweater dress that I *know* comes from this year's winter line at my boutique. "Why do you have this?" I check the tag and sure enough, it's in my size. *Everything* in the closet is my size. There's not a single scrap of menswear to be found amidst the dozens of outfits.

"This end has casual wear," Rage explains, shoving the majority of winter coats and cute blouses to the side to show me the leggings and tank tops hidden at one end of the closet. "While the other end is mostly outerwear— jackets and gloves for when you go outside. The middle section has more formal attire for events, but I'm clearing the hall closet for the more expensive pieces."

I look between the clothes and Rage, trying to absorb what he's saying. "You bought these for me?" My heart flutters while my mind struggles to catch up. Even the shoes range from winter boots to sparkling heels, meaning that he not only took into account my size, but he also coordinated the outfits. Everything is brand new with tags still attached. "All of this is mine?" I glance up at Rage, and my breath catches.

His eyes spark like embers in the night, glowing as softly as the gentle curve of his lips. "Yes, *krosotka*, these are all yours."

I break away from his gaze, clear my throat, and busy myself with inspecting the clothes. Not a single garment is the wrong size or color for my complexion. There are no unflattering boxy shapes or irritating fabrics—it's as though I hand-picked everything myself.

How well does Rage know me, after all?

"Pick something." He watches as I put together a workout ensemble, complete with black leggings and a hot pink sweat band for my forehead. "We'll have to make room for maternity clothes, but I'm thinking we can renovate, tear down some walls, expand the apartment across the entire wing instead of only these few rooms." Without warning, he presses his palm to my stomach and releases a long breath. "It's only a matter of time before our family starts to grow. We need to be ready."

Placing my palms over Rage's, I hold my breath as tears threaten to surface. *A family.* He really wants one— with *me.* Part of me has spent the past two weeks believing he only wants kids to bind the two of us together, but what if he truly wants to be a father?

A good one?

Lifting my chin, Rage stares into my watery eyes. "What's wrong, mama?"

I swallow hard and shake my head. "Nothing, I—" Taking a quick breath, I force myself to be honest. "I didn't know you cared so much about... this."

About *me*.

He smiles suddenly, and it's so radiant that it takes my breath away all over again. "Of course I care, Celia. Haven't you been listening?" Leaning close, he brushes his lips over mine. "I take care of what's mine. And you, my beautiful, stubborn woman, are *mine*." He captures my lips in a warm, sensual kiss that makes my knees shake, but just like Rebel's kiss at the breakfast bar, this one ends as soon as it's begun. Rage brushes a hand over my hair as he straightens. "Now get dressed, *krosotka*."

Neither Rage nor Rebel leave while I change clothes, but for once, I don't mind. Their eyes never leave my body, but rather than find it an intrusion of privacy, it makes me feel safe.

It makes me feel *loved*.

That feeling is what carries me out the door and across the hall to the training hall Rage insists actually exists. He accompanies me the entire way there, either for the honor of delivering me to his brother or to ensure I don't run down the grand staircase and out the front door. Either way, I still don't mind his presence.

That's what scares me most of all.

After he fucked me in the cage yesterday, I was sure that I could never stand to be around him again. The things he said to me—the way he fucked me—nice men don't do or say those things to the people they care about. But the man walking beside me this morning isn't the same one that choked me out or threatened to lock me back up in his gilded cage if it turns out that I'm not pregnant.

They can't be the same person.

Because there's no way that violently possessive man would smile this gently as he tugs on the edges my hoodie pocket and pulls me in for a kiss. It's tender and sweet and makes my head spin.

As he pulls back, his lips ghost over my temple and the crisp scent of his aftershave washes over me. "It's a good idea, the training." He tilts my chin up and stares into my eyes. "Exactly what the mother of my children needs to defend our family. You have my blessing to come here as often as you want. *With* supervision," he clarifies. "I don't want you getting hurt by lifting more weight than you can handle or misusing a machine. Understand?"

I swallow the lump in my throat and try to calm my fluttering heart. Rage is *actually* giving me room to breathe, like I wanted. Yeah, I'll have supervision, but it doesn't have to be his. It could be Thanatos. Or Rebel. Or *Ruin*. Shit. I could be here all hours of the day if I wanted.

A shiver rolls down my spine as I picture the gleaming golden bars waiting for me across the hall. I need to do everything I can to avoid staying another night in that prison.

Including getting pregnant.

"I understand." Lifting onto my tiptoes, I press a chaste kiss to Rage's lips. "Thank you."

Surprisingly, I genuinely mean it. I'm grateful for this. The training, the clothes, the sense of normalcy.

The way he runs his fingers through my hair before letting me go.

"I'll be back in a few hours. Rebel will come pick you up if I'm running late."

I watch as Rage walks away and disappears like he always does, leaving me to deal with the aftershocks of his attention. My hands shake. My heart races. My mind is like a live wire—snapping from one idea to the next so fast that I can't keep up.

The room remains silent until Thanatos clears his throat. Between us lies a pale blue training mat that covers the floor from wall to wall, with an extensive catalog of weight-lifting and bodybuilding equipment waiting behind him. He steps onto the mat barefoot, and my gaze travels up the expanse of his legs—full, round calves and thick thighs corded with muscle—as I marvel at the heavy tattoos disappearing beneath his shorts. The fabric is tight on his body, leaving little room for imagination as they curve over the bulge in between his thighs.

And down one leg.

My face flushes bright pink as I hastily flick my gaze up to his face.

Unlike Rage, Thanatos isn't smiling.

"Take off your shoes," he orders, "and get on the mat, Princess." He pulls his hoodie over his head, giving me a glimpse of washboard abs before his black tank top falls back into place. The vertical scar running through his upper lip deepens as he scowls. "Hurry up."

I kick off my boots and meet him in the middle of the mat. "Thank you for breakfast—"

The look he gives me would freeze fire. "Shut up and hit me."

My eyes widen. "I'm sorry, what?"

He takes one step closer, then another when I don't move. "Hit me."

I gape up at him. "I'm not going to hit you!"

Thanatos narrows his eyes, looking eerily similar to Rage in his worst moments. "In this room, you'll do exactly as I say, when I say, or you can walk away right now before you waste any more of my time. You asked me to train you, and that means following my rules. I don't need you to question my methods or make small talk. I need you to pay attention to what I tell you to do and learn how your body reacts, or you won't be able to control your movements when someone's running at you with a knife."

"How comforting," I retort, but Thanatos still isn't smiling. He's grabbing my wrist and pulling it high over my head, then quickly spinning me around so that my back is pressed to his chest. He grabs my hip with his other hand, gripping tight enough to hurt, and hisses in my ear. "*Pay attention.* I've got you trapped, Princess. What are you going to do now?"

Hot panic surges through my limbs as my fight or flight response kicks in. I grit my teeth and follow the first instinct that kicks in—slamming the back of my head into his face. The collision rocks my brain, but Thanatos is the one cursing as he tosses me to the ground and jumps on top of me. Pinning me onto my back, he exhales hotly across my face. "Hit me again."

This time, I don't hesitate.

I hit the motherfucker as hard as I can, throat punching him and finally earning a crooked smile. It's then that I see the greatest resemblance between Thanatos and his brothers. It's not the dark hair or midnight eyes or endless tattoos covering his body—it's the way his mouth goes slack as he glances down at my lips, a flicker of desire flashing in his eyes.

He catches himself and recovers instantly, exemplifying the lesson he's trying to teach me.

Learn how your body reacts, then control your movements.

How hard can it be?

CHAPTER 16

THANATOS

EVERY HEAVY BEAT of my heart kicks like a bass drum, the cadence fast and hard, drowning out the thud of my feet on the pavement as I round the corner to Celia's boutique. It's midday but overcast, meaning that despite the hour, there shouldn't be too many customers in the shop to notice my entrance. The bells jingle overhead as I swing open the front door, and not a single head turns my direction.

There's no one here after all.

A giggle from the back of the shop catches my attention, and I make my way towards the sound. Hidden amidst rows and rows of neatly-organized boxes of supplies, a woman twirls a strand of her brunette hair in her finger while she talks to someone on the phone. "No, she isn't here. It's just me again. Yes, of course you can come hang out with m—" As my shadow falls over her, she turns and gasps. "Oh gosh, I gotta go." Hanging up the call, she smiles up at me. "I'm sorry, sir, but this area is for employees only. Can I help you with something?"

This must be Sara, Celia's employee. College student, undecided major, a sophomore. Originally from Kansas, but she moved in with her aunt to attend Harlin Heights' community college at the outskirts of the city. Works part-time with Celia, although with how little Celia has been around, she may be working full-time hours.

None of that really matters, though it's information I keep filed away for moments like these.

"Celia asked me to pick up a few things," I lie easily, looking over Sara's head to the decorative boxes lining the shelves. Leave it to Celia to avoid a simple metal rack and cardboard or plastic to store all of her materials—she had to go with professionally-labeled, floral print designs for every box on the custom, built-in wooden frame. Of course. I don't actually know what Celia needs from here, but I make my best guess and reach for a box labeled *color swatches—A-F.* Do I need the entire alphabet?

"Oh, do you need the binder too?"

Sara turns around and grabs a thick binder. Inside, hundreds of fabric types and colors are neatly displayed with both a picture and a square of material. "Here you go! And her office is right over here." She leads me to the room with a kind smile that tells me more than her portfolio ever could.

She's way too trusting of strangers.

"So how do you know Celia?" Sara sticks around as

I slide various items inside my backpack to bring back to the apartment. "Let me guess—" Sticking out her tongue, she hums while she looks me up and down. "Are you related to her boyfriend? A brother, or something? Maybe his dad?" She shakes her head with a laugh. "Man, you look familiar. Have you lived in the city for long, or are you visiting? Maybe we've met before."

Damn, she's talkative.

I open all four drawers in Celia's desk, find little of interest, and look up to meet Sara's curious stare. She's got that lovestruck puppy look that shouldn't be anywhere near me. I'm not interested in children half my age. But I understand that she's infatuated with her boyfriend and likely seeing him everywhere—even in men like me. *Something* is bound to bring her thoughts right back to the man she's falling in love with.

Maybe I need a new haircut.

"Does she have a laptop?" Celia has to do her bookkeeping online, right? And all of her orders, too? I scratch my neck while Sara flits around the room for a set of keys that opens the filing cabinet in the corner. "Shouldn't you be working the front?" I ask, unimpressed by how poorly the girl is doing her job. "Are you the only one here?" I glance up at the ceiling, grateful to find a camera. At least Celia has a security system in place. "You shouldn't be here alone."

Sara is shorter than the murderer's M.O., but easy access is easy access. She shouldn't be alone, even while working.

"Oh, I'm okay! It hasn't been as busy since Celia's been on vacation."

That isn't comforting.

"You said that your boyfriend was coming over?" I zip up my bag and throw it over my back. I have enough stuff, I think, for Celia to pick through. I may have Rebel go to her house while I check the perimeter around the club—*again*—to make sure the area is secure. We've recruited a few of our best men to keep an eye on the street, but there are multiple abandoned buildings a few blocks away that I'd like to keep an eye on.

If my father is in hiding, he won't be above squatting in a rat-den to stay alive.

"Oh, well I—uhh—I mean, he might—"

"I won't tell your boss," I clarify, holding my hands up. "I just want to make sure you're safe."

Celia would freak out if anything happened to Sara because of our father's obsession with her.

Then again, maybe she deserves it.

The thought sours in my mouth, and I swallow the bitter taste before it settles. There are a lot of things that I think Celia deserves—a hard reality check and an even harder spanking—but heart-wrenching guilt over her employee being brutally murdered?

Maybe that's a bit of a stretch, even for me.

Sara smiles brightly. "Oh, okay. Then yeah, he'll be here later today. He likes to bring me lunch and—"

I tune her out. "That's nice." Walking past her to the back door, I check that it's secure. One dead bolt is hardly break-in proof, so I quickly pull out my phone and put in an order for a second one to be installed. "I'm having a contractor come out to do some repairs today. How long will you be here?" While Sara rattles off her work schedule for the entire week, I save the details on a note in my phone and inform my guy to beef up the security at the front, too.

I'll have to ask Rage if he's tapped into the security system here, or maybe we should replace it with our own...

Interrupting Sara's monologue, I give her shoulder a squeeze. "Stay safe, Sara. Lock all the doors when you're alone—I mean it—and keep an eye on who comes into the shop."

She blusters loudly, clearly missing the gravity of the situation. "You make it sound like there's a murderer out there or something."

"Or something," I murmur, sighing. "Look, just be careful, okay? Do you have a gun beneath the counter?"

"We—" She looks up at me owlishly. "We have a panic button."

Unholstering one of my pistols, I give her a basic run down of its mechanics, how to aim and fire, and slide it into her palm. "Keep that hidden, but close."

"I don't need a gun!" She cries, trying to give it back to me.

"You never do until it's too late," I counter, shoving the weapon against her chest. "Hold onto it. Does your boyfriend know how to shoot?"

"I—I don't know." Biting her lip, she holds the gun

like it's a bomb about to go off. I guess to her, it might be.

"Put it away," I say again, "but don't forget where you stash it. I'll check in on you every few days." With that, I step out into the afternoon gray, cold raindrops wetting my face.

What I should be doing instead of playing delivery boy is searching for my father. Running a hand down my face, I text Rebel to pick up supplies from Celia's house and take my backpack to her.

REBEL

what r u gonna do?

There's only one real answer.

Hunt.

CHAPTER 17

REBEL

RUIN'S IDEA of babysitting is sitting across the room from Celia and watching her flip through magazines all afternoon. *Booooring.* He might as well be a ghost for how little he says to her. I'm sure if he suddenly moved, he'd spook her like one, too.

The man doesn't have a stick as far up his ass as Rage does, but he sure doesn't know how to let loose, either.

Or, more likely, his idea of *letting loose* involves a lot more slicing and screams than mine do. To each their own, but at least I'm not dragging Celia to a corpse-carving fest for fun... which I wouldn't put past him, honestly.

But I have much better things in mind to make Celia scream.

"Baby, wanna go for a ride?" I jangle the set of brand new car keys in my hand. "You can driiiive."

Celia's head whips up from the magazine in her lap. I can feel the excitement from across the room as she jumps up and practically runs into my arms. Although she doesn't fall into me like a grateful girlfriend should, I wrap my arms around her body and tuck my hands in her back pockets. Ever since Rage gave her the new wardrobe, she's been rocking pale blue jeans and cute, cozy sweaters that never fail to give me the hard-on of a lifetime. I grind my throbbing length against her stomach, enjoying the way she blushes and squirms.

Rage will have a hissy-fit if I fuck her, but she hasn't been letting any of us into her pants since her workouts with Thanatos started a few days ago. *Too sore*, she says, jumping into the shower for hours at a time.

If it weren't for the video footage of their training sessions, I'd swear that *he's* the one fucking her into the mat, but no. They really are just working out.

Hardcore sparring and weight-lifting, sure, but working up a sweat regardless.

You'd think her hormones would be raging for some dick by now, but she's out like a light every night. At least I'm the one sleeping beside her. In that arena, I'm clearly winning against my brothers.

It feels fucking *good*.

I glance over at Ruin. "Wanna come with us?" He's been sleeping in my bed, too, naked like the rest of us. It's a little weird to share a bed with him every night, but Celia seems to like the extra warmth, and although Ruin doesn't say as much about it, I know he's enjoying it, too. He likes to watch Celia in her sleep, the creepy fucker.

What better way to do that than lie beside her every night?

"C'mon, you can ride shotgun." Which means he'll have a better view of her than me, but I'll throw the man a bone. He's been going hunting with Thanatos before dawn every morning, and they've been coming up empty for days. My little brother needs a win, too.

Ruin peels himself off the wall and stalks over to us, crowding in behind Celia like a second skin. She gasps, her pretty emerald eyes going wide as we sandwich her between us. Grabbing her chin and tilting her head back, I stare into those gorgeous eyes, admiring the way they dilate as her body reacts to ours. Thumbing the bow of her lips, I smile. "Want a kiss, baby?"

She licks her lips, swiping her tongue against my fingertip. *Fuck*, I'd kill to see her taste my cock exactly like this. "Yes," she breathes, lifting onto her tiptoes and parting those perfect lips for me.

Fucking *breathtaking*.

With a hum, I claim her mouth in a slow, measured kiss that leaves me buzzing. Alcohol doesn't touch this feeling—neither does E or blow or any other drug on the street. *Nothing* compares to the way Celia fires me up from one nerve ending to the next, lighting me up like a damn Christmas tree. I pull off of her mouth with a reluctance that's only rivaled by my eagerness for the alternative. "Now, lean back and close your eyes." I gently push Celia back onto Ruin's chest and place my hand on her throat to keep her still. Her pulse jumps beneath my fingers, and my body trills from the thrill of knowing how much we affect her.

We. Not just me. But the both of us.

It's becoming its own kind of addiction, seeing the two of them together. It's different than when she's with Rage—the two of them are explosive—but with Ruin, there's a tenderness that can't be matched. Even with me, we lick each other up like fire to gasoline, but with Ruin...

There's something different about them, and I'm itching to explore it.

Celia obeys without comment, and a rush of pride rolls through me. "Good girl," I tell her, squeezing her ass. Fuck, that's gonna turn me on. My cock twitches and swells at the memory of her rasping *good boy* to me in Fox's Ferrari. I could blow right now, spilling in my skinny jeans like some teenager getting his first over-the-pants handie.

Ruin handles her compliance much more gracefully than me, staring down at her without moving. He's a master of restraint, knowing when to withdraw and when to go in for a strike. Slowly, his hands circle her hips, and I have to wiggle my own free from between their bodies. "Stay still, baby, and you'll get another kiss for being so good."

I lift an eyebrow at my brother. Can he do it?

Does he even know how?

Once it becomes clear that he isn't going to throw his mask off and devour her lips like he should, I press a soft kiss to her lips. A moan catches in my throat, and I have to hold back before slipping my tongue inside her heat. Damn damn damn. Ruin better get in here soon, or I'll—

The little *snap* from one of the clasps on the side of his mask makes my muscles twitch. Slowly, he lifts it just high enough to free his mouth. I know that he's self-conscious about the burn scars, but I can barely see them curving down the side of his cheek. A smooth edge from the longest patch of scars on his face touches the edge of his lips, and I know it's that exact spot he's thinking about when he twists his mouth into a frown.

He wants to kiss her. He's tempted. She's right here, ripe for the taking, if only he could—

Celia reaches up and touches Ruin's neck, fingering his t-shirt collar and brushing her fingertips over the scars visible there. "Ruin," she breathes, her chest rising delicately, "can I see?" Her hands wander higher, curving around his throat and across his jaw. She keeps her eyes closed, but her brow pinches in concentration as she brushes her fingers over his jaw, his chin, then finally, his lips.

Ruin's throat bobs on a swallow. "*Krosotka—*" He grimaces, his voice laced with pain. I hardly breathe as he takes Celia's hand in his and presses a kiss to her palm. "It hurts."

"Shh, it's okay. It's going to hurt a little at first. It'll get better." She caresses his face, blindly smoothing her palm over his mottled skin.

"She's being so good for you, Ruin," I interrupt, desperate to refocus on the purpose of this exercise. "Doesn't she deserve a reward?"

Celia's lips twist into a frown. "Rebel," she hisses in a whisper, "don't."

I squeeze her throat gently. "C'mon, baby, don't you want another kiss?" Looking back up at my brother, I nod. He can do this. He *needs* to do this. For fuck's sake, this'll go on forever if he just keeps staring at her—

Slowly, he lowers his face toward hers. Celia's fingers catch in the hair at the nape of his neck, and I watch as he brushes his lips over hers. It's the barest of touches—hardly a kiss at all—but he groans like a man buried balls deep inside of her as his body spasms and his grip on her hips tightens. Celia locks her hands around his neck and pulls him closer, sealing their lips together in a *real* kiss.

And, holy fucking shit, this is what I've been waiting for.

They're delicate with each other, testing the waters with a fluidity and grace that's damn near angelic. She gives a little more *oomph*, and he absorbs the impact with a bone-weary sigh that belies how much he needs this.

I almost feel like I'm intruding.

Curving my body over hers, I press my lips to Celia's throat and skim my teeth over the cut that mysteriously appeared the other day. It's healed by now, but the tiniest sliver of a scar remains. A little time at the beach in the sun and sand will likely scrub it off, but for now, we all know that it's there.

I think Ruin likes the idea of having marked her for good.

She shivers, and it goes right through her body and into both of ours. I hum against her neck, sucking on the tender spot until I leave a new mark. "Tell us how good you feel, beautiful." Finding her breast, I knead it in my palm, enjoying the weight of her flesh.

She gasps, her eyes clenching shut. "R-Rebel," she whines, and *fuck me*, that's hot.

"Mmm, baby, you're gonna get me going, talking like that." That's a lie—I'm already hot and heavy for her. I'll always be hot and heavy for her.

One of her hands wanders my body, the other still rooted firmly in Ruin's hair, until she brushes against the keys in my pocket.

Oh, yeah, we were gonna go for a drive.

She gasps, and at first I think that Ruin's grabbed her ass, but then she whips the keys from my pocket and shoves them into my gut. "Car ride," she demands, snapping her eyes open. Ruin retreats and pulls his mask back into place before she can see anything, but she's too caught between the two of us to give either her full attention. Her gaze pings back and forth, her eyes shining brightly. "Car ride," she says again, digging her nails into my abs. "Right now."

My responding grin is wolfish. "Okay, baby, you win. Let's go for a ride."

Reaching behind her, she grabs Ruin's hand and smiles at him. "Ride with me, okay?"

I can't see Ruin's face, but I don't have to. He stumbles out the door behind her, as whipped as I am and just as ready for whatever she throws our way next.

CHAPTER 18

RUIN

SOMETIMES, I think my body doesn't work like it should. I watch the men in *Midnight* fuck around with their tongues and cocks out, wetting people's lips and driving into each other with an energy that can only be described as violent. They sweat, they curse, they spill their seed all over the floor and all over each other, not caring to clean up the mess that's left over, rolling around in it like pigs in the mud.

I know that Rebel shoots off like a rocket when he comes. At night when Celia's asleep, sometimes he'll stroke his dick, breathless and desperate, writhing beside her. I think he wishes she would wake up and tend to his body, but she never does.

Thanatos is wearing her out in the mornings—that, or she's pregnant and spending all of her energy supporting the life starting to grow inside of her.

I don't mind that she's too tired to have sex, but my brothers miss it. I can see it in the way Rage flexes his entire body, tightening every single muscle to divert the blood flow from his cock. Or how Rebel kisses her like she's his favorite addiction, stealing the air from her lungs just as quickly as she's stealing his heart.

But there are pieces of me missing, and I think this is one of them. I don't come in an eruption of heat and bliss like my brothers' do. It's a quick burst, a rush of fluid, and a bone-deep weightlessness that lets me forget how broken my body is for that brief moment.

I wonder what it feels like for Celia when she's with us. I've seen her come dozens of times now—I dream of the way her face turns bright crimson, the blood quickly rushing to the surface, and of the softness of her pink pussy, slick with her desire as she comes on her fingers *and* on mine—but I haven't felt it the same way my brothers' have. They bury themselves inside her heat and feel her body welcome them deeper, begging to be filled.

If I put my dick inside of her, will her body beg for it, too? Can I make her come as hard as my brothers' do, or will she realize that I'll always be this broken tangle of sharp edges and limbs that can't make her feel the same way they do?

Even if she comes to understand this about me, it won't matter, in the end. My brothers will keep her in their own way—and I'll keep her in mine.

Bound in the most decadent crimson rope, tied up tightly, her body as marked as mine once the rope digs into her flesh.

I keep these thoughts to myself, but it's getting harder to avoid the temptation to carry her up the stairs to my bedroom and put her body on display. Under the warm spotlight, I can see everything. Every reaction to my touch, every pebbled inch of flesh, every whisper of desire I elicit from within.

Tempting, but not impossible to ignore.

The itch to touch her with my knife, though—that's a song that's sweeter than honey, and I'm *desperate* for another taste.

While she chats idly with Rebel on our way down the grand staircase to the garage, I imagine the glide of the handle inside her pussy. The heat radiating from her cunt, the slick desire building on the polished metal, the rich scent of her body filling the air. I lick my lips and imagine kissing her there, at the apex of her thighs, the way she'll squirm and gasp and—

A high-pitched scream catches me off guard, and I blink to clear my head. In front of us is a gleaming, pale blue sports car that I've never seen before, and hovering in front of it is Celia with her arms spread wide and a cute little hop in her step.

"Ohmygod!" She shrieks, still bouncing on her heels. "When did you get this?"

Rebel grins like a cat eying its next meal. "Bought her just this morning and drove her over." He pats the hood before pulling Celia over, easily setting her down on top of it. With a whistle, he steps back to admire her. "Damn, you're gorgeous. Wait, let me take a picture!" He snaps what looks like a dozen photos, each of them focusing on different parts of her body. The first few are of the whole picture, Celia's body on full display in front of the car, but the next few are zoomed in on her chest, her lips, her hips and thighs. He groans and slips the phone back into his pocket. "God, you're crazy beautiful."

Celia blushes a deep crimson and idly plays with the waves of her hair falling loosely over her shoulder. "You mean it?"

"Of course I mean it." Sliding up to her, Rebel slots his hips between her thighs and pulls her to the edge of the hood, easily fitting into place. Brushing his hand over her cheek, *he* blushes. "You're the most beautiful thing I've ever seen, Celia."

They fold into each other's arms, and it's impossible to look away. Unlike when she's with Rage, she melts into Rebel's touch. Little gasps catch in her throat with each pluck of his lips on hers, and she wraps her arms around his waist to pull him closer.

"Gonna dent the hood," he warns, exhaling harshly, "but fuck it." Climbing up on top of her, he leans Celia back and lifts onto his knees. "Ruin, get over here. Watch this."

I don't know why he thinks I'm not paying attention, but I walk closer and get a perfect view of Celia's tender blush trailing across her cheeks and down her neck. It dips into her sweater and out of sight, but Rebel slips his hand up her shirt and lifts the fabric over her breasts. Bright pink blossoms across the stripe of skin visible on her chest, and she bites her plush bottom lip as she looks up at me.

"You think Celia is beautiful, too, don't you, Ruin?" My brother glances over at me, expecting an answer.

"Yes."

That doesn't please him. His mouth twitches into a frown. "C'mon, man, she's on the hood of a Lamborghini. She's gorgeous."

"Yes."

Shaking his head, he laughs ruefully. "*Shit,* you're bad at this."

I don't know what he wants me to say, and my skin pricks with discomfort. I shift my weight from foot to foot and clear my throat, my body feeling too tight.

Celia tosses a glare at Rebel before reaching for my hand. She squeezes it and tugs me closer, forcing me to brace myself on the hood of the car. I lean over her body and breathe in her scent. She smells like summer, full of warmth and sunlight and something cloyingly sweet. "He doesn't have to say anything if he doesn't want to."

I have plenty to say but not enough words to say them.

Grasping Celia's hand, I lower it to her thighs and rub the soft denim covering her skin. This is different than crawling on top of her while she's sleeping in bed, but the effect is the same. Her breath catches and she spreads her thighs wider to make room for me. Without my leather gloves in the way, I can feel the warmth of her hand and how much hotter her thighs are. Have I been missing out this entire time?

Is there more that I can feel?

"Fuck me," Rebel groans, rocking back on his heels. "I should have never bought you this car. I'm gonna wanna fuck you in it—*on it*—every day."

Biting her lip, Celia pushes her breasts together with her arms. "How is that a bad thing?"

Cursing, Rebel runs a hand through his messy hair. "We're *seriously* gonna dent the hood."

"We already are."

He grins and presses a quick kiss to her wrist. "I guess there's no point in stopping now, then." Undoing his belt, he drops his pants and boxers to his knees and frees his cock. It's already full, and Celia wraps her hand around the base. Hissing through his teeth, Rebel rocks into her palm. "Fuck, baby, that feels good."

Next, Celia reaches for *my* belt. She fumbles with it one-handed and manages to undo it, but the button and zipper prove too challenging. "Ruin, help."

Slowly, I unbutton my pants and mimic my brother's movements, dropping them below my hips. Celia reaches inside my boxers and pulls my cock out, squeezing it gently. She might be stroking Rebel's dick, but she's staring at mine. Her lips part and she scoots closer, like she wants a taste.

A bead of precum slips free as I imagine what that would feel like, having her soft tongue pressed to the sensitive underside.

She spreads my precum with the pad of her thumb, then begins stroking in earnest. Pleasure zings up my spine, and for the first time in my life, I think I understand the appeal of jerking off. As she tugs the skin over the tip and maintains a steady amount of pressure, more precum leaks out onto her palm. Taking a shaky breath, I lower myself to my forearm and thrust my hips in time with her movements, the cool metal of the car spreading goosebumps down my thighs.

"Shit, shit, shit," Rebel rasps, trembling beside me. "I want your mouth—*fuck*, no, your pussy. I want your pussy, baby, *please* milk my cock." She nods breathlessly, and that's all the permission he needs to drag her jeans down her thighs and thrust harshly between them, grunting as he slots himself inside. Her hot pink panties turn deep magenta as Rebel thrusts in and out of her heat, staining the fabric with their need for each other.

But it's not her pussy I'm enthralled with—it's her mouth and all the pretty cries spilling past her lips. She grips my cock hard as my brother rocks into her. Each time their bodies meet, she tugs my shaft and pants in my ear, her moans growing louder by the second. I know that it's my brother that's pleasuring her, but it sounds like she's moaning for me, and that's all it takes for me to slip over the edge.

I come without warning, gasping as it ricochets through my body like a gunshot. My legs quake as ropes of cum spill into Celia's hand, too much for her to hold, and spill all over the hood of her new sports car.

She doesn't seem to care about the mess as she throws her head back and cries out in bliss. The sound goes straight to my loins, and another wave of pleasure crashes over me. Gritting my teeth, I hiss as my cock spills once more, flooding Celia's palm, smearing my seed all over her fingers and wrist.

Rebel comes next, slamming his hips into hers and groaning as he pumps her full of cum. He cups her face in his hand and turns her towards him, capturing her lips in a sloppy kiss. I wonder what that's like, too—looking her in the eyes and filling her up, leaving a piece of yourself so deep that it can't be removed.

I've already fingered my blood inside of her pussy, satiating a need to claim her like my brothers do.

But maybe I can do *this*, too.

The way she threads her hand in Rebel's sweaty hair and pulls him into an embrace sends a twinge of jealousy through my veins. But then she smiles—a radiant show of warmth and affection—directly at me, and the jealousy snaps out of existence.

I may not fuck her like my brothers do, but that smile—that smile is just for me.

CHAPTER 19

CELIA

THERE'S a certain kind of power that's addicting. I used to think that having social status, being the name on everyone's lips, and having the power to influence others' opinions was the height of my existence. Hosting dinner parties, attending lavish private events, and catering to my ex-husband's every whim were my arena, and I was at the top of my game.

But *this*—this is another level of satisfaction that I never knew existed.

I whip around a sharp corner with a shriek of pure joy, the tires hugging the road in a perfect balance of control and power. We zip down the road faster than anything I've ever experienced before, the wind roaring in our ears as I punch the gas. Rebel pumps his fist against the roof of the car with a *whoop*, holding onto the two front seats to keep himself steady. I insisted that he wore a seatbelt, but the man wouldn't be deterred. If he isn't in the front seat with me, he'll still get as close as possible

—which, for now, means hugging the middle console. Most sports cars only have two seats, but somehow Rebel found a four-seater *and* had it delivered in record time.

If I didn't know any better, I'd suspect he wants to have an orgy in the backseat.

Laughing at the mental image of the gymnastics required for that feat, I can't believe any of this is real. *I just jerked off two men!* At once! Past Celia would have been mortified, but the new me wonders what's next. The Eiffel Tower, isn't that a sex position with the woman framed between two men? Could we try that?

After seeing both Rebel and Ruin drop their pants beside each other, I'm willing to bet that they're open to more than they ever imagined, too.

The thrill of endless possibilities is a high of its own, but that thrill being partnered with Rebel's glowing grin in the rearview mirror and the peaceful tap of Ruin's fingertips on the dashboard heightens the feeling. Today feels like a perfect day, and I don't want to waste a single second of it.

"Oh, Than wanted us to stop by your house." Rebel points to a street a few lights down the road. "Take a right, and we should hit North Side again. Then we can cut across the river and be there in no time."

"What for?" I follow the directions, eager to head home no matter the reason. Despite how nice it's been sleeping in Rebel's bed, I miss my own. Maybe I can convince the boys to let me stay the night at home—and if they agree to join me, they might actually say yes.

Rage won't like it, but Rage isn't here to tell me no.

"Supplies pick up," is Rebel's reply. "He dropped off a package for us."

"At my house?"

He nods. "At your house."

As we drive over the largest bridge in the city, the river sparkles like a bed of diamonds. I glance down the waterway to the ocean glittering in the distance, marveling at how beautiful the city is. Waterfront on one side, mountains on the other, with a sprawling metropolis in between. Harlin Heights really is beautiful —it's the perfect place to raise a family. I've always believed that a robust childhood filled with beachy weekends and movie nights and camping under the stars would enrich my future children's lives in a way that mine was lacking.

I won't enroll my children in finishing school or force them into ballet if they don't want to point their toes or wear tutus. We'll go camping or fishing or hunting—assuming their father knows how to do those things—and spend hours at the park on the swings, or attend the annual fair in the fall to pet the cows and ride the ferris wheel.

We'll ensure that our children have a better childhood than we did.

Rebel hums a tune for the rest of the drive to my house, and to my surprise, Ruin picks up the tune in a gravely, low pitch. I listen intently but can't pick up the melody. It's only when we've pulled up the driveway that I recognize a Russian word on Ruin's lips, but by then, they're both already stepping out of the car. Rebel opens my door for me and greets me with a smile that ignites sparks in my heart.

Things might be turning around for the two of us. My first night back when we visited the diner feels like a lifetime ago, but I still remember the salt on his lips and the cool night air clinging to our skin. It's the first time he asked me to trust him—to let ourselves figure things out between us—and I think I'm ready to know what that means.

I'm grateful that the idea of having a child doesn't scare Rebel off. He might not vocally talk about becoming a father like Rage does, but if he weren't at least open to the idea, I think he'd be running for the hills instead of holding my hand as we walk up the path to my front porch. "How old are you, Rebel?" I ask, watching as he grabs my spare house key from its hiding spot behind one of the porch columns. He really *has* made himself at home here.

He licks a stripe across his teeth as he unlocks the door and lets us all inside. "Twenty-eight, but my birthday's in a few months." He jabs his thumb in Ruin's direction. "Ruin's twenty... five, right?"

Ruin grunts, which apparently means yes.

"Yeah, twenty-five. And Rage is the oldest until you bring Thanatos into the picture. He's got us all beat by about five or ten years, give or take. He was already in school when our parents got together and had Rage."

I do the math in my head to piece together their family tree. "Thanatos is in his forties?" He sure doesn't look it. I guess the grays streaking through his hair or his bleak outlook on life could give it away.

Rebel shrugs. "Something like that, yeah. He's pretty old."

I nearly choke. "Forty isn't old!" I'm rounding the corner to thirty in a few weeks—I don't need my boyfriend thinking that *I'm* old next!

"How old are you?" Rebel asks.

Ruin answers for me. "She is twenty-nine."

"Damn, crossing the bridge into your thirties, huh?" Rebel whistles long and low, laughing when I smack his arm. "I'm just kidding! Hey, stop it! I'm *kidding!*" He grabs my wrists and pins me to the wall in the entryway, grinning as he presses his body against mine. "Easy, baby, easy. I promise, I'm into older women." To prove his point, he licks into my mouth and teases my tongue with his, groaning as he tilts my head back and deepens the kiss. Cupping my face, he sighs against my lips. "Your age doesn't matter, Celia. Older, younger, I don't care. Because *this* is real."

His kiss lingers in my system long after he's stepped back to give me space. My body thrums with the intensity of it—of this feeling growing between us. I find myself smiling as I reacquaint myself with my house. Throwing out old food from the fridge, sifting through the mail piling up on the kitchen counter, tidying up the rooms. "Have you been getting my mail from outside?" I toss the junk mail into the trash and flick through the bills with disinterest. "Rebel?"

Voices float down the stairs, meaning that he's

rummaging through my things again, likely through the panty drawer, knowing him. Rolling my eyes, I follow the sound and walk up the flight of stairs to the second floor. A shiver rolls down my spine at a smear of blood on the wall—is that mine? Or my attacker's? I haven't forgotten about the break-in, but I've been able to avoid thinking about it with everything that's been going on. Swallowing the lump in my throat, I push open my bedroom door to find both men standing in front of my dresser, the top drawer pulled open in front of them.

"I'm telling you, this one has to be her favorite."

Something vibrates, and panic makes me yelp. "*Rebel!*" Storming over to them, I yank the vibrator from his hand and hold the button to turn it off. "Stop playing with my things!" A blush breaks out across my face. "I thought we were here for supplies!"

"Oh, we *are*. I'm packing your stuff for you. The most important things go first, and *that* is very important."

"It is not!" My face burns with embarrassment. "*Please* stop stealing my things."

Rebel smirks, not sorry in the slightest. "Alright, *krosotka*, I'll play nice. You can pack your vibrators yourself. I'll grab the package Than left downstairs."

I breathe a sigh of relief. "Thank you."

While he disappears downstairs, I throw random things into my suitcase, too frazzled to pack anything with intent. It feels like I'm saying goodbye, and that's not at all what I want. This place is my home. It has been for half a decade, at least.

"What do you think about staying here for a while?" I ask Ruin, glancing up at him. He's been silently watching me pack for the last few minutes, not nearly as interested in my belongings as his brother. He doesn't respond, which isn't helpful. Sighing, I sit on the edge of my bed and press the heels of my palms to the backs of my eyes. Merging worlds with them is easier when I can pretend my old life doesn't exist.

I glance around the master bedroom and see all of the memories I'd hoped to build here. A baby's cradle in the corner by the window. A spring breeze fluttering past the curtains while the baby laughs in my arms. My husband —who no longer looks like my ex-husband Ted, but a dark-haired, tattooed figure—bouncing a toddler on his knee from the bench seat at the foot of the bed. This house was meant to be a home full of life and vibrancy, with children's laughter bouncing off the walls and silly little crayon drawings hidden on the closet walls.

Instead, the house has become a memorial to the life I thought I'd have. The one I always wanted to build. And that thought is *very* sobering... and downright depressing.

"What is wrong?"

I blink tears from my eyes and look up at Ruin. His fingertips ghost across my cheek, brushing a stray tear away. If it weren't for the mask obscuring his features, I could almost picture the frown on his lips.

Lips that I've kissed.

Sighing, I shake my head. "It's nothing. Just reminiscing, I guess." There's no sense crying over what could have been. My life was never meant to turn out how I imagined, and I need to come to terms with what's real and right in front of me. Taking Ruin's hand, I lace our fingers together. Tattoos peek around his knuckles, symbols and numbers that seem random to the untrained eye. "What do these mean?"

He spreads his fingers for me to see his tattoos. Pointing to each of them, he rattles off various things. "My first kill. My second. The weapon that made this scar—" he lifts his shirt and points to a jagged cut along his abdomen—"and the one I used to kill a difficult target." He doesn't expand on any of these stories in detail, but I don't push him for answers. It's not like he pushed me to divulge what I'm sad about. I need to respect his boundaries, too.

Lifting his knuckles to my lips, I kiss each one in order from his thumb to his pinky. A sound catches in his throat, and he pinches my chin between his thumb and forefinger. "Why?"

I meet his eyes, unsure of what to say at first. "I know that you've done bad things in the past. I want you to know that it's okay. We don't always have a choice. Sometimes, the choice is made for us, and we can't control what happens next."

He presses the pad of his thumb to my lips and pulls them apart, feeling for my teeth. "Pretty words," he muses, "but not true. I have done bad things, *krosotka*, because I am good at them. Every kill I've made, I chose to follow through. I could say that I was following orders, that the choice was made for me, but that is not true. I've looked Death in the face and smiled as his friend." Slipping his thumb over my tongue, he pinches my chin harder, digging his fingers into the soft flesh beneath my jaw and making me flinch. "You may think you understand, but you don't. There are things stronger than flesh, things I have seen, that I have felt, that no one else has, and no one else will." He releases my mouth, and I fall back onto the bed, cupping my throbbing jaw.

Ruin towers over me, his hand hovering over my thigh. "There are things stronger than flesh," he repeats, grabbing my leg and lifting it higher on the mattress, "but the body is the gateway to finding them."

My heart pounds as he spreads my thighs wide and exhales harshly against his mask. He stands there staring at me for a long moment, like he's unsure how to proceed. I guess in the past when he visited me at night and touched me, I was in a nightgown, not jeans. He had easier access to my pussy.

"Is that what you've been doing? Searching for something?" It sounds a little insane, but I'm trying to understand. I *need* to understand if he's going to be a permanent fixture in my life.

He grunts, which I think means yes, and pulls the hunting knife from his belt. The same one he pushed inside of me before, in the bathroom back at his apartment.

I scrabble up the bed away from him. "Oh, no. Not again. Put the knife away, Ruin." I keep my eyes on him while I shout for his brother. "Rebel! Ruin has a knife!" I'm not opposed to a little kink in the bedroom, but a knife in the hands of an unrepentant killer might be pushing my boundaries a little too far.

Something shatters downstairs and thundering footsteps storm up the stairwell. "Ruin! I already told you, no knives!" The moment he spots his brother from the doorway, Rebel flies across the room and tackles him. "Drop it!" He grunts as he tries to force the knife from Ruin's grasp, but he's got a death grip on the handle. There's no prying it free.

I jump up from the bed to put more distance between us. I like Ruin, I've always been intrigued by him, but I think he's got a lot of trauma to unpack, and when he pulls out a knife...

Ice chills the blood in my veins.

I'm scared of him.

Rebel gives up on forcing Ruin to drop the knife. "Fine, just put it away! You're scaring her!"

"I need to see," Ruin murmurs, "I need to see it."

"Not today, buddy, not yet."

I scoff. "Not yet? Don't I have any say in this?"

Rebel ignores me. "Here, look into my eyes. Can you see it? You know it's there."

Ruin shuts his eyes and shakes his head. "I want to see *hers.*"

I look between the two of them, unsure what to do. "What is he looking for?"

"That's a hard question to answer," Rebel huffs, "but it has something to do with our—"

"*Shut up!*" Ruin snarls, pushing his brother off of him. "I won't find it if it knows I'm looking for it!"

Holding his hands up, Rebel sighs. "Okay, okay. I won't tell her. But promise me that *when* we do this—because we will, just not right now—that you won't do it alone. I have to be with you when you look for it. Okay?"

Ruin clenches the knife handle tightly. "We can look right now."

"*No,* man, we can't." Rebel glances over at me, and in another first for the day, he looks defeated. This isn't a battle he's going to win in the long run. Whatever it is that Ruin wants to do with me, he's going to do it. All Rebel is doing now is stalling for time. "She's not ready yet. If you look now, you won't find it."

I flinch as Ruin looks in my direction. But he doesn't step any closer; he slips the knife back into the holster on his hip and rumbles deep in his chest. "She's not ready," he agrees, clenching his fists. "But when she is, I'll find it."

The look Rebel gives me next is solemn, but it's clear whose side he's really on. It won't be long before he lets Ruin do whatever it is he's trying to do to me. If a knife in the pussy is considered foreplay, I can't imagine what comes next.

I wrap my arms around my stomach and try to calm my racing heart. No matter what it is that Ruin ultimately does to me, Rage and Rebel won't let Ruin hurt me.

If they're around when it happens.

And when they're not, I need to be ready for Ruin.

Whether that means defending myself... or surrendering.

Chapter 20

Celia

WHILE REBEL SMOKES a cigarette on the front porch, I keep my distance from Ruin. Thankfully, he has the same idea, staying out of whichever part of the house I'm inhabiting long enough for me to pretend he doesn't exist and that everything is back to normal.

But even *normal* doesn't feel quite right.

I stare at Rebel's silhouette through the window and wonder when that changed. Was it the moment I came home after work one day and found him rummaging through my kitchen cabinets? Or before even that, when Rage first appeared at my shop door with a cocksure grin and an unshakable belief that I was his girl?

How long have these men been so intertwined in my life that I can no longer imagine it without them?

Sighing, I stare at the canvas backpack sitting on my dining room table. It's not mine—but apparently the contents within it are.

Thanatos got these for you, Rebel said nonchalantly

once we returned downstairs, *something about doing you a favor.*

I flip open the top and unzip the main pocket, surprised to find my laptop case nestled snugly inside with the binder I use to catalog different color swatches sitting beside it. Digging further, I find various items from my office tossed inside at random. One of my favorite pens. A half-used sketchbook. Old invoices and magazine clippings of inspirational designs I meant to scan onto my computer.

Thanatos went to my boutique.

He got these things... *for me.*

I worry my bottom lip between my teeth and slump into a kitchen chair. Things have been tense during our morning training sessions, and we've only had a few of them. Thanatos doesn't speak—not with words. He uses his body as a language, spinning me around and around, throwing me to the mat, forcing me to fight to get back up again. It's brutal and unrestrained and nowhere near ethical, but even when Rage stands watch or lifts weights from the other side of the room during our sessions, he doesn't question his brother's methods or tell him to take it easy on me.

It's like he approves whatever Thanatos deems effective for making me stronger.

The thing is, it's working *too* well.

I'm learning Thanatos' movements. His mannerisms. And he's learning mine. Showing me how to maneuver around a man twice my size, or how to use my weight and flexibility to my advantage. I don't know much about martial arts, but I gather that he's well-versed in various disciplines, using them all to his advantage not only to take me down, but to give me a well-rounded foundation for attack.

Because not only am I defending myself from his advances, I'm learning to strike back, too.

I'm grateful for the lessons. If their father comes after me, he won't pull his punches or go easy on me because I'm a woman. He'll go in for the kill, and I need to be trained accordingly. I wouldn't receive this kind of training anywhere else—or from anyone else.

It's becoming clear, however, that as calm and collected as Thanatos thinks he is, he lets out some of his frustration on the mat. He pins me on my back, on my front, wraps his arms around my body from all different angles, forces me into pretzel-like positions and pushes the limits of my flexibility, all because he likes seeing—and feeling—what my body is capable of.

The perpetual hard-on gives him away.

But unlike his brothers, he doesn't tear my leggings off and dive between my thighs. He keeps his impulses to himself, keeping the dick-to-female-body contact as minimal as possible.

Still, I notice his body's reaction to mine.

And still, he doesn't talk about it.

I've been grateful for the silence since it means there's at least one man's problems I won't have to detangle, but *this*—the backpack filled with supplies from my boutique—speaks volumes.

It's a kindness that I never asked for, one that I don't

want. Not if it comes with heartstrings attached. I already have three men—three very complicated, chaotic men—to contend with. I don't need a fourth man added to the mix.

I can only handle so much trauma-laced testosterone.

Dropping my head onto the kitchen table, I groan loudly. My relationship with these men was meant to be a fun, easy little fling, but it's getting more complicated than I ever imagined. Ruin's a hot mess with a hard-on for knives, Rebel's currently chain smoking to cope with his stress, and Thanatos is in denial about his physical attraction to me. At least Rage seems to be coming around in his own way. He hasn't tried to have sex with me since the cage incident, and he's been gentle in the mornings we spend together.

If Rage can put in genuine effort to change for the better, I know his brothers can, too.

I lean back in my chair and look down at my stomach. "Your daddies have issues," I admit, whispering to the little life growing inside of me, "but I know they're trying to be good for us."

It feels silly to talk to a bundle of cells, but—

A cell phone rings from inside the backpack, making me jump in my seat. "Um, Rebel?" I look over my shoulder, but he's still smoking outside. Unzipping the front pocket of the pack, I reach inside to find the phone. "Is this your pho—" A pale pink case, complete with a swirling rhinestone pattern on the back, means that the phone isn't Rebel's.

It's *mine.*

I quickly flip it over and check the caller ID, jumping up so quickly that my chair clatters to the floor. The doctor's office is calling.

My test results are finally in.

I swipe to answer the call, my heart racing inside of my chest. "Hello?"

"Miss Monrovia," a familiar voice greets.

"Dr. Sakovia," I stammer, surprised to hear his voice. It's rare for the doctor to call a patient himself, but then again, I've known Wren Sakovia for years. He probably wants to give me the good news firsthand. Hope blossoms inside my chest, and I clutch my cell phone tightly.

"How are you, Celia?"

"I—I'm fine. Do you have my test results?" There's a pause across the line, and my stomach drops. My bottom lip trembles as I try to hold myself together for the next two minutes of this agonizing phone call. "It's negative, isn't it?"

Dr. Sakovia sighs heavily. "I'm sorry, Celia. Truly. I know you've been trying for a while—"

"That's okay, Doc," I wheeze, bending at the waist to keep from collapsing. It doesn't help the raw pain lancing through my chest, and I have to gasp for air. "I'll go back on the supplements. I'll try again."

"It's good to hear that you're optimistic. You're still young, so the odds are in your favor."

"Of course. Thank you for calling. I—I need to let everyone know."

"Stay positive, Celia. These things can take time."

We say goodbye, and the phone slips from my hand

and clatters to the floor. I walk numbly out of the kitchen into the living room and take a seat in one of the barrel chairs, wrapping my favorite throw blanket—the fuzzy one with silver hearts—around my shoulders. After tucking my feet under my legs, I stare out the bay windows overlooking the backyard. Ted insisted that we keep a willow tree out back, but I've always hated the wispy thing.

Every time I get another negative pregnancy test, I can't help but stare at its hideous, drooping branches. It's mocking me—mimicking my own tears as its limbs blow in the wind.

I'm sick of that fucking tree.

I jump up from my seat and rush to the garage. Finding the pruning shears hanging on the wall is easy, but hacking away at the willow's branches proves tougher than I imagined. Either the shears are dull or the branches are thick, or I'm just *that fucking weak* that I can't cut off a tree limb, but I end up throwing the stupid shears against the trunk and screaming.

I scream myself raw, finally crumbling into a ball on the dead, dry grass.

Ruin comes up beside me the moment I finally quiet down, silent as a shadow as he takes one look at me, then at the discarded shears, then at the branch I failed to cut dangling like a snapped toothpick. He takes out his knife and slinks closer to the willow. First, he slices through the branch I attempted to snip in half, cutting it away until it drops to the ground. Then he carves the rest of the tree bit by bit. It takes a long time, long enough that the sun dips below the tree line, but he doesn't stop until the tree is naked and ugly and as rotten-looking as I feel inside.

He wipes his blade on his pants before stabbing it into the dirt by my feet. "You can stab it in the heart."

"That'll kill it."

I think. I don't know much about trees.

Ruin grunts and sits on the ground beside me. "Will it make you feel better?"

I hug my knees to my chest and fight another wave of tears. Sorrow radiates deep within me, making it hard to breathe. Still, I manage to choke out a reply. "I don't think anything is going to make me feel better right now, Ruin."

He stares at me, then at the naked tree. "That's fair."

Closing my eyes, I try to calm down. This isn't the end of the world—not really. It's just another disappointment in a long line of disappointments. I'm used to those. I can overcome this.

I can still get pregnant and raise a child. I can still have a family of my own. Adoption is an option, too, if it comes to that. But I've always wanted to carry my little one inside of me, and losing that experience feels like losing a piece of life itself.

A hand touches my cheek, turning my head to one side. I open my eyes and stare at a watery image of Ruin. It takes him a minute to say anything, but when he finally speaks, there's a reverence in his voice that soothes some of the ache in my heart.

"I can see it," he whispers, barely loud enough for me

to hear. "In here." Cupping my face, he leans in to get a deeper look into my eyes.

"See what?" The bitter, hurt part of me wants to say something sarcastic, like, *how pathetic I am?*

But Ruin can't sense my cynicism. When he answers, he's serious, the deep timbre of his voice making me tremble.

"Your soul. It's weeping." He gently brushes away the tears streaming down my cheeks. "It's beautiful, *krosotka*."

I stare into his dark eyes and wonder what exactly he sees that's beautiful, because right now, I don't feel like something beautiful. I'm a broken shell of a woman, too weak to successfully carry my own child, cursed with a body that doesn't work. "It's all my fault," I murmur, my voice breaking on a sob. "I can't get pregnant even with *three* boyfriends!" I grab Ruin's knife and stab it into the ground, tearing through the grass, the roots, scraping the blade against rocks and carving deep gouges into the earth. It doesn't make me feel better, but it gives me something to do with my hands.

It lets me grieve in a new way, and for that, at least, I'm grateful.

I hide in my bedroom for what feels like an eternity, wrapped in a cocoon of cotton and down feathers. Maybe if I wait long enough, I'll undergo metamorphosis and emerge as something better. Something whole.

Something that can nurture a life inside my body.

I know it's foolish to think that I'm broken—but all of the evidence points to it as fact. I couldn't get pregnant with Ted. I haven't gotten pregnant with Rebel or Rage. I'm too scared to have sex with Ruin—at least, I think I am. I play the scene in my head, wondering what kind of a lover he's like. Will he keep the mask on and hit it from behind, or will he finally let me see his face as he fulfills my greatest desire?

Would he look into my eyes and claim to see my soul? And if he does, would it still be a sad, lonely little thing, weeping and scared? Or could our broken bodies finally become whole again if we work together to fix them?

I fix his body, and he fixes mine.

Sighing, I roll onto my back and flip my comforter off of my face. The room is dark with the lights turned off, but a sliver of warmth peeks through the crack beneath my bedroom door.

Someone's pacing in the hallway outside.

Once Rebel finished his last cigarette and found me and Ruin in the backyard, I told him that I needed space. He's giving it to me, albeit reluctantly.

Everything is okay, baby. Nothing's changed. I promise.

I know he's being sincere, but he's only able to speak for himself.

Rage is the one I'm worried about.

My stomach twists, and I imagine for the hundredth time how Rage will react to the news that I'm not pregnant. Will he be as disappointed as I am? Excited at the prospect of fucking me day in and day out until his sperm actually takes? Or could he be angry with me for getting his hopes up to begin with?

Will he punish me for failing?

I stare up at the ceiling as headlights shine through the windows and a car door slams shut. It's Rage finally arriving—I know it is. Rebel must have called him. Or the doctor, Wren. Shit, has Rage known this entire time? Was he expecting me to call him or come home crying into his arms?

My anxiety spikes as footsteps climb the stairs.

Rebel's the first one to speak. Something thuds against the wall, and I can feel his anger through the door. "I called you two hours ago! What the fuck was more important than this?"

I can't hear Rage's reply, but I'm not sure that I want to. I've been in here for two hours, and Rage never bothered to come check on me until now.

That speaks louder than any words ever could.

The door handle rattles. "Unlock the door, Celia."

I ignore Rage and pull the comforter back over my head.

"Celia, please. I need to see you. I need to make sure that you're—" Something bangs against the door. It could be his fist, or it could be his face. Either way, the sound makes me jump. "Please let me in."

Sitting up, I glare at the closed door. "Why? So you can lock me up again? Throw away the key this time?"

Rage hesitates before responding. "I won't lock you in the cage. I never should have in the first place."

I scoff. "Too late for that."

"Celia—"

"I'm not interested in anything you have to say to me. Please leave."

The door handle suddenly snaps and falls to the ground as Rage breaks the lock. He pushes the door open and steps inside my bedroom. "I'm not going anywhere."

It's too dark for me to see his face, but it makes rejecting him easier. "You're off the hook. I'm not—" my voice cracks—"I'm not pregnant, so you don't have to pretend anymore, okay? You can leave. You can all go back to your lives, and I'll go back to mine."

Three long strides is all it takes for Rage to reach my bed. He kicks off his shoes, tears the tie off of his neck, and pops the buttons on his shirt as he strips down. "You *are* my life, Celia Monrovia. Stop pushing me away, because I'm not going anywhere." Once he's completely naked, he crawls on top of the bed and tears the comforter off my body.

I gasp and kick out at him, landing a hit square to his gut. The air punches from his lungs, but he grabs my foot and pushes it back down. "*Celia,*" he growls, "stop. You're going to hurt yourself."

Agony rips through my chest and tears well in my eyes. "I'm already hurting!" A sob catches in my throat as my vision swims. "I thought this time—I thought for sure, I had to get pregnant. If anyone could knock me up, I thought it would be you! You said it would happen! You promised that you'd give me a baby!"

Rage crawls on top of me and smothers me with his body, trapping me against the mattress. His body heat seeps into my muscles and down to the marrow of my bones, making me tremble.

Fuck, he smells good, too. Like fire and smoke, cinnamon and clove, like warmth and comfort and everything I suddenly crave.

I gasp for air while he holds me tight. "I *will* give you a baby. I swear on my life, I'll do everything in my power to make you happy. Just breathe. Breathe with me." He takes a deep breath, and I can feel his chest expand over mine.

"Maybe I don't want to breathe! Maybe I want to drown!"

It's not true—there's so much I still want from this life. So much love that I have yet to give, but it *hurts.* The waiting hurts so much.

"Don't you dare quit on me." Rage's voice shakes. He grabs my face in his hands and forces me to meet his eyes. "I need you. My brothers need you. And our baby needs you—*yes, you*—because you're the only one who can put up with our bullshit and actually make things better—make *us* better. I won't accept anyone else, because there's no one I'd rather do this with than you. This is our fucked up little family, but it's *ours,* and I promise you can handle it. So stay with me. I know it hurts, I know you're tired, but I'm here now. I'm *finally* here. So please, let me in, let me take your pain away, because it's my turn to carry it. You are never alone anymore. I am here with you—and I will *always* be here with you. Breathe, baby, *please*. Please breathe. I've got you. We've got this. I promise."

The tears won't stop, and I sob into Rage's chest as he holds me. In the before, back when I was trying to get pregnant with Ted, he'd disappear into his office with a bottle of brandy and let me cry on my own. That's what I was expecting this time, too—to carry the pain alone, like I always have.

But Rage is here with me, begging me to let him in. Holding me while I smear saltwater and snot all over his chest, not caring in the slightest that it's disgusting or that I sound like a banshee wailing in the night.

He's *here*.

Not just for the good times, but the bad ones, too. And if he is a man of his word, he'll be here for all the good, bad, and in-betweens from here on out.

A heavy feeling collapses inside my chest, and I can finally take a deep breath. The walls I've built to keep my heart safe crumble as Rage runs his hand through my hair and murmurs sweet encouragement, holding me tight and refusing to let go.

I'm not sure when Rebel and Ruin climb into bed with us, but when I've finally calmed down enough to breathe without feeling like I'm on the verge of collapse, I feel their presence. The weight on the pillow beside my head. The hand hooking around my calf. The gentle brush of fingertips down my spine. I can hear them all breathing in time with each other, deep and calm and strong.

Alone, I am fallible. I regress into painful patterns

and responses that aren't healthy for the life I want to build.

Together, however... Together we might be strong enough to overcome our weaknesses. Rage can hold me tight when my strength and confidence wavers. Rebel can keep me smiling and bright and carefree. Ruin can keep me true to myself and to others. And Thanatos... I'm not sure how he fits in yet, but I know he has a place.

Rage is right, this is *our* family now.

Even though the odds seem stacked against us, we'll pull through stronger than ever, because we have each other.

That might be all it takes to keep pushing through another day of wanting to find the sunrise waiting just over the horizon.

CHAPTER 21

RAGE

WHEN I FIRST MET CELIA AT the Baranova wedding, I knew she was the woman for me. Fierce in the face of adversity, loyal to those she cares about, and strong enough to hold the line against armed, dangerous men who were threatening the peace. She was willing to fight men like me to protect others.

And yet for years, no one has been willing to put up the same fight for her.

It's why breaking through to her has been an uphill battle this entire time. She isn't used to people fighting to keep her. Her twin brother Mikhail may be the exception —the *only* one—but he hasn't been around as often since he rose the ranks of the bratva. Celia has been on her own for years now, and when she finally found a man she thought she could trust, he bailed on her. Got his secretary pregnant and left Celia to clean up the mess from their shattered marriage on her own.

She may have been expecting me to do the same, to

cut and run the moment I realized that she couldn't give me what I needed in our relationship.

It's a bullshit expectation, but I can understand it.

I can even forgive her for running away when she realized how serious I was about us. I'm not the kind of man she ever imagined marrying or raising a family with. I'm not *anyone's* first pick. But the difference between me and other men is that I'm okay being her second love—as long as I'm her last love. It's why I'm okay with her getting close to Rebel or learning all of Ruin's shadowed secrets—I'm not going anywhere, no matter how hard or fast she falls for my brothers.

I'll always be right here when she needs me.

Which is why being late tonight is something I'll never forgive myself for. The moment I walked through the front door, I knew that I'd fucked up. Rebel shoved me into the wall and should have done much worse. I wasn't here when I should have been, and Celia wrapped herself in her pain for much longer than should have been possible.

This isn't my first fuck-up, but it *will* be my last.

Swallowing my pride isn't something I'm experienced with, but I'll do whatever it takes to earn Celia's heart. I kiss her shoulder and watch the sunrise drift lazily through the curtains, painting her in an ethereal pink glow. Her mouth twitches in her sleep, and it takes all of my willpower not to slant my lips over hers and kiss her awake.

She laid awake for hours after we all climbed into the bed with her last night. I won't be the reason she's restless and tired throughout the day. She needs rest to heal her aching heart.

Rebel, on the other hand, has other ideas. He props up onto an elbow and studies her face, his gaze wandering lower as the sunlight plays across her body.

"Don't," I warn.

He frowns. "She needs a pick-me-up. What better way than morning sex?"

"She will *not* want to have sex right now."

Rolling his eyes at me, he brushes his knuckles across her breast, teasing her nipple into a tight peak. "The best way for her to move on is for us to remind her of what's waiting right around the corner. Not just the sex, but the *after*. And that only comes *from* having sex."

He blows air across her chest, smiling at the goosebumps trailing down her arms. "She's always so responsive." Chuckling, he kisses her collarbone. "Even in her sleep." Within seconds, he's gently licking and sucking her tit and palming her waist. Her back arches and her eyelashes flutter.

Fuck.

I will *not* be outdone by this fucking asshole.

"Fine," I hiss, slipping the blankets over Celia's hips, "but when she wakes up and starts crying again, you better stay to help her work through them."

Rebel hums in the back of his throat as he plucks her nipple between his lips, quickly moving to kiss the other peak while palming the abandoned one.

Shifting my weight lower on the bed, I gently spread

Celia's thighs wider. She's wearing panties which is annoying, but it's easy enough to slide them—

A sharp blade appears beside my face, and with a flick of his wrist, Ruin cuts the fabric away to grant me access. He plants his hand behind her knee and lifts, tilting her hips up toward my mouth. "Tell me how she tastes," he rumbles, hovering closer than I'd like.

"Taste her yourself," Rebel mutters, clapping a hand on Ruin's shoulder. "Rage, move, let him eat her out."

"No." I glare at the both of them. Fucking meddlers. "This is *my* morning ritual. Get your own."

She's glistening down there when I spread her perfect lips. *Fuck.* It really has been too long since I tasted her. With a growl, I dive in, licking a long, wet stripe up her tight channel. Celia keens, her back arching far enough that her hips lift off the bed. I reach beneath her thighs and grab her hips, pulling her pussy onto my mouth. Closing my eyes, I bury my tongue in her sweet cunt and devour her one mouthwatering lick at a time.

"Here," Rebel murmurs, "you suck this tit while I suck on the other."

Great, now he's coaching our little brother on how to please a woman.

Actually, that might not be a bad idea.

I lift my gaze to the scene above me and my dick jumps to attention. Celia's eyes are barely open, but she's got the most *fuck-me* look on her face that I've ever seen. Cheeks flushed. Lips parted. One nipple in Rebel's mouth while Ruin pinches the other between his knuckles. That's not quite what Rebel meant, but it's enough for Celia to cream all over my face. *Fuck*, she's dripping.

My fingers slip right inside her molten core, and within seconds of rubbing her G-spot, she's riding my face in earnest.

"O-oh, ohgod, *ohmygod, Rage!*"

That's fucking right, you're gonna moan my name. *Mine.*

"Does that feel good, baby? *Mmm*, fuck, you're gorgeous."

I could do without Rebel's voice in my head right now, though. Thankfully, Celia's moans drown out whatever filth he's muttering in her ear, because she gets louder and louder and *louder*, her moans pitching higher the closer she gets to coming.

"You're gonna come all over his face, aren't you, pretty girl? I can hear how wet you are. Can you hear it, baby?"

She pinches her bottom lip between her teeth and nods frantically, coating my hand in her desire. It drips down my wrist and onto the sheets. Which means she might actually—

Quickly, I shift the angle and go *hard*, pressing and rubbing faster and faster until I feel it start—she *explodes*, drenching my mouth in her squirt. I groan as her taste bursts on my tongue and fills my mouth, streaming down my chin and drenching the bed in a delicious mess.

"Oh shit, did she just squirt?"

Licking my lips and wiping my face on my forearm, I grin. "Yeah, she fucking did."

"Fuuuuck," Rebel groans, jamming his erection against her thigh. "That's so fucking hot. Goddamn."

Celia's face is frozen in shock, her blush deepening to crimson. "I don't—I've never—I'm so sorry!"

"Don't be." Rebel tips her face towards his. "It's fucking hot. We love it. Don't we?"

"Yes," Ruin rasps in my ear.

Jesus, I didn't realize he'd gotten so close.

He reaches out and runs his fingers through her slit, mesmerized.

I can't blame him. Her lips are swollen and hot, begging for more. Slowly, Ruin slides a finger inside, down to the first knuckle, and her pussy sucks him in greedily, taking not just one finger, but *three* all the way to the base. He tries to slip his pinky inside, but Celia cries out and pushes herself up toward the headboard.

"N-no way, I can't—it's too much—"

To my surprise, Ruin lets his fingers slip out and doesn't push them back in. But then it becomes clear what his real goal is—he slides his mask to the side and pushes his fingers into his mouth to taste her.

Celia's mouth falls open as she watches him suck his fingers clean. She can't look away, and frankly, neither can I. To my knowledge, he's never been with a woman before. This could be a first for both of them. When I tear my gaze away to check Celia's reaction, she's swallowing hard and biting her lip—which means she's nowhere near done yet.

Squirming, she looks between the three of us. "Um, good morning. I see that you're, ah, awake."

The throbbing ache in my balls only grows with her shyness. I can tell Rebel's raring to go, but she should be the one to decide what happens here, if anything at all. "Do you want to keep going?" I ask, *praying* that she says yes.

If I've ever earned anything in my life, dear God, let it be this.

She worries that bottom lip between her teeth as she covers her chest with her arms and cups her breasts. "Um, how?"

My brain stalls as she tries to close her legs. Holding them open, I caress her inner thighs, careful not to touch her pussy yet.

"We could take turns," Rebel suggests, glancing at each of us to make sure both of our dicks are hard.

Yeah, dipshit, we're hard as fuck.

Ruin's already leaking jizz all over the sheets.

Celia's eyes widen. "Turns?"

"Yeah," he continues, caressing a hickey on her neck with his thumb. He leans in and kisses the spot, humming against her skin. "Think you can you take three loads, baby?"

I glance over at Ruin and know that there's no way he'll last long enough to come inside of her. His whole body's quivering, like he's barely holding on as it is.

But I play into the fantasy, knowing that we all need to get used to the idea. We've all already thought about it, I'm sure, but I don't know if Celia has. "We'll knock you up," I tell the room, making sure to meet each of my brother's gazes before nodding at our woman, "all three of us."

"Together," Rebel confirms, kissing her jawline. "Is that what you want, baby?"

Celia takes a moment to process, but then she's wrapping her hands around the base of Rebel's neck *and* Ruin's, pulling them both closer. She looks each of them in the eye before whispering, "do you think it will work this time?" Tears shine in her emerald eyes, and she hastily wipes them away. "I really want it to."

Pride swells inside my chest. If there's anything my brothers and I can do, it's complete a mission together. We're experts.

"I know it will." I close the distance between us and kiss her hard, aligning our hips and grinding my length against her pussy. She's slick and hot to the touch, moaning into my mouth and wrapping those perfect thighs around my waist. I slide into her slowly, stretching her walls, the tight embrace of her body making mine tremble. "I've got you," I promise, kissing her deeper, making sure she understands. "I'm not letting go."

I relinquish her mouth to Rebel and lean back on my knees to drive my cock deeper, reveling in the way her tits bounce with each measured thrust. She moans as Rebel tilts her head back and slips his tongue between her lips, claiming her mouth.

"He's gonna fill you up," Rebel rasps, biting her lip, "and then it's my turn."

She nods, clinging to his neck and panting in his ear. Blindly, she reaches to the other side and grabs Ruin's arm, pulling him closer. "You, too," she cries out, digging her nails into his flesh. "I, a-ah, need you to—" she gasps and grinds her hips, muttering and moaning as I drive harder into her heat. Ruin turns her face back toward him and stares into her half-lidded eyes, groaning weakly as his cock jumps against his stomach. A burst of semen pours from the tip, and his shoulders curve inward as he comes early—way too fucking early, but we'll work on that—gasping behind his mask. He reaches up and claws at the clasps, breaking one as he snaps the mask in half at the nose and throws the bottom half away. Celia reaches up and cups his scarred cheek, a smile playing on her lips for a split second before I slam home and derail her entire being, tearing a high-pitched scream from her throat. Her nails scrape his cheek, drawing blood, and that's what does him in more than anything else that's happened this morning.

Ruin grits his teeth as cum shoots from his cock, striping Celia's neck and tits in streaks of white. A *huge* fucking load, going on long enough that I come, too, filling up our girl's pretty pussy with a groan that I can feel in my bones. I've barely finished when Rebel is shoving me aside and crawling on top of Celia for his turn.

As he thrusts, he bites onto her neck and moans, his shoulder muscles rippling as he pumps in and out of her nice and slow. I know he's trying to hold on, but it's pointless.

She feels like Heaven every time.

"You're gonna come for me, right?" Celia's gentle

voice washes over me, and I do a double-take as she brushes her palms up and down Rebel's back in soothing strokes. Ruin's blood smears over Rebel's shoulder, but neither Rebel or Celia notices. They're too wrapped up in each other.

Rebel moans, a soft sound that can't be real. I have to be imagining it. But then he does it again, and Celia kisses him with the brightest smile. "That's it, baby," she cries, pushing her tits into his chest, "God, you're such a good boy, coming for me—filling me up—" Her voice breaks off on a whine that's breathtakingly beautiful. I commit it to memory and know that each of my brothers is doing the exact same—memorizing every detail of this moment.

Our girl is *ours* in every way imaginable.

Rebel convulses over her, crying out as his hips jerk into the cradle of her thighs. "Fuck, baby, yes, I'm coming so hard for you," he moans, thrusting deep. He collapses and she's quick to wrap him up, holding him as close to her body as possible.

The tiniest flare of jealousy fires inside my heart, but it's gone as soon as it's born, because my girl is smiling up at me so beautifully that I know she's going to be okay.

We're all going to be okay.

CHAPTER 22

THANATOS

IT ONLY TAKES ten minutes after Rage suddenly leaves our latest crime scene for me to decide to follow him to Celia's house. I idle in her driveway in the cold night air, contemplating my next move.

I shouldn't be here.

I should be tracking a killer.

Yet here I am... aching for a chance to see her again.

Our morning trainings have been long and arduous, testing my own limits as much as hers. I've never wanted someone so badly while simultaneously knowing that she's bad for me.

So, so fucking bad for me.

She's bad for all of us—nothing but trouble wrapped in an expensive cashmere and silk satin. It's no wonder my dad wants to kill her. Maybe he's obsessed like the rest of us, unable to look away despite the inevitable train wreck on the horizon. She can't *really* be okay with sharing her body with all three of my brothers. Something's going to break them apart. She'll pick a favorite, or Rage will take over and demand that she's *only* his, or Rebel will laugh while he drives her over a cliff for the thrill of the fall.

I stare at the sleek sports car beside me in the driveway, knowing exactly who gave it to her and why. Rebel's never been what I would call *subtle*. The car is proof of that. And if he's falling for her? Truly head-over-heels lovestruck?

He's going to do something impulsive.

I just don't know what to expect.

Spending five years away has taken its toll on my relationship with my brothers. Rage is easy enough to understand—we're the closest in age, and after my stepmother passed away and our father skipped town, we both took up the mantle to take care of our younger brothers. But Rebel and Ruin are another story, born from the chaos sewn by missing parents and a fucked-up past. Ruin in particular, I know very little about other than the pieces I've put together from the stories on the streets.

None of them are pretty, likening him to a monster more than a man. Carving up bodies for fun and muttering to himself as he tears sinew apart with his bare hands.

I can't fully blame those tendencies on our father's shit parenting. Ruin has always had a fondness for blood. It's what tipped my dad off in the first place. The moniker *demon* didn't come from the bullies on the playground—it passed our father's lips when Ruin was still in elementary school and going by his birth name.

Sometimes, I think that all the tragedy in our lives comes from our names. My brothers chose theirs after gaining a reputation within the bratva, but my name was given to me by my mother, a women I hardly remember. *Thanatos*, a reference to the grim reaper in Greek mythology. I track my targets much like I imagine Death himself would—it's the one thing that Ruin and I have in common, aside from the beatings our father used to give us.

We both know how to end a life efficiently.

It's why I don't understand his fascination with Celia. She's not a target for him to pursue. He doesn't get to shove his knife between her ribs and watch the light leave her eyes. But something is keeping him interested, just like something is keeping *me* interested.

Maybe we have more in common than I thought.

I unsnap my helmet and hook it to my motorcycle. There's no sense waiting around out here for the sun to rise. Rage seemed worried the minute he checked his cell phone, like he couldn't get away fast enough. The trouble is that we were on the outskirts of the city, on the opposite end to where we are now. It takes at least an hour to drive across, and we still had a body to manage.

Another pretty daughter of a politician mutilated with Celia's initials carved into her back.

We can't keep the press quiet about the murders for much longer. I can feel the clock ticking in time with my heartbeat, every second becoming a moment of agony. As the clock winds down, so too does the time between this moment and the one when I see my father again for the first time in years.

Will he recognize me? Or can I kill him before he realizes that it's his son holding a gun to his head?

I don't know which I want more—the satisfaction of surprise in his eyes, or the knowledge that he never saw it coming.

I drag my feet up the walkway to Celia's front porch. The door is locked, but it doesn't take an expert to shimmy the handle until it unlatches. I lock it behind me just in case I've been followed and slide a dining room chair beneath the handle for good measure. "Rage?" I call out, peering around every corner of the main floor to look for my brother. He isn't here, and neither are Rebel or Ruin.

Voices float down the stairwell, and I follow them to the second level. No one notices as I stand outside Celia's bedroom door, witnessing their collision. I see everything, from the way Rage handles her grief, to how she lashes out at him in her anguish, up until the moment when every jagged emotion suddenly slots into place. The tension in the room shifts, softening with her waning cries. I watch as both Rebel and Ruin slip onto the bed with Rage, all three of my brothers taking turns stroking Celia to sleep.

Even as the seconds pass into minutes, then into an hour, I don't think they realize I'm here.

A wave of emotion washes over me as I realize that I'm a stranger within my own family. Longing grips my heart and squeezes tight, but I'm not sure if it's longing for the woman in their arms or for a closer connection with my brothers.

Most of my life has been spent watching over my brothers. When our father used to go on a bender and raise his fists, I'd take the hardest swing just so that they could go to school without a black eye. I'd complete my rounds on the streets, peddling drugs or muscling my way into the fighting pits to earn enough money to put food on the table. My father sure as shit wasn't feeding the family while nursing a booze problem, and my step-mother was too busy trying to soothe his perpetual anger to find a job.

The bratva took care of us in its own way, but it was still a tough life.

I stare at the outline of Celia's body on the bed for another moment before finally turning away. While my brothers work together to soothe her, I shift my attention to the luxury of her house. The bedroom is massive, fully furnished with two sets of dressers, a vanity, a desk that looks more decorative than functional, and hundreds of shiny trinkets and nicknacks that likely cost more than I used to make in a month. I wander down the hallway to inspect the framed photographs on the walls. Pictures of her and her brother Mikhail are the most prominent, the twins seeming inseparable while attending school. *Private school*, too, with a pleated skirt and button-down shirt as part of the girls' uniform. I move on to the more recent pictures, finding a few of her parents, then a few more of her ex-husband Ted. A wedding photo sits on a bookshelf in the office downstairs, the glass broken and its metal frame bent. Someone had a fit of rage while staring at this picture. It could have been Celia after her husband left her, or it could have been Ted when he realized he made a mistake marrying her. Hell, it could have been Rage when he first came to her house and saw the bastard's face grinning at him.

The office is bare save for a few things, so I move on with my tour of the house. The moonlight outside illuminates a professionally-detailed backyard, with one of the ugliest stumps of a tree that I've ever seen sitting dead center on the lawn. I stare at its whitewashed trunk for a long time, wondering what it means. Everything in this house is painted white or gray. Modern, chic, expensive. But with silver moonlight blanketing the room in an eerie glow, everything also looks dead.

How could Celia ever be happy in a house filled with ghosts?

I picture her radiant smile in the summer sun, the video I found of her at the beach burned into my memory. She was wearing white then, too, a bikini that showed an endless canvas of tanned skin. The wedding ring from her late marriage was missing, Celia likely having been too young to have met Ted yet.

She was happy then. What would it take to make her happy now?

Beyond that, can my brothers actually pull this whole thing off? Making a woman like Celia—who seems light years out of their league—happy enough to start a family with them?

I think about that for a long time as the night wears on. Walking the perimeter of her house becomes second nature, and I learn each dip in the yard and crack in the driveway. As the stars start to fade with the oncoming morning, I find myself standing in front of that ugly white tree in the backyard. It's been freshly cut into ribbons, its branches spread across the ground like thick straws of hay. I've never seen a tree so heavily scarred, its trunk gouged with deep cuts, chunks of its bark littering the ground.

I used to think that Celia was as ugly as this tree, with a rotten core hidden beneath all the money and makeup. She abandoned the bratva that raised her, married a man without a drop of Russian blood in his veins, and couldn't even do *that* right. He left her heartbroken and alone, and I used to think that she deserved it.

But just like my brothers and I didn't choose to have a shit father, Celia didn't choose to have a shit ex-husband. Sometimes, things are simply out of our control. Like how attracted we are to the way someone smiles, or how shitty we feel when that smile cracks like it's made of the thinnest pane of glass.

When I first learned that Celia was messing around with my brothers, I thought that she was a gold-digger looking for her next sugar daddy to take care of her, or that she was trying to worm her way back into the brat-va's good graces so that our *pakhan* would forgive her for her transgressions and allow her back into high society. But I couldn't have been more wrong. She fought my brothers' advances as well as she could. I've seen that footage, too, of all the mornings Rage visited her at the boutique and pushed her to love him back. She never sought my brothers out. They're the ones that forced themselves into her life.

She never wanted to be a bratva wife, or she would have accepted the role the second she turned eighteen. All she's ever wanted is a family to call her own, and somehow, she ended up joining mine.

The sun starts to crest over the horizon, and I rub my aching eyes. There was no activity on the property all night, but it gives me peace of mind to know that had anything gone down, I would have handled it. Still, it's careless of my brothers to forget to watch their backs, no matter how tempting the woman is lying beneath them.

I triple-check that all the windows and doors are locked before walking back upstairs. Surely, they're awake by now. It's less than an hour until eight o'clock, and I've been conditioning Celia to be an early riser. She should be waking up any minute now—

A heady moan fills the air, and I freeze in my tracks. My heart rate spikes, jumping to a thousand in a millisecond. *That's* a sound I've never heard before. In all of my research into Celia's past, I found not one illicit photograph or video of Celia Monrovia. I've been using my imagination for days—*weeks*—wondering what she sounds like when she's on the verge of coming.

And now, after groaning into my pillow and coming into my fist more times that I'll ever admit, I hear it.

The sound she makes when she comes.

My cock stands to attention immediately, painfully

hard within seconds. Time moves in slow motion as I step into the master bedroom doorway and witness a scene I'm sure that I'm not supposed to see—but I can't look away.

I've been waiting for a glimpse of what it might be like for Celia to whisper my name in the throes of passion. We get close during our training—both of us sweating and panting as we roll around on the mat, her cheeks flushed and tendrils of soft, wavy hair clinging to her skin. I've been rock-hard every morning this week, aching for her to submit to me.

To let *me* be the one to make her forget her own name.

But even though this isn't quite how I imagined, even though it isn't my face buried between her thighs or kissing the sweat from her skin, it's close enough for me to pretend.

My cock is in my hand before I realize I've undone my belt and pulled down my pants, but by the time Rage is balls deep inside of her, I'm stroking my shaft like my life depends on it, the moan caught in my throat barely restrained. They're too caught up in each other to notice me standing in the doorway, but I take in every detail.

Amazed.

Completely, utterly enthralled.

Not only is she sharing her body with them, but it's clear that this is more intimate than how I'd imagine your typical foursome would be. Tears shine in her eyes as she looks between each of my brothers, a smile curving on her lips as she touches them with gentle strokes and hushed whispers.

I still don't know why Rage tore across the city to get to her, but if *this* is what waits for him every time he comes home, I think I understand.

There's love inside this room.

I suddenly crave a taste of it more than I need air. More than sleep, or food, or whatever else I need to survive. My body can starve if it means I'll receive a drop of the magic playing out before my eyes.

It's more than physical intimacy. It's something deeper, an unspoken bond that I've never experienced before.

Love.

None of them say it aloud. There are no hushed *I love you*'s shared between them. But I know that if I can feel it standing ten feet away, they have to feel it, too.

All three of my brothers come, two of them inside her body and one across her chest. I come for her, too, clamping my teeth on my fingers to keep from making a sound as thick ropes arc toward the bed, staining the beige carpet white.

I'm an intruder to this precious, vulnerable moment between them, and I don't feel a shred of shame or guilt for taking a piece of it for myself.

That's the worst part of all, the lack of remorse.

Because if I'm willing to take this special moment from them, what's going to stop me from taking something else, too? How far will I go for my taste of happiness—and will I steal it from the people I've sworn my life to protect?

A heavy weight settles in my chest as I zip up my pants and back out of the room. I shouldn't be here. I knew that before I ever walked through the front door.

But I've learned that I crave more than Celia's body —I crave her love, too.

And that's the most dangerous desire of all.

CHAPTER 23

CELIA

I BARELY MANAGE to keep from moaning as sinfully hot water cascades down my back. Showering alone after an eventful morning with three naked men takes an act of God to accomplish, but I manage to keep all of them out of the bathroom long enough to soak in the hot water and wash all the cum and sweat off of my body. If any one of them had slipped into the room behind me, I'm sure I'd have a dick pressed against my ass the whole time I'm washing my hair... until inevitably, he manages to push his cock between my thighs and fuck me against the tile wall.

A familiar ache blooms between my thighs, and I have to ignore the urge to slip my hand between them and take care of business.

I really *am* sore down there.

My muscles have gotten used to the push and pull of my intense morning workout sessions with Thanatos, but my pussy isn't on the same page with being stuffed full of throbbing cock every day.

I bite the inside of my cheeks as a wave of desire washes over me, turning my body *hot*. Taking a quick breath, I turn the water temperature way down and let it cool my heated skin. I'm sure the boys aren't faring much better, but if they smell even the slightest hint of sex on me, they'll try to start round two in a heartbeat, and this mama needs a break for at least a few more hours.

Once I've turned the water off and toweled myself dry, I slip into a pair of silky pajama shorts and a matching top, complete with an oversized, knit sweater to fight off the morning chill. The sweater falls past my hips and should deter my men from touching the goods underneath... *if* they have any self control.

I'm not sure they do... but I can't imagine them any other way.

Funny how the things I used to complain about are now the features I might miss if they suddenly stopped.

By the time I make it into the kitchen, Rebel is attempting to flip a pancake without using a spatula while Ruin stares out the window at the backyard. The willow tree he carved up last night is an eyesore, but I feel better knowing that it can't mock my failures anymore. It seems silly, letting something as simple as a tree impact me so strongly. I don't know how I let it go on for so long.

He must see my reflection in the window, because he turns toward me the moment I arrive. The smooth, flat mask that usually covers his face is still broken in half, leaving his mouth and cheeks exposed, but progress has been made between us. I'm not sure how far things will go or if I'll ever fully understand his reality, but I can try.

I join him at the window and nod toward the scarred willow tree. I watched as Ruin cut the branches off yesterday evening, but the morning light reveals that deep gouges have been scored in its trunk since then. Mist clings to its flesh, making the wounds look wet as they drip with condensation. I hold back a shiver and wonder if that's what he sees—just another dismembered corpse. "It looks worse than it did yesterday. Did you—"

"I stabbed it," Ruin confirms. He taps the windowpane with his fingertips. "So you don't cry anymore."

An odd gesture, but it fills my heart with warmth. I take his hand and lace our fingers together. "Thank you." Ruin's trying to connect in his own way, so I'll try, too.

He stares at our joined hands, finally squeezing mine back, and grunts.

Rebel whistles loudly and interrupts our conversation. "Alright, everybody, come get it!" Slapping a plate full of folded and torn pancakes onto the breakfast table, he grins. "Some of my finest work."

The pancakes are pale and unappealing to look at, but I smile back anyway. He's trying, too. "Thanks." I head into the kitchen for the butter and syrup, but he wraps his arms around my waist and pulls me into his chest.

"Mmmm, good morning, beautiful. Go sit down and I'll feed you." He steers me toward the table and kisses my cheek. "Eat up so we can go for another drive today."

Smacking my ass with a smirk, he retreats to grab toppings and utensils. "Rage! Than! Get your asses in here before I feed Celia your breakfast!"

Wait, Thanatos is here, too?

I tell myself not to get nervous about it, but butterflies flutter in my stomach anyway, oblivious to my desires. I hadn't expected a full family reunion so soon after I—

Swallowing hard, I fight the flicker of sadness turning every fluttering butterfly into dead weight, dropping them like stones into the pit of my stomach.

So soon after learning I'm not pregnant.

I busy myself with breakfast instead of dwelling, sitting gingerly on my stinging buttcheek and making a plate for Ruin, then for myself. "I didn't know you cooked, Rebel." I slide the first plate across the table, and Ruin picks up a plain pancake and shoves it into his mouth. No butter. No syrup. *Nothing.* He swallows, but it looks difficult. Glancing over my shoulder, I watch as Rebel tries to balance every possible pancake topping from the fridge in his arms. "Let me help—"

He rushes over and dumps everything onto the table. "I've got it." Once he sits down beside me at the table, he takes my plate, slathers my pancakes in whipped butter and drowns them in syrup, then cuts off a bite with his fork. Holding it up to my lips, he smiles brightly. "Open wide, baby."

Despite the dry pancake, the syrup makes the food edible. I let Rebel feed me two entire pancakes, licking sticky syrup from my lips while he grabs a third. His hair is still messy from last night, falling into his eyes and making him look boyishly charming. He rolls his snakebite between his teeth as he pours more syrup onto my plate. "Gotta fatten you up," he murmurs, "so you're ready for the baby."

I choke on my glass of milk. "That's not how it—" The word *works* dies on my lips as he turns back toward me with the goofiest smile on his face. He's *happy*, thinking about our future with the baby.

I can't take that away from him, no matter how adorably misguided he is about how pregnancy works.

As I chew on my third and final pancake, Rage and Thanatos appear from the garage. Both of them seem tense. "They've been strategizing," Rebel explains, rolling his eyes. "On how to tell Ezra how bad it's gotten."

"How bad what's gotten?"

"The bodies," Ruin clarifies.

"They found another one last night, near the community college."

I grab Rebel's wrist to keep him from shoving another bite in my mouth. "Sara goes there! Is she okay?" I glance at my phone on the kitchen island and wince. I haven't kept in touch with her at all after Thanatos kidnapped me from my father's safe house. I'm lucky if she's still working at my boutique at all. "I need to call her right now—"

"She's fine," Thanatos grouches, rubbing the back of his neck. "I gave her a gun to protect herself."

My mouth falls open. "You *what?* You can't just give a girl a gun!"

He shrugs one shoulder, avoiding look my direction. "I showed her how to use it first."

I stand from my chair and grab my cell phone. Two dozen missed calls and over one hundred messages. Wincing, I scroll through the phone calls, glad to know that most of them are my brother Mikhail. We haven't spoken since he showed up at my shop and scared Rage off, but that doesn't mean he's let my silence go. If anything, he's likely *more* worried that he hasn't been able to get in touch with me.

"I need to make some calls." First to Sara, then to my best friend Lilith to let her know I'm not dead in a ditch somewhere, then maybe... to Mikhail. He's not going to be happy that I'm in a relationship with three men. At least Lilith should be ecstatic for me. She knows how miserable I've been since my divorce.

Dick every day keeps the doctor away! she used to say, laughing as she snagged another man to warm her bed at night.

Wait until I tell her that I'm trying for a baby again—that'll prove her little theory wrong.

"Don't break anything," I tell the men, stepping into the living room to place my first call. "No stabbing or punching or shooting. And don't steal any more of my stuff, Rebel!"

"Only your heart, baby, I promise!"

I can't help but giggle as even better butterflies flutter in my stomach. Not from nerves, but from giddy excitement. *Butterflies*, like I've got a crush who likes me back. Laughing as I step into my office, I click *dial* on Sara's name in my address book, praying that she picks up. When she doesn't answer, I leave her a five minute voicemail, apologizing for my radio silence and promising to come by the shop soon with a huge bonus for her. Once that's done, I send Lilith a text and invite her to lunch to explain everything that's been going on. Thankfully, she immediately fires back a winking kiss-face emoji, followed by an eggplant and a blushing face.

Yeah, we're still good.

The canvas backpack filled with things from my office sits on my desk, and as I start to unpack it, an idea strikes like lightning. I quickly shoot a text to Valentina, my brother's girlfriend and the wife of our bratva's *pakhan*, to ask if she's attending the upcoming gala.

I could make the most beautiful dress for her. I already have her measurements from her wedding, and designing another opulent gown will keep my mind off of being targeted by a murderous psychopath.

I'm already sketching the dress in my mind when there's a knock on my office door. Rage idles in the doorway, wearing one of Ted's old shirts that he left behind in his office. I crinkle my nose at him, and his mouth curves into a smirk.

"Not my color?"

"Not your style." Walking over to him, I straighten his already-perfect collar and smooth down the front buttons. The shirt's a tight fit across his chest, but it should get him from point A to point B without bursting at the seams. When he flexes his arms and the corner stitches bulge, however, I start to rethink that.

"Where are you going this time?" I force a smile on my face, but he sees right through me. Things might be better between us, but I haven't forgotten about everything he's done. I'm not sure if I'm going to forgive him yet.

But my heart has other ideas.

"Will you miss me, *krosotka*?" Planting his hands on my hips, he sighs against the curve of my neck. "I always miss you." He trails soft kisses up to my jawline, then mouths a sensitive spot that wasn't there yesterday. I gasp as he nips my skin and sucks, bringing blood to the surface to leave a mark.

"W-what are you doing?" My fingers thread through his hair, holding him in place as pleasure warms deep in my belly.

"Until you let me put a ring on your finger," he rumbles, "I need to make sure everyone knows that you're mine. When the baby starts showing, no one will dare touch you, but until then—" Growling, he grabs my ass and pulls me against his body. "I'm going to mark you up, mama, every chance I get."

My knees shake, and he palms my ass and lifts me off of the floor. Pressing my back to the door, he grins as he claims my mouth in a greedy kiss, grinding his hard length between my thighs. I gasp, and he slips his tongue between my lips, groaning as I kiss him back just as hard.

"Do you have to go?" I bite my swollen lip. "You always leave during the day." I've spent countless hours with Rebel by now, but all of the time I've spent with Rage has been in the evenings or with his face buried in my pussy. Neither of which have really allowed me to get to know him beyond how his body feels when pressed against mine.

Regret ripples across his face. "Oh, *krosotka*, you have no idea how much that—" He presses his forehead to mine and closes his eyes. "How much it means to me that you want me to stay. But I'm trying to keep everyone safe, and I can only do that by putting that bastard into the grave where he belongs."

I understand it, but I don't have to like it.

"I'll wait here for you." I have work that I need to do, anyways, so staying home will be good for me.

Rage grins and pecks my lips. "That's my good girl." He lowers me to the ground, and I follow him to the front door. After giving me one more kiss, he turns to leave again, and my heart trips inside my chest.

"Rage, wait." My heartbeat hammers like a kick drum as he turns around, a curious gleam in his eye.

"Yes, *krosotka*?"

Clearing my throat, I close what little distance remains between us. "Thank you for..." *Don't blush, don't blush, don't blush*—my face warms, but so does my stuttering heart. I take his hand and lace our fingers together, wrapping his visible scars around my invisible ones. There are a lot of things I could say to fill the space between us, all of the distance I've built when pushing him away over the past few weeks, but before I can summon the right words, his lips curve into a soft, little smile that mirrors my own. Slowly, he dips his head to brush his lips against mine, clutching my hand so tightly that I almost doubt he'll leave.

I don't want him to. Not after last night.

"I'll be back this evening," he promises, kissing me again. This time, he cradles my jaw and melts into me, pouring whatever words we've left unsaid into this one, tender gesture. When he finally pulls back and looks deep into my eyes, I'm reminded of a time when I thought that his were empty pools of black, threatening to swallow me whole. But now I see the warmth hiding in their depths, woven throughout all of the dark, shadowy parts of himself that I was too scared to explore. But where there's shadow, there's also light, and the peaceful look on his face rivals the warmth of the sun.

He brushes his thumb across the corner of my lips. "Do me a favor," he murmurs, "and stay inside today. Lock the door behind me."

My eyebrows furrow together. "Is something wrong? Like, more than usual? I know Rebel said there was another body—"

A muscle in his jaw tics. Instead of answering my question, he presses a kiss to my forehead and backs away from me. "Lock the door," he reminds me, "and don't go outside no matter what Rebel says to tempt you."

"Something *is* wrong."

"Not for long. I'm taking care of it."

Thanatos suddenly appears from the dining room holding an empty crystal vase with rotten flower petals stuck to the sides. Curving spirals, jagged and sharp, wrap around the base. It's the same one I found filled with roses the day someone broke into my home and attacked me.

I wrap my sweater tighter around my body. "Why do you have that?"

"Do you know what this is?" Thanatos isn't asking me—he's asking Rage. The cut of his jaw looks sharper than I remember, the dark circles under his eyes more pronounced. Did he get any sleep last night, or was he searching for their father until dawn?

"A vase," Rage replies, unimpressed. "What about it?"

"This was your mother's," Thanatos snaps, slamming the vase to the floor. It shatters around our feet, the heavy base the only piece remaining whole. The remaining pieces skid across the foyer and tumble into the walls, some of the larger pieces sliding beneath the antique grandfather clock in the corner, with the more fragile ones breaking into invisible little slivers that will take days to properly clean up.

As the glass breaks, I cry out in shock and jump back, but I'm not fast enough to avoid getting hit. Blood streaks across the tops of my feet and on the side of one of my ankles. "Ah!" The cuts sting, but it's nothing compared to the *crack* of Rage's fist meeting Thanatos' jaw.

"What is *wrong* with you?" Rage snarls, shoving him into the dining room table. "You've been a dick all morning. Why show up at all if you're only going to make things worse?"

Someone lifts me from behind and carries me into

the living room, setting me down on the edge of the couch away from the glass. Ruin walks around to my front and kneels at my feet to inspect the damage, careful to remove the remaining shards off of my skin.

"For fuck's sake," Rebel huffs, stomping into the dining room after his brothers. "Can't you two stop measuring each other's dicks long enough to actually accomplish something? What's the problem—you missed your little foreplay session this morning and had to beat your meat without any spank bank material? Get a grip!"

Spank bank material?

Embarrassment hits me like a freight train. Ruin disappears to grab the medical kit under the kitchen sink, but as soon as he returns, I grip his shoulders to keep myself from shaking. He doesn't react, too focused on pouring peroxide on my cuts and wiping them clean to pay attention to the argument brewing in the other room.

But I hear everything loud and clear.

"She asked me to train her," Thanatos grinds out, his voice pinched like he's in pain. "So that's what I'm doing. Training *your* girl, watching her like a fucking hawk all hours of the day, listening to you guys have sex with her over and over again—"

I cover my mouth with my hands.

"I never took you for the jealous type," Rebel sneers, kicking a piece of glass hard enough that it clatters across the hardwood. "But I guess it makes sense. You finally roll back into town and can't wait for your piece of the pie. Well guess what? I'm not sharing her with someone who can't control his fucking temper. You hurt her, *again*, and I'm sure as shit getting tired of it."

"I'm never meant to—"

"Rebel's right," Rage sighs, sounding exhausted. "You need to apologize. Not just for the vase, but for the things you said to her before."

There's a beat of silence between the three of them, and then they all appear from around the corner. Ruin just finished wrapping my feet and both ankles in a bandage, tucking the end neatly inside one of the bands. It's overkill for the amount of damage taken, but he seems satisfied with the job, idly rubbing his thumbs down the arch of my foot.

I run my hand through his hair, scratching his scalp as he stands up. "Thank you, Ruin." He slips out of the room without saying a word, but I have no doubt he's watching from a safe distance.

"Apologize," Rage demands, pushing Thanatos closer to me.

The oldest brother cuts his gaze to the window, the deep scowl on his lips making him look more like Rage than ever before. Finally, after a few minutes of tense silence, he stares at my feet and unclenches his jaw. "I shouldn't have thrown the vase."

I fold my hands in my lap and wait for him to continue.

He flicks his gaze up to mine and winces. "I didn't mean—I don't want to hurt you."

That hasn't always been the case, but this time, I think he means what he says. "I believe you."

Some of the tension in his shoulders relaxes. "Thank you."

Rage doesn't look pleased, but at least he isn't as angry as he was five minutes ago. He claps Thanatos on the shoulder and spins him around. "If you hurt her again, intentional or otherwise, I don't care that you're my flesh and blood. You're *dead*, and she's going to decide how long we make you suffer. Do you understand?"

Thanatos nods, his mouth pressed into a grim line. "I understand."

"Don't you fucking forget it, asshole."

Rage runs a hand down his face and turns back to me. "You don't have to forgive him. Hell, you don't have to forgive *me*. I've been—" He grits his teeth—"*stubborn*. Demanding."

"A dick," Rebel chimes in, smiling cheekily.

"I have," Rage admits slowly. "I've hurt you, too, and although I don't regret the things I've done to keep you, Celia, I'm—" He kneels at my feet in the same spot Ruin did moments ago. Taking my hands in his, he presses a kiss to each of them. "I'm a better man than I've shown you. I *will be* a better man, for you and for our family."

I don't know what to say to him. To any of them. None of this feels real—I could wake up any moment and still be locked inside that cage, cold and angry and afraid—

Rebel leans over Rage's shoulder and kisses me,

soothing my worries away with practiced ease. "Nothing's changed, baby, I promise." He winks, repeating the same turn of phrase he said yesterday when I found out I wasn't pregnant. Except everything *does* feel different—like we're about to step into a new chapter together.

Not just the four of us, but the *five* of us.

With both Rebel and Rage's help, I stand up and wrap my arms around Thanatos' shoulders, lifting up onto my tiptoes to press a chaste kiss to his cheek. "Thank you for the apology."

Hesitantly, he returns the embrace, holding onto me as though I'm made of glass. Only after I don't immediately let go does he relax, sighing into my hair as he engulfs my body in his.

I don't know what the future holds for us, but no matter what happens next, we have one more fierce fighter willing to protect this family at all costs. I never imagined finding hope for the future within the bratva, of all places, especially after my father died, but I'm starting to realize that life with these battered, brutal men might be where I've always belonged.

CHAPTER 24

REBEL

ONCE RAGE and Thanatos finally leave, I enlist Ruin's help in cleaning up the broken glass in the entryway. Neither of us talk about where the vase came from or who brought it inside Celia's house. But if I know my younger brother like I think I do, he's thinking about it just as much as I am.

There was very little that survived the house fire that tore our family apart. My brothers and I made it, obviously, but not only did our mom perish in the flames, so did all of our belongings. Not that we had much to lose to begin with, but that stupid fucking vase—the one Dad filled with flowers any time he sobered up enough to suck up to our mom—somehow emerged unscathed.

It's a sick fucking joke that it's still covered in ash like the fire happened only yesterday, but what's even more fucked up is that it reappeared at all.

Dad brought Mom flowers the day she died, and the

sick fuck decided to do the same to Celia the day he tried to abduct her.

I can't wait to gut the bastard.

Glancing over my shoulder at Celia, I find her perched on the couch watching me and Ruin clean up. She's sipping on one of those sparkling waters bougie girls love and idly wiggling her toes on the coffee table. "You good, baby?" I ask, handing Ruin the dust pan. She hasn't said a word since Rage and Thanatos left, stuck in her head with whatever's on her mind. Ruin, similarly, is quiet as a mouse, focusing on the task at hand.

Man, *fuck* this.

I toss the broom to the floor and hop over the last pile of glass shards to get to Celia. She looks up only when I'm standing directly in front of her. "C'mon, let's get out of here. Rage doesn't have to know."

Celia purses her lips. "He put a tracker in my phone, Rebel."

"So leave it here." I pluck the cell phone from her lap and toss it onto the couch beside her. "He'll never know you're gone. It'll be just like last time." Then, I snap the heart-shaped collar from her neck and drop it onto the coffee table.

Let's see Rage find us *now*.

Celia's eyebrows knit together. "But the last time he followed us, he showed up right when we were—" Her pupils dilate as the tiniest, little breath catches in her throat.

I can't help but grin at my horny girl. "That's right, baby, you gave him quite a show." Licking my lips, I rub my palms up her thighs. She has the softest skin. Warm and pliant and so fucking sexy—

An ear-shattering ringtone, some kind of popular pop song, pierces the air as Celia's cell phone comes to life. She jumps a solid inch off the couch, but I clamp down on her knees to keep her still. "Go out with me. On a real date this time."

The little wrinkle on her forehead drives me crazy. She's overthinking things again. "But Rage told me not to leave the house. He says it isn't safe."

I click my tongue against my teeth. Such a goody-two-shoes. It's fucking adorable. I gesture for Ruin to come over and join the convo, hoping that he'll say something to convince her to go out with me.

With us. Whatever. He can come, too, as long as he stays in the car.

"Pleaaase," I beg, giving her my best pout. It's been years since I've had to literally beg for a girl's attention, but thankfully, I'm cute as fuck, and Celia loves me.

My heart kicks into overdrive, revving up every part of my body like an engine. Damn, damn, damn, do I like the sound of that.

Celia loves me.

I repeat the phrase in my head, going over how nice it will be to hear her say those words out loud, while she checks her phone.

I love you, Rebel.

Stay with me, baby.

Please fuck me.

Okay, so there are a lot of things I'd love to hear her say, but the most important one is the evergreen I-L-Y.

Ruin finishes sweeping the broken glass into the trash and comes up beside Celia to peer over her head at her phone screen. She's gone pale while checking her messages. "Who is it?" Ruin asks, sliding onto the couch beside her. Together, they read whatever's on her screen, Celia's lips moving as she pieces through the words.

Must be a long fucking message.

Suddenly, she jumps up and loses her grip on the phone. It crashes into my chest, and I have to scramble to catch it before it hits the floor. "Whoa, hey, what's wrong—"

"We have to leave *now!*" She squeezes around my body and rushes to the car keys hanging up in the kitchen. Once they're in hand, she fumbles for her purse and slings it over her body so that it rests against her hip. "Come on, let's go!"

Ruin is already jumping into motion, but it takes me longer to gather my wits. I don't even have shoes on. "Celia, hold up." I know that I was the one to suggest we get out of the house, but *goddamn.* Growling in frustration, I grab one of my shoes from under the kitchen table —where the hell is the other one?—and follow them into the garage. She's already got the car running with Ruin riding shotgun.

Great, looks like *I'll* be the third wheel.

I snag my missing Converse from the doorway and jump into the backseat. "When am I gonna ride up front?" Slipping on my shoes, I don't bother hiding my annoyance. I bought her the car—I should get to sit up front one of these days!

"Read the text," Ruin instructs, unmoved by my plight, "and buckle seatbelt."

"You buckle your seatbelt," I grumble under my breath. Flipping the phone over, I squint to read the latest voicemail while Celia backs out of the driveway. It's from Sara, the chick Celia pays to mind the shop. The message doesn't make sense, though, the speech-to-text system only picking up pieces of Sara's voice rather than the whole thing. Another message comes through, this time as a text.

It's a blurry picture of a woman tied to a chair, a raging inferno blazing behind her back. I read the previous messages as fast as I can, my stomach dropping. Sara isn't the one sending these messages.

The killer tearing through our city is.

Another text comes through.

> HURRY UP IF YOU WANT TO SEE
> HER ALIVE

Pinpricks of fear skitter down my arms as I lift the phone to my ear. There's only one way to be sure that it's our dad sending these messages, and that's by playing the voicemail.

But... it might not be him. It could be anyone—a prank!—or a butt dial!—seriously, *anyone* could have stolen Sara's phone. I bet it's a bunch of college kids smoking pot in the science building, having a real laugh about scaring some stranger they've never met—

A gruff, male voice crackles in my ear. He laughs, *fucking laughs*, as a girl in the background screams. "We miss you, Celia," the man taunts, breathing heavily into the receiver. "I keep asking Sara when you're coming back from your vacation, but she won't stop screaming to answer me. I think she might be broken." He chuckles again, making my skin crawl. "You shouldn't have taken so long to come see us."

"For fuck's sake." I pause the voicemail and go back to reading the automated text translation. I can't stomach another second of that man's voice crawling in my head.

> I've been dying to see you again. I
> have a big surprise… don't wait…tell
> my sons…

With a hiss, I slam my fist into the back of the Ruin's headrest. "Goddammit!" Our bastard father *did* break into Celia's house. He set up the red roses in the crystal vase—the twin taper candles on the dining room table— the broken glass pane in the back door.

He assaulted our woman and tried to kidnap her. "I'll never forgive him," I snarl, slamming Celia's phone against Ruin's shoulder. He takes the device from me and reads the message again, remaining silent. If anyone has a reason to hate our father, it's Ruin.

But if anyone should be scared of him, that's Ruin, too. The evil bastard has tried to kill him at least a half dozen times—some of which Ruin doesn't even know about, because Rage and I got in the way. Some of the scars on Rage's body aren't from street brawls or collecting bratva debts—they're from our fucking father going into a drunken rage and attempting to beat his kids to death.

"We should have emptied a clip in his gut the day he showed back up." My anger flares bright, burning me up from the inside.

"We did not know where he was hiding."

I grab my head in my hands. "Fuck! We still don't know where he's hiding!"

Celia slams on the breaks and narrowly avoids getting into a wreck. "I knew I should have gone to check on her. This is all my fault." Her voice is strong but unstable, warbling on her vowels. "Now she's been taken, and he's going to—" Her voice cracks this time, and the sound is a dagger straight to my heart.

It won't be long before she goes into a full-blown panic at this rate.

"Breathe, baby, just breathe."

"I *am* breathing!"

Ooookay, wrong choice of words.

"Pull over. Let Ruin drive."

"We don't even know where to go!" She isn't wrong —we've been driving aimlessly through the streets, having jumped before we checked where to land. At least Celia is coherent enough to pull over and switch seats for to Ruin take the wheel. As she buckles up and Ruin adjusts the mirrors for his height, I think back to what I know about my father.

Aside from being an emotionless sack of shit, he's

smart. It's how he avoided capture after he set the fire that killed our mother and the *pakhan* tried to panel him for it. Thanatos has been tracking him outside the city for years, traveling the country to stay on his trail.

I pad my pockets, but I don't have my phone on me. "Call Than." When Celia continues tapping her fingers on the dash, I realize she hasn't heard me. "*Celia*, call Thanatos!"

"I don't have his number!"

"Bullshit." The man is almost as anal as Rage. He'll have saved his number in her cell. I take the phone from Celia and flick through her contacts, surprised to see that he's saved himself under the name *Thanatos (Riot)*. Since when did he take on an R-name like the rest of us?

Dialing his number, I read the street names as we pass by. "Where are we going?"

"To the store," Ruin replies, turning onto a street without using his blinker. "There will be camera footage."

Celia sits up straighter. "It's her shift right now. She should be there."

Thanatos picks up on the third ring, sounding as confused as I feel about how he answers. "Princess?"

"What did you just call me?"

His tone shifts in annoyance. "Rebel? What are you doing with Celia's phone?"

"What are *you* doing, calling her Princess?"

"*Rebel!*" Celia snaps, turning around to glare at me. "Not now! Send him the fucking voicemail!"

With a sigh of frustration, I follow orders and send

everyone a group message with not only our father's creepy-as-fuck voicemail, but the subsequent text and picture. The image is potato-quality, so it's hard to see the woman's face, but she's definitely tied up and there's definitely a fire blazing behind her back.

Thanatos curses in heavy Russian. "Don't move. Stay at the house. We're coming."

I snort. "Fuck that, we're already on the road."

Rage's voice booms in the background like canon fire. "You're *what?*" Their phone changes hands, and Rage is suddenly yelling into my ear. "Get her back to the fucking apartment. Lock her in the goddamn cage and don't let her out of your sight."

My pulse pounds in my ears as I put my brother on speaker. "No fucking way, we're not going home. We're going to find the bastard and kill him." My brothers have taken ages to catch him and *still* haven't found him, so it's obvious that they need more men on the job.

"We're saving Sara!" Celia shouts, grabbing the phone from my hand. "We can kill him after she's safe"

Fuck, she's hot when she's pissed. I'd nearly forgotten how drop-dead-gorgeous that fire inside her heart is.

"I won't let him get near you," Rage hisses. A car door slams, and I hear their car engine turn over across the line. "Go home, Celia. You'll be safe there until we figure out where he's keeping Sara."

"Listen to the voicemail! She's screaming, Rage! He's torturing her!" Celia's voice pitches with her anger. "Don't you dare tell me to go home when it's my fault she's been dragged into this."

Thanatos speaks next, the only calm one aside from Ruin. "Take a deep breath, Celia. Where would Sara be right now?" He walks her through a few questions to try and pinpoint Sara's location, and it helps calm Celia's emotions. She's razor-sharp by the third question, recalling details about Sara's life that I never realized she would know. Thanatos doesn't seem surprised by this—or by the information itself—as he walks us all through multiple possible scenarios.

The voicemail could be a recording of someone else screaming.

Our dad could have pickpocketed Sara's phone.

Sara could be on a date with her boyfriend, none the wiser to any of this.

The list goes on, each possibility seeming more far-fetched than the last. Finally, we pull up to Celia's boutique and jump out of the car. The lights are on inside, but we can't see anyone unless you count the mannequins in the windows.

Ruin grabs Celia from around the waist before she can run inside the building and pulls out a Glock from a holster strapped to his hip, then pushes her back toward the car. I trade places with him as he steps into the building, carefully wrapping my arms around Celia's torso to keep her from doing something reckless.

Like walking into an ambush.

"He can't go in alone! *Please*, Rebel!"

My brother is a professional. He can handle himself. But when Celia says please...

There's only so much I can do to resist.

With a hiss, I run a hand through my hair and tug on the ends. Her presence in my life makes these kind of situations much more complicated than they used to be. "Baby, listen to me. I'll go inside with Ruin, but you have to promise to stick by my side the entire time. We are *silent.* We are *quick.* And for the love of God, don't fucking scream, no matter what happens."

But Celia is determined. Her jaw is set and her eyes are steely, reminding me of why Rage fell in love with her at first sight. Once she's in the zone, she's fucking unshakeable.

I reach inside the car and grab the gun I planted inside of her glovebox. She's checking our surroundings while she waits for us to follow Ruin inside the boutique, but *fuck.*

I love this woman too goddamn much to let her go in there unarmed, and I only have one gun.

Before she can react, I grab the handcuffs I stashed beneath the passenger seat and clip them around one of her wrists, cinching the cuff while I drag the other one to the passenger side door. I hook it onto the inside handle of the door and lift her up, setting her down on the seat as carefully and quickly as I can. Then, I place the gun in her free hand and wrap her fingers around the grip, making sure she's holding on before I let go.

Her eyes are blown so wide with disbelief that I can't bear look at her.

"Rebel, wait—" She tries to grab me, but her arm snags on the cuffs. "Don't do this without me."

Slamming the door shut, I yell, "fuck! Lock the doors!"

"What's going on?" Rage's voice roars from inside the car. Celia must have dropped the phone in the floorboard. "Talk to me, dammit!"

Instead of answering, she stares directly at me, her stone cold gaze piercing my heart. It bleeds all over the pavement with each step I take away from her. "Hurry up, Rage," I growl, "because if I die without seeing our kid, I'm haunting your ass for eternity!"

Celia doesn't speak to me again, but it's for the best. If she had said please and begged me to stay with her, there's no way I'd ever have walked away.

But I'll never forgive myself if my little brother dies and misses out on his happy ending. That's what Celia is for us—the happy ending we never thought we'd find. He's the one who deserves it the most.

Over my dead fucking body is he losing it on my watch.

As I walk to the shop's front door, I catch a whiff of gasoline. My body reacts on instinct, recoiling from the smell. "What the hell?" I spot a shimmering liquid trailing through the shop, splattered across the walls and all over the floor. *Shit.* Ruin's sense of smell isn't what it used to be. He might not have noticed before he went inside.

I yank open the front door and call out my brother's name. "Ruin! Get the fuck out of here! Something's not right!" I watch through Celia's office window as my brother enters the room, and something over his head sparks bright orange.

"Oh, fu—"

A flash of light and searing heat kicks me back, glass shattering all around me. I land on my back on the sidewalk, the air punching from my lungs. When I breathe in, all I taste are chemical fumes.

I jump up to my feet and the first thing I see is Celia's face obscured in flame. They dance across the windshield, reflecting the damage behind my back. Embers cascade all around us, turning to ash as they sweep the ground. I swivel back around to face the burning building and lunge forward to find my brother, knowing that he's trapped inside, knowing that I can still get to him, knowing that there's no possible way our dad finally succeeded in taking him out.

I won't fucking let him.

Book three, *Bound by Ruin,* arrives May 2025.

Thank you so much for reading *Tempted to Rebel!* If you enjoyed your time with Rebel and his brothers, please leave a rating or review. 🩶

For a sneak peek of *Bound by Ruin,* join my newsletter!

Haven't met Valentina Baranova yet? Read *Rule of Three* in ebook, paperback, or Kindle Unlimited here:
Amazon US

For another dark read, check out my MFM serial killer standalone romance coming in July 2025: *Theirs to Take*

Two unhinged brothers make me the target of their twisted game. The ending? *Death*.

If I thought being a college student was hard enough, adding in two psychotic misfits definitely ups the ante. They're both obsessed--one with hating me, the other with teasing me. At first, I think it's a flirting game to get into my pants.

Then someone brings out a mask, a knife, and an ultimatum, and the alarms bells in my head start screaming. This isn't just a game--it's a death sentence.

There's only one way to win:
Know Your Enemy
Seduce Your Enemy
Don't Fall for Your Enemy

Meet Kane, Zane, and Mercy in the preview prequel on my website:
https://mistiwilds.com/pages/theirs-to-take-preview

About the Author

Just a smut-lover listening to angsty love songs on repeat.

Misti Wilds loves watching characters pine after one another from afar--until a tall, dark, brooding alpha male says *fuck this* and claims his woman. But one man isn't enough these days--Misti's got her hands full when it comes to writing multiple dark and delicious men with violence in their hearts and a declaration of love etched on the barrel of their guns.

Why choose one when you can have them all?

Baranova Bratva:

Rule of Three

Reign of Four

Brutal Beauty (prequel)

Claimed by Rage

Tempted to Rebel

Bound by Ruin

Serial Killer MFM:

Meet Mercy, Kane, and Zane in the free Prequel

Theirs to Take

www.ingramcontent.com/pod-product-compliance
Lightning Source LLC
Chambersburg PA
CBHW032355310726
48973CB00007B/2017